He jerked  he
growled in her , how.
Please."

He didn't even sound breathless, and her heart pounded in her chest, her breathing loud.

"Where?" she managed to choke out.

"Back." He whirled her around and nudged her back in the direction they came.

She obliged, what fight she had abandoning her.

"Why don't you just kill me?"

"It matters not to me," he murmured. "I will get you back there one way or the other. But it would be far easier if you just come willingly. You'll see that. You will. I promise."

"But where?" she demanded.

"You really don't know, do you?"

His voice held a hint of awe.

Was he so surprised? She opened her mouth to ask, but his grip fell away and his cry of pain echoed in her ear.

"Run, Evelyn!"

She whirled to stare wide-eyed at her rescuer.

David & Katie,
May you always
find each other
in the hardest of times.
xxx

Through the Veil

by

Kyra Whitton

Breaking the Veil, Book 2

Through the Veil

Cover Art by *Kristian Norris*

The Wild Rose Press, Inc.
PO Box 708
Adams Basin, NY 14410-0708
Visit us at www.thewildrosepress.com

Publishing History
First Fantasy Rose Edition, 2019
Print ISBN 978-1-5092-2793-8
Digital ISBN 978-1-5092-2794-5

Breaking the Veil, Book 2
Published in the United States of America

Dedication

For Steve, my partner in all things

Also By Kyra Whitton

Breaking The Veil series
Into The Otherworld

Chapter One

"This is amazing." Evie Blair looked out over the little medieval town, a cool, salty breeze coming off the North Sea blowing her dark hair into her eyes. She tossed her head, clearing her vision. "Why did you wait so long to force me up here?"

"You kept telling me you were afraid of heights."

She snorted. "And you listened?" She gazed out over the water, searching out the white-tipped waves unfurling toward the shore like rolls of lace. When he didn't answer, she spun around.

"Oh!" she squeaked, clasping her hands over her mouth.

Nestled on a velvet cushion, a diamond ring glittered in a rare glimpse of sunlight.

Her heart slammed into her chest "Are you—?"

"Evie, will you—?"

"Yes!"

"Oh."

Calum Baird blinked, his expression frozen, mouth slackening. But as a lop-sided grin slowly split his face, he lifted the ring out of the box and slid it gently onto Evie's outstretched finger.

"I had more of a speech. I could—"

She launched herself at him. Arms wrapped around his neck and toes strained to add enough height, she kissed him through the grin she couldn't wipe off her face. His own arms slipped around her waist, hugging her until her toes no longer touched the ground. As if he never wanted to let her go.

"You ready for a real holiday?" he murmured next to her ear.

She pulled back only enough to look into his blue eyes. "There's more?"

"Oh, Evie lass, there is so, so much more," he purred huskily.

She giggled and gave his lips another quick peck. "Then what are we waiting for?" She wiggled out of his arms and whirled away, disturbing the parcel of crows dominating the north side of the tower.

Calum grabbed her hand as she stepped down into the dark stairwell, and slowly they made their way down the narrow, twisting steps.

As they emerged back into the warm summer morning, Evie looped her arm in his, and they strolled down North Street.

"Where are we going?" she asked, her gaze on her left ring finger, the weight of the ring foreign, but not unpleasant.

But he didn't answer, instead pulling the passenger side door of his car open so she could slide in.

She buckled the safety belt as he jogged around the front to the driver's seat, and raised an eyebrow in question when he made no immediate attempt to answer.

He pushed a pair of dark sunglasses onto his hawk-like nose. "A grand tour of the Highlands." He grinned.

Shoulders drooping, she slumped back into the seat. Hitting every tourist stop between St Andrews and Inverness topped her bucket list, but there was no way she could fit a holiday into her schedule.

"I can't be gone that long. I have so much to do here, and there are deadlines I have to meet. You know I—"

Calum reached across the center console and squeezed her leg just above the knee. "I've already spoken with your professor, Evie." He gave her thigh a pat and then pressed the gear shift into reverse.

"You-you what?"

"She's known for weeks. Even made suggestions for stops along the way." He grinned and nudged the small car out into traffic, heading west out of town. "We have five days, love. I thought we would start at Tay and work our way north."

Her jaw slackened. "Are you serious?" Was it possible to adore this man any more?

He chuckled and tossed his head toward the rear of the car.

She glanced over her shoulder. In the small back seat, two overnight bags sat propped on the narrow bench, a cooler wedged between them.

"How did you—? I don't know what—?" She snapped her mouth shut. "Calum Baird, I can't believe you kept a secret like this from me!" she half-heartedly admonished him.

He shrugged modestly and reached for her hand, weaving their fingers together and resting them on the gearshift. "I'd planned to ask on the shores of Loch Lomond," he admitted. "But then, seeing you there, up on St. Rule's with the wind in your hair, I couldn't wait any longer."

Evie tried not to smile, pulling her lips down, but pleasure bloomed across her face, anyway. "It was perfect," she murmured, gaze returning to her left hand.

She settled down into the seat, leaning her head against the window. The landscape pulled her attention away, and she stared at the waving grasses carpeting the rolling hills, clear blue skies frosted with thick, heavy clouds. It was true. That morning was perfect. He was perfect. For her, at least.

She nestled down in her seat, his thumb idly stroking the back of her hand. Was this not the future she planned for herself? Settling somewhere full of history and beauty with someone she loved? With someone who loved her? When she'd come to Scotland, she never would have predicted this. Or him. But now that she had both, she never wanted to let go.

A flash of sunlight on glass in the rearview mirror caught her attention

"Calum!" she wailed as the car thrust forward with a sickening crunch of metal. Their hands broke apart as his arm swung wide to brace her.

Beneath them, the tires screamed. The nose of Calum's car buried itself in the truck ahead and the last thing she saw before her head cracked against the window was the inflating airbag. Metal and fiberglass shrieked as blinding-hot pain tore through her.

And then there was nothing but darkness and the distant cawing of crows.

Chapter Two

One Year Later

By the time she realized the pounding wasn't in her head, Evie could no longer ignore it.

"Mom!" She groaned as she pulled a pillow over her eyes. "Door!"

But there was no answer.

She slunk out of bed and crept down the back stairs, leaning around the corner into the main hall. The grandfather clock in the corner bonged once, quickly going back to its rhythmic ticking, but otherwise, the house was full of stillness and silence.

"Mom?" she called again, and when no one came running, she peeked out the back window into the alley.

Both of her parents' cars were gone.

Sighing heavily, she opened the back door, yanking it when it stuck. "What?"

A uniformed man stood in front of her and her gaze instinctively went to his chest. His rank, two black bars signifying he was a captain, stood out against the ghastly green and brown pattern of his uniform. She raised her stare to his face, but it was hidden in the shadow of his patrol cap. Evie crossed her arms over her stained t-shirt, its collar ripped out so it hung over only one shoulder.

He didn't say anything.

She lifted an eyebrow.

He mumbled. "I, uh, found your dog in the middle of the road."

Her gaze traveled down his arm to where he grasped a black Lab by the collar.

"Uh…"

"Someone almost hit him crossing toward the hospital. I didn't want him to get lost or hurt."

"Um, no, I—next door. This is 2711A." She pointed around the corner to the other half of the stately, historic duplex. "B's over there."

"Okay. Thanks. Sorry to disturb you."

"Yeah, no problem," she muttered as he turned away and she shoved the door shut. But it was a problem. Was it too late to go back to bed?

Groaning, she padded barefoot into the kitchen and eyed the clock on the microwave. One-oh-six blinked back.

Definitely too late to go back to bed. Eyes drooping and head pounding, Evie pulled down a single-serve cup from the cupboard and shoved it into her father's fancy coffee brewer. She dumped a liberal amount of both sugar and cream into the bottom of a soup bowl, slid it into place, and hit the start button.

At exactly the wrong moment.

"Are you just now coming downstairs?" her mother Laena asked as she pushed through the back door.

Evie resisted the urge to bang her head on the kitchen cabinet. Over the past few months, her ears had become finely turned to pick up the sound of her mother's car in the driveway. Most days, she could pick up the crunch of tires over old, cracked concrete and gravel. It gave her exactly forty-five seconds to make herself scarce. But the spurt of the coffee maker must have droned out the high-pitched hum of the car's hybrid engine and the scrunch of rubber on rock.

In answer to the question Evie grunted and grabbed the bowl, clutching it to her chest like a life preserver.

"I have groceries in the car." Laena set a paper bag down next to the sink.

"That's nice," Evie murmured as she shuffled unevenly out of the room, making her way to the TV and the sofa.

She sank down on the dark brown leather and pulled a fuzzy gray throw over her legs as she curled them up next to her. Using the remote left on the side table, she flipped on a rerun of an old sitcom.

"Damn it," she muttered as her mother fell into the chair a few feet away.

"There was a black car in the back when I came in. Who was that?" Laena asked, crossing her legs as she leaned back.

Evie grunted. "Oh. Yeah. The dog next door got out, again."

"Ah. No more details are needed. The black Lab is found wandering around the neighborhood more often than he can be found inside his own fenced yard. You'll never guess who I ran into at the commissary."

Evie had no desire to guess.

"Evan Griffith," Laena said.

Evie's ears pricked up at the name.

"The kid who dumped mustard on my head?"

She didn't have to see her mother's face to know she was rolling her eyes.

"Really, Evelyn, that was fifteen years ago. He's a lieutenant, now."

"Well, whoop-de-doo," Evie muttered and turned her attention back to the television. She'd seen the episode several times before, but it was far more interesting than anything Laena could tell her about her childhood nemesis.

"I invited him over for dinner."

Evie shot straight up, spilling coffee on the floor. "Why the hell would you do that?"

Laena quirked an eyebrow. "He's new to the area, he probably doesn't know anyone, and we've been friends with his parents since before we were married." She sighed heavily. "Come on, Evie, you were what? Eight? Nine?"

"Seven." She seethed.

"That was more than fifteen years ago." Laena shook her head and slapped her thighs with her palms then stood. "Time to get over it."

Evie rolled her eyes, but stood and turned toward her mother. "Does Dad know you're fraternizing with the junior officers?"

Laena continued toward the kitchen. "You should probably take a shower and put on something that doesn't look like you fished it out of the dirty laundry."

Evie scrunched up her face, but once she was sure her mother was unable to see her, she lifted her t-shirt up to her nose. It did smell a little stale. And there was a sizable coffee stain just above her right breast from splattering herself a few days ago. Sighing, she trudged toward the stairs, her slippers slapping on the polished hardwood floors.

Stairs still gave her some trouble. Her gait was still uneven. A year before, she would have been taking the steps two at a time. Now she had to grip the railing and lean against it as she dragged her bad leg up to meet her good one. The pain had subsided considerably; unless there was a storm rolling in. Or if it was particularly cold. Or she spent too much time on it.

Yet the skin grafts were mostly healed. Although if she stretched or turned wrong, they would pull. It was uncomfortable, but not debilitating. And her dark hair was finally growing back over the spot where it had been shaved. If she ran her fingers over her scalp, she could feel the slender ridge where doctors cut through the skin and drilled through her skull. Even the tracheotomy scar was fading.

She was lucky to be alive, they told her. A miracle. She shouldn't have lived.

Most days, she wished she hadn't.

The upstairs bathroom was nothing special, a remodel to the historic house that left it feeling like a new build. The fiberglass tub and faux-marble countertops were littered with her toiletries and a few her sister left there when she was visiting for spring break. The bar of green soap their brother brought with him was stuck to the tiles, dried out and cracking.

She turned on the hot water, avoiding the mirror over the sink. The reflection she knew she would see wasn't anything she had any desire to see. When she did catch sight of the whey-faced young woman in the glass, it only served to remind her that she wasn't herself. Not anymore. The surgeon had tried to duplicate her features, and to anyone who hadn't known her well before the accident, he succeeded. But she could see every slight perfection that was once an irregularity, symmetry where there had been none. She was a more perfect version of herself.

It was a slap in the face.

She climbed into the shower and stood under the spray until the water pinkened the healthy skin and puckered the scarred areas. Shampoo and razors were luxuries she hadn't taken advantage of in almost a week, and by the time she was done with both, she felt raw and bare.

Why was she even putting forth an effort? Evan had once been one of her favorite people. Her best friend. They had been inseparable in kindergarten, but then, when several families left and new ones moved in, families with other boys their age, she lost her friend.

She stepped out of the shower and toweled herself off. She'd tried everything to get them to allow her to play. She could be a ninja or a warrior or a soldier, too. But they would only let her play if she was the princess. Conceding, she agreed. She just wanted to play with her friend.

It wasn't Evan who came out with a plastic bottle of yellow mustard, but he was the one who uncapped it and spread it over her head. Because princesses needed golden hair and hers was only dark like a witch's.

The other boys laughed as it seeped into her eyes.

She could only cry.

No, she wasn't cleaning herself up for him. She was doing it to prove to her mother she could look put-together when she wanted to.

Evie reached into one of the drawers and extracted the makeup her sister left behind while she was at school. She turned the half-empty foundation over in her hand before uncapping and applying it. It almost felt strange to go over her old routine, to smooth shadow over her eyelids, to brush her long, thick lashes even longer and thicker with mascara.

The last time she put make up on her face, she was meeting Calum at Saint Rule's tower on a beautiful, summer day.

The old clock downstairs chimed six as Evie descended back downstairs, the echo of her father's boots on the hardwood floor coaxing her out of hiding. By the scents rising up the two-story foyer, it seemed dinner wouldn't be long, but she hadn't wanted to brave seeing Evan Griffith with only her mother around. Staying upstairs indefinitely had temporarily tempted her, but it would only have been a matter of time before Laena dragged her out of the converted guest room.

Colonel Jamie Blair hung his patrol cap over a hook on the tree stand before shrugging off his jacket. He could easily pass for a man ten years his junior, his hair still thick and full, though he had it cut once a week to keep it military-short.

She descended the last step as he turned toward her with a twinkle of mischief in his eyes. It was often accompanied by a crooked grin, and as he leaned in to give her a hug, it bloomed across his clean-shaved face.

He dropped a kiss to the top of her head. "How ya feelin', kiddo?"

She grunted and leaned into him, breathing in the starchy scent of his uniform. "Do you remember Evan Griffith?"

He quirked an eyebrow as she pulled away. "Of course I do. Dan and I have been friends for more than twenty-five years."

"Mom invited him to dinner."

"Dan? I thought he and Jen were in Hawaii."

"No, Evan, Dad."

"Evan is here? That's great." He paused and turned back to Evie with a frown. "He isn't under my command, is he?"

Evie shrugged. "How should I know?"

He patted her shoulder and strode for the kitchen, calling her mother's name as he went.

Evie made a bee-line for her spot on the sofa, lowering herself into the deep dent in the cushion just as the doorbell chimed. Cursing, she pushed herself back to her feet and limped to the front door.

She pulled it open.

She blinked, eyes widening. Evan wasn't at all like the tow-headed boy she remembered. He wasn't *that* much taller than she was, and she wasn't particularly short, not tall, either, but somewhere in the middle at five-six. He may have skimmed five-foot-eleven on a good day, maybe even made it to six feet when in his boots. He was nearly as broad in width as he was in length, his shoulders comically wide, his arms thick with over-large muscles. His scalp was shaved smooth.

He grinned and held up a bottle of yellow mustard.

Evie's eyes narrowed and her mouth pinched. She gripped the door handle to suppress the urge to slam it in his face. "Is it my turn?"

His smile faltered, but he held the bottle out to her with one hand and self-consciously rubbed the curve of his scalp with the other. "I suppose you could try, but there isn't much to work with."

The corner of her mouth twitched and she crossed her arms before stepping aside so he could enter. "You know, most people bring wine."

He chuckled and placed his hands on the waistband of his jeans. Her dad usually stood the same way, his thumbs usually tucked into his belt loops. Most officers did, rules strictly forbidding them from putting hands in the pockets of their uniforms.

The buttons of Evan's shirt pulled at the holes. It's a wonder they didn't pop off.

"I would have hated to make an inappropriate pairing."

Evie raised an eyebrow. "Oh, yes, well, yellow mustard is always a perfect match for every meal." She smiled, tight-lipped.

His face fell. "Oh, I… Look, I just wanted to tell you, you know, I'm, uh, sorry. For what happened when we were kids."

The apology was unexpected. How was she supposed to respond to it? She attempted a smile, but words failed her, and she turned abruptly for the kitchen.

She dropped the mustard on the counter as Laena pushed past her, arms wide as she welcomed Evan. He wrapped his gorilla-thick arms around Laena and placed a kiss on her cheek.

Laena pulled back first. "Jamie will be down in just a minute. Can I get you anything to drink? Beer? Cola? Sweet tea?"

"A beer would be great."

She grinned, the corners of her eyes creasing, and pointed at Evie. "How 'bout you take Evan out to the porch and I'll be right there with that beer."

Evie sighed heavily and led him through a side door to the screened-in porch. She motioned him to the wicker loveseat overlooking the parade field as she gracelessly flopped into one of the matching chairs. Overhead, antique fans churned the summer air, its heat heavy with humidity and the scent of freshly cut grass.

Evan clasped his hands together between his spread knees. "I, uh, I heard about your accident."

"Ah, yes, most people have." She sighed and waved her hand dismissively. "I'm sure it was the talk of holiday and New Year's receptions the world over."

He chuckled, an uncomfortable look crossing his face. "You, uh, you look good." He cleared his throat and ran a hand over his head.

"Yup. Not too hideously deformed. I guess I should thank my lucky stars for that."

He squirmed.

"Stop making our guest uncomfortable, Evelyn."

She glanced up at her father as the screen door clattered shut behind him.

His stern look gave way to a wide grin when Evan stood, hand outstretched. "How are ye, son?" He leaned forward, clapping his hand on Evan's shoulder.

Evie rolled her eyes as they moved to the usual military prattle. "What unit?" and "How are they treating you?" and "Are you a platoon leader, yet?" She could never escape it.

But she'd never really wanted to until, now. The military had always fascinated her, every battle, every tradition. She loved the social implications, the technology, the history.

She pushed away their conversation, unable to avoid the anger that bubbled up anytime the accident was brought up. It simmered just underneath the surface, ready to erupt. She clenched her teeth as tears burned the corners of her eyes. No one ever mentioned Calum. They didn't shed an ounce of sympathy for the man she lost or the future he would never have. The one she lost when she lost him.

To them, it was like he had never existed. She might as well have been in the car all by herself, and she suspected her mother preferred it that way.

Chapter Three

"I'm supposed to meet some buddies in Manhattan, if, uh, you want to, uh…" Evan trailed off.

For someone who seemed so confident in his outward appearance, the guy sure had a hard time stringing simple sentences together.

"Going to scam on college girls?" Evie quipped. She leaned back against the arm of her chair, her legs curled up on the seat.

He grinned sheepishly. "I am sure we can scrounge up some college boys for you."

She shot him a disgusted look.

"Or girls!" he held up his hands. "Whatever you want."

"I think it would be good for you to get out of the house," he father called through the open kitchen window.

She should have known they were eavesdropping. She started to protest, but he came through the door.

"Have you even left the house this week?"

Evie opened her mouth, but quickly snapped it shut, again. After some contemplation, she nodded. "I brought you lunch on Tuesday."

"You didn't even get out of the car."

"No, but I did have to walk through the rain to get to the car."

"It hasn't rained in two weeks."

"Fine, the heat and humidity, which is practically the same thing."

"How do you figure?"

"Both are extreme conditions."

Evan watched their exchange with bewilderment, his gaze bouncing back and forth between the two of them like those of a tennis spectator. "So, does that mean…?"

"She's going," Jamie answered before Evie could get a word in edgewise.

She pursed her lips. "And my father is picking up the tab."

Jamie crossed his arms over his chest and narrowed his eyes. "I'll pay for your cab home."

"Oh, I'm designated driver, sir." Evan held up a hand. "Low man on the totem pole and all that…" he trailed off.

Jamie's gaze didn't leave Evie's. "I'll give you a fifty."

"A hundred."

"Sixty."

"One ten."

"That's not how bartering works," Jamie said with wry amusement.

Evie shrugged. "I haven't been out in months. I'm in no rush."

"Seventy-five," Jamie sighed.

"Eighty and we have a deal."

The colonel nodded and reached into his back pocket for his wallet. He pulled out a couple of bills and handed them over. "I expect change."

Evie swiped the two fifties and shoved them into the pocket of her jeans. "Sure thing, Dad." She turned to Evan. "Ready?"

Evan nodded dumbly and stood. "Thank you for having me, Sir. Mrs. Blair," he added as Laena remerged from the kitchen.

"It was our pleasure, Evan. Please come back. *Any time.*" Laena hugged him, patting his back.

Evie rolled her eyes. "Let me get my purse," she muttered and disappeared into the house. She returned and walked out the screen door, leaving Evan to follow.

Outside, the deep-throated frog calls mingled with the whine of cicadas in the waning light. The sun had nearly set, turning the sky a vibrant, electric blue run through with shards of purple and pink. Evan led her down the street to a large, pristine pick-up truck sitting under a leafy oak. He pulled open the passenger side door, offering his hand so she could climb up. She hated to admit she even needed the assistance, but the step up was high and balance was no longer her star subject.

Anxiety climbed up her spine like an angry phantom as she pulled the seatbelt snugly around herself. Every time she strapped herself into a car, it gripped her, but the acceleration of her heartbeat was always quickest when she wasn't behind the wheel. Giving up control was a difficult task, even when it was to her own parents, but placing her life in the hands of someone she hadn't known in almost twenty years had her nails digging into the supple leather armrests.

"So, you told them you were bringing a date, didn't you?" she asked after as Evan maneuvered the truck away from the curb and down the tree-lined street.

He had the good sense to try to look like he had no idea what she was talking about. "What? No, I would never—"

"Save it." She waved. "What if I had been hideous? What if I had to drag my leg behind me like a horror movie villain? What if I *drooled*?"

He kept his gaze on the road, but blinked a few times. "Uh…"

She crossed her arms over her chest and sank a little further down into the seat. "You just mentioned my father's name, right?"

He turned bright red, the color growing up from his ears until it covered his perfectly smooth scalp. He almost looked like a red billiards ball.

"Look, I'm just the new guy." He shot a glance her way. "And you didn't even want to come in the first place. The col—your dad had to pay you to get you out of the house."

Evie smirked. "Yup."

"So, me asking you to come out benefited you quite a bit. You should be thanking *me*."

Oh. There was the muscle-guy confidence. It came complete with self-appreciative grin and painfully blinding teeth.

Evie sighed. "All right. What do you want?" She released the armrest to point a finger at him. "And don't you think for a second I have forgotten about your little mustard stunt."

"I thought that was behind us," he grumbled. "Just pretend like you don't completely hate me?"

"Now you're asking for the impossible." She sighed.

"Gotta start somewhere, I suppose."

She laughed and relaxed a little.

His was one of the only cars on the road, only a

few headlights running in the opposite direction, a pair of red brake lights glowing in the distance. The drive would have been nice if darkness hadn't snuffed out the rolling green hills. For someone who was so new to the area, Evan seemed to know exactly where he was going.

She shouldn't have been surprised; he was a single male in his early twenties living and working within twenty miles of a college town. It was like a moth to a flame. A paperclip to a magnet. Her mother to paperback romance novels. Every imaginable cliché rolled up into one.

He turned up the radio as they cruised into town and took a residential street toward the campus. The bar where they were meeting his coworkers was a block away from the football stadium in a little area filled with local restaurants, bars, coffee shops, and bakeries. Evan searched for a close parking spot, but had to park around the corner, the only available space near the bar being too small for the truck. He didn't think much of it until she joined him on the sidewalk, her limp more pronounced than usual due to being stuck in the same position in the car.

He stopped short as she joined him on the sidewalk, stiffness from the long ride making her limp more pronounced. "Oh, shit, I didn't even think, I'm sorry, do you want—"

She waved him off. "It's fine."

"Are you sure? I could carry you?"

She chuckled and lifted an eyebrow. "You want to carry me?"

"Well, if you need me to, I can."

She shook her head. What ridiculous offer. "I'm

fine. Really."

He shoved his hands in the pockets of his jeans and they continued in companionable silence down the sidewalk. As they approached an Irish-themed establishment, four leaf clover logo painted on the brick wall, Evan trotted ahead to pull the door open for her. Inside, the décor was exactly what she expected of a college town: billiards tables, dart boards, and a wall full of dollar bills. She followed Evan to a crowded table of short-haired men and a single female.

Evan introduced Evie around, but she could barely hear any of the names. She held her hand up in greeting and shook a few offered her way. Only one avoided looking at her, his head bent over a beer, one hand cupping the sweaty sides.

She pulled out empty chair next to him.

His gaze shifted beneath hooded brows to take her in as she looked up at Evan. "I'll take whatever beer's on tap."

She lifted an eyebrow when the stranger continued to eye her around his long, straight nose.

"I'm Evie," she half-yelled at him over the noise. "Sorry, I didn't catch your name."

His gaze shifted again, a muscle in his jaw ticking. "Iain."

"Do you work with Evan?" she asked. She hated sitting back and feeling uncomfortable. She would rather *talk* and feel uncomfortable.

"In a manner of speaking."

"Oh. Well… what do you do?"

He stared at her for a beat too long, his brows pulled low over his eyes. "I'm a scout."

"Oh." She chewed on her lip. "I have no idea what

that means."

He shrugged and turned away, giving her the back of his head.

"Okay," she mouthed and huffed out a breath.

Swiveling in the chair, she scanned the bar for Evan. He leaned against the bar, his head bent toward a girl with a long, sweeping curtain of black hair. The other woman matched him in height and regarded him through heavily-made up lashes. A short dress hung from her mostly exposed shoulders, the silhouette just shy of elegant.

She had once been that girl.

Evie sighed and looked down at her soft jeans and simple blue shirt. Not anymore. Not with her scars.

She turned back to face her momentary companion then dropped her chin into her palm. "Well, I guess I can give up the expectation that the beer would be cold," she muttered as she reached for the drink menu.

"I take it that means you aren't really his date." Iain canted his head in her direction.

"Is that what he told you?" she asked slyly.

"He intimated as much," he said with a shrug.

"Yeah, well… No. I am here giving him the moral support only a friend can give." She fluttered her eyelashes in his direction, but couldn't even muster a bland upturn of the lips.

She shouldn't have agreed to this, even if it did make her a wad of cash she really didn't need.

"And you? What is it you do?" Iain yelled over the loud humming conversation around them.

She waved her hand off-handedly. "Oh, you know, just the proverbial leech on society."

His expression didn't change, but he watched her,

waiting for her to explain.

Evie sighed, propping her elbow on the table and dropping her chin into it. "I'm sort of taking a break from life right now."

"Taking a break from life? That doesn't sound like a thing."

She grimaced. "I was in an accident last year. I'm living with my parents while I recover and, you know, figure out what the hell I am supposed to do next." She let her empty hand drop and it smacked onto the smooth surface of the table.

"I would imagine you just pick up where you left off."

"Mm, not that easy." She looked back over toward Evan, wondering if he would ever bring a beer. He was still enthralled by the black-haired girl and her long, slender limbs.

"Oh? And why not?" He turned in the direction of the eager young lieutenant and smirked before returning his gaze to Evie.

How much did she really want to tell him? On the one hand, she hated talking about it. Hated remembering it. But on the other, it was one of the rare opportunities for her to tell her own story to someone who hadn't already received the highlights from her mother.

"I was engaged," she finally answered. "He was driving and… didn't make it."

How did she sound so collected? How was her voice so even and emotionless? She still felt like she was being pulled apart on the inside, the pain no different than it had been the moment she learned she would never see Calum, again. She hadn't talked about it. With anyone. Not her mother, not her father, not the therapist she now refused to go to, the loss of Calum was something she kept locked inside.

It was a pain she felt she was owed for being the one to live. And she kept her punishment to herself. Not that anyone had really tried to get her to open up about the good ole days, anyway. It felt oddly liberating to have told someone—anyone—about her engagement and subsequent loss.

"I'm still trying to figure out if I should strike out and do something completely new, go back to plan A, or just give up, entirely." She let out a shaky breath.

"Giving up sounds like a cop-out." There was a bite to his tone. A challenge.

"Oh, really? I take it you've lost a lot of fiancées in your time?" She scoffed.

He didn't look at her. Instead, he kept his gaze on the glass in front of him, his fingertips running over the condensation, his thumbs wiping at it absently.

Evie wasn't sure he would ever answer her when he turned his attention back, his eyes steely.

"I just see a fire in you. It would be a shame if you snuffed that out."

"You see that, huh? After five minutes?"

"Some people just make it obvious." He took a sip of his drink, gaze moving back to an invisible spot on the wall behind the bar.

Or perhaps it was the model-thin beauty who was wrapping her arm around Evan's neck.

"What was Plan A?" he asked after a moment.

She shrugged. "Grad school. I was going to finish my PhD, sit in a dusty office, and read all day." She couldn't help the small smile that pulled at the corners of her lips.

"So why not do that?"

"It would just be hard to go back there."

"It might not be as hard as you think."

She lifted an eyebrow. "You're awfully philosophical for a scout."

But he only regarded her with an amused twist of the lips.

****

She couldn't shake what Evan's coworker had said.

Evan disappeared from the bar sometime around midnight. He never made it back from the bar with her beer, instead standing with his head bent close to the leggy beauty.

Around midnight, she finally broke away from his group of co-workers to look for him, but he was nowhere in sight. So much for being the designated driver.

She had to call a cab, anyway.

The night out had done her good. She almost felt like the Evie she was before the accident. The Evie who went out for drinks at the local pubs. The one who planned day trips to Edinburgh or nights doing club crawls. The one who agreed to go to Monaco with her flat mate last minute. The Evie who smiled and laughed and played. The Evie who didn't watch daytime television and hid in her room.

She leaned her head against the window in the cab's backseat, gaze fixed on the stars hanging in the sky. They were fairly bright in the middle-of-no-where, Kansas, but not as bright as they were at the end of the pier in St Andrews.

They'd sat at on the edge of the stone, staring up at

them the night Calum kissed her the first time. It had been cold, but the sky had been clear as the waves lapped below their dangling feet. They left the Chinese restaurant for a stroll down the old streets, talking about, well, everything. Her irrational fear of volcanoes, his obsession with orange chocolate. Her newfound love affair with Scottish war history, how he had grown up in St Andrews, the only child of a single mother. And then she was teasing him about the way he dropped half of his consonants, and he was kissing her.

They were interrupted when her mobile phone went off, singing out into the near silence of lapping water and calling seagulls. Calum gave her a quizzical look and made fun of her taste in music as she had answered the phone to her incredibly drunk flat mate.

The corners of Evie's lips lifted at the memory, and then regret flooded over her, cold and heavy. She hadn't talked to Sarah since she left Scotland. Sarah was always calling and emailing, but Evie found it difficult to reciprocate. What was she supposed to say? "Glad you're doing well, my life is shit?" She wondered if she had let it go for too long, if she could contact Sarah and not have it be weird.

Before she could regret it, she dug her phone out of her pocket and pulled up her email. A few taps of the screen, and "I miss you," buzzed through the airwaves to the other side of the world. She didn't expect an answer, but… Maybe she would get one.

The cab dropped her off in front of her parents' house, the front porch light still glowing. She expected they went to bed hours before, but when she let herself in, it was to find her father sitting in the living room, a book open, his glasses perched on his nose. He didn't wear them often, only for reading, watching television and at the movies. Jamie took the wire rims off, folding them up and setting them on the side table when he saw her. He shut the book, but didn't stand up.

"Have fun?" he asked.

She gave a little shrug of one shoulder, but her lips crept up at the corners.

"Where's my change?" He grinned.

She made no move to pull out the change stuffed in her back pocket. "Can I borrow your car, tomorrow?"

"Sure, kiddo. What's up?"

"Nothing, I'd just like to get out, I think."

"You got it." He rose and pressed a kiss to her forehead. "I'm proud of you, Kiddo. See you in the morning."

"Night, Dad."

Chapter Four

Fort Riley was smack dab in the middle of a wasteland. A major state university and an Army base should have warranted more in the way of shopping chains, regional stores, or even cute local shops. But the prairieland between Topeka and Salina was only dotted with farmland and the basic necessities.

How did people survive it?

Evie had seen a lot of the world, *lived* in a lot of the world, but she couldn't remember chain stores being so under-represented at any of the other major bases. Sure, Fort Lewis in Washington had sorely lacked any sort of popular chain restaurant options; Fort Lee in Virginia had been in the center of it all, though just a few too many miles away; their time in Germany had been full of travel, so if anything was missing, she had never had time to notice. Living in St Andrews, she became accustomed to having everything she needed, just on the miniature. But the same could not be said of Junction City and Manhattan.

For awhile, she just drove aimlessly, looking for anything that caught her eye. Gun shops and faith-based furniture stores were not it.

But when she came to a little bookstore not far from where Evan took her the night before, she felt the first prickles of interest. It was just off the main footpaths of the university's campus, perhaps only a block, if she remembered correctly.

She found a parking spot and strolled in its direction, her step light, her limp almost undetectable. Rolling bookcases were pulled out onto the sidewalk, reminding her of the Saturday morning sales in St Andrews, the booksellers hawking their wares in the middle of Market Street.

Evie pushed inside, the familiar scent of old books enveloping her. Ah, yes. She could get lost in here.

Most of the books were used, but she didn't care. She hadn't read anything since the accident. She was always a voracious reader, her tastes spanning across all genres. She was suddenly overcome with the desire to own as many of these books as she could carry. The remainder of the money her father had given her was suddenly burning a hole in her pocket, and she was drawn to the shelves like a crow to a discarded picnic lunch.

In no time, she cradled a stack against her chest, a mystery, a young adult novel, a fantasy novel several of her friends had been raving about a few years ago. She found a particularly steamy romance that had her intrigued, but nearly nude bodies were splashed across the cover. She tucked it between the mystery and the fantasy, hoping no one would see she wasn't above purchasing smut. She was just about to head to the counter when a name caught her eye.

Sylvia Bascomb-Murray.

Dr. Bascomb-Murray was her mentor. Evie spent months as her graduate assistant. She made the historian's copies, highlighted her notes. She organized bibliographies and pulled books from the library. And Dr. Bascomb-Murray was the one to give Evie the long weekend that destroyed her life.

Evie swallowed and reached for the book. "*Women of Culloden: Taking Up The Tartan*," she whispered.

It was published a few months before she took the research assistantship, and this particular copy looked like it had been read through a few times. She had meant to read it, but she was too busy helping with the follow-up research to find the time.

She ran the pad of her thumb over the slick cover of the paperback, brushing over images of the Carlisle tartan and crest: lavender and blue with threads of white, tree and crown, and motto "Eternal."

The book hit each of her interests: feminism, war, Scotland. Her obsessions. Not the Carlisles, per se, but the Scottish resistance. It's why she applied to work with Sylvia Bascomb-Murray. Why she had applied to St Andrews. She became fascinated by the subject as an undergraduate after taking a course on Britain before the 1830s. Was there anymore more romantic than taking on the most powerful Army in the world? And a full generation before the American Revolution? Their determination was so strong to self-govern they clashed against the English muskets with swords and knives and pitchforks.

The book brought back the memory and excitement of having an idea or hypothesis no one else had ever published. It reminded her of the smell of the library and the white gloves used in the rare books section. A tingle ran up her spine as she imagined the paintings of Highlanders and the feel of the magic in the mountains and lochs of Scotland.

Maybe she should go back.

Her pulse accelerated, and the tickle of anticipation

dripped into her stomach until a knot formed. She wasn't ready for that, yet. Maybe she should just read the book.

She added it to her pile and turned, barreling right into someone.

The books fell to the floor, one of them landing squarely on her foot. She sucked in her breath, and then knelt to pick up her requisitions, but quickly drew her hand back when her fingers brushed against another's.

"Sorry," she muttered, and then lifted her face to see him—because, *of course,* she had run into him—looking quizzically at her.

She was instantly drawn to him, as if some invisible thread connecting them pulled taut. As if she was destined to be there at exactly that moment. Time stood still with the beating of her heart, and when they caught up, she felt shy, tongue-tied. She'd never felt shy and tongue-tied, before. At least not like this.

He stared at her with pewter gray eyes and something akin to shock. His eyes were wide and his lips parted before they turned up in a ghost of a smile. Did he feel it too, that tug? No, she was being ridiculous.

"My apologies," he murmured, books outstretched.

She could only gape at his mouth. Soft, almost feminine, pouty. It seemed misplaced on his rectangular face and firmly set square chin.

When she didn't respond he canted his head to the side. "Do I know you?"

Blushing, she shook herself out of her silent reverie, and took the books from him, their fingers brushing. Again, a spark of awareness raced through her and she realized the smutty romance novel was on top, the half-naked hero and heroine glistening in sweat at they clung to one another.

Heat flooded her face as her eyes grew wide. "I-me, too. I mean. Um. No. Thank you."

She stood, but a twinge of pain pulled at her thigh, and she reached out a hand, grasping his forearm, to keep from falling. His hand wrapped around her elbow, steadying her, and she stammered her thanks, again, even more embarrassed than she had been for not only running into him, but staring at his mouth. Her gaze caught his and she couldn't look away.

"Are you okay?" He looked concerned, his eyebrows pulling together.

She readjusted the books in her arms and gave a weird little head-shake-shrug. "Just a, just a bad leg.," She tried to smile and roll her eyes, but probably just looked like she had some sort of tick.

"Here, I can get those." He held out one hand. In the other, he cradled the Bascomb-Murray research.

"No, really, I'm fine. But thank you." She cleared her throat and cut her gaze away only for him to draw it right back. Why did he have to be so tall? He had nearly a full foot on her, and she was five-and-a-half feet in her bare feet. And why did he have to smell so good? Like toasted wood and spices.

He smiled again, the corners of his eyes crinkling, and warmth reflecting in his eyes. It wrapped around her insides until her pulse fluttered, and her skin tingled.

She was staring. Again. *Shit.*

Evie focused on the book he carried and held her hand out for it. Confusion briefly crossed his features, and he followed her gaze. "Oh, this is yours." He offered it over, cover facing up. "It's not bad. Interesting hypotheses."

She added it to the pile, quickly covering the romance, and pressed it into her chest. Hopefully, he didn't notice.

"You've read it?"

He shrugged, a non-answer.

"I was her graduate assistant," she said.

"Really?" His eyebrows shot up.

She nodded slowly. "Yeah. It was after this, though. I just never got the time to read it. I mean, I know what she was working on, but it was already in publication when I came along, and so what I helped with was… different."

His head canted to the side. "You're an historian, then?"

She shook her head. "I was going to be, but…"

She didn't want to tell this stranger her problems. There was clearly such a thing as oversharing, and she'd already crossed that line. She wished she could sink right through the floor and disappear.

Yet, he held out his hand. "Alec."

She leaned back to take the burden of the books into one arm and held out the other. He grasped it, his long fingers curling over her, his palm warm.

"I'm Evelyn. Well, Evie."

"You don't often hear that pronunciation," he mused as she let her hand fall. It was true; Eve-lin was not nearly as popular as Ev-ellen.

"Oh, yes. I know. Weird parents and all that." She rolled her eyes and grimaced around a blush.

He grinned. "I couldn't buy you a coffee, could I?"

Her shocked expression had him immediately

backtracking. "Sometime. Whenever," he added.

"S-sure." She forced herself to breathe.

The left corner of his mouth lifted in a half-smirk. "Are you free now?" he asked shyly.

She tried to wrack her brain for anything she could be doing, but all she could think of was the curve of his lips, the dimple in his cheek, his broad shoulders, and the way his t-shirt pulled across his chest. She just nodded dumbly.

"Let me just…" She motioned to the cash register manned by a spectacled college student.

"Of course."

She scurried to the counter, glad her back was to Alec so he couldn't see the besotted grin spreading across her face. Most of the leftover cash went to the books. The clerk carefully lifted them into a paper bag with the store's logo rubber stamped on its side before passing her the change. She shoved the wad of paper and coins into the pocket of her cropped jeans and moved to the side for Alec. He paid for a small, black book using a credit card, slashing his signature across the bottom of the receipt with a wiggle of his fingers.

He turned down a bag, instead tucking his copy of the receipt between the pages. He joined her by the door, pushing it open so she could walk through ahead of him.

"There's a coffee shop down the street on the next block." He pointed with his book. "Are you okay to get there?"

Ah. He had seen the limp. "Oh, yeah, I'm fine. Just an old battle wound."

He frowned. "Were you…"

She quirked an eyebrow as they started down the

street next to each other. "In the service? No. In fact, hell no," she grinned up at him. "Car accident."

"I'm sorry to hear that," he murmured.

"What about you?" she asked quickly, wanting nothing more than to change the subject.

"No major accidents recently."

She grinned. "I meant are you in the service?"

She really didn't need to ask, she could already tell. His hair was short and well groomed. His face clean shaven, even on a Saturday. The metal dog tag chain hovered just above the collar of his red t-shirt. It was in the way he stood and the way he walked. She suspected it was in the way he talked, but their conversation had been somewhat limited, so far.

"How did you know?"

Evie grinned at his sarcasm. "Well, it was either that or well-paid student, and those are like giraffe-spotted unicorns. Or were-pigs."

Were-pigs, he mouthed, followed by a soundless chuckle. "Are you working at the university, then?" he asked.

They came to a standstill at the street corner and waited for the lights to change and walk signal flash.

"What?" The idea seemed ridiculous. "Oh, no. I'm just sort of… in holding, I suppose."

He gave her a questioning look.

For the first time in a year, she *wanted* to answer. Avoiding it became second nature, but perhaps opening up about it the night before had cured her reluctance. Or perhaps something about him made her want to open up. To tell him everything.

And then strip him naked and have her way with him.

35

"I'm staying with my parents. The accident left me… in need of a lot of help." She sucked her lips between her teeth and bit down on them. "I was working on my PhD overseas, you know, with Dr. Bascomb-Murray who wrote the book? And had no one nearby who could really be at my beck and call while arms and legs and face were in casts."

"Face? Really?"

She nodded. "Yup. My whole face was screwed up. What you see now is a masterpiece created by one surgeon Cho of Edinburg and contains little to no resemblance to my former genetic self."

"Now that I find hard to believe." He came to a stop outside a glass door and smiled down at her.

Her insides turned to liquid.

She pulled her gaze away and stepped inside, falling into line next to the case of pastries. The scent of hot coffee and warm sandwiches wafted through the air, filling the space their conversation had briefly occupied.

She focused on the menu board to distract from the uncomfortable silence and gnawed on her lower lip. From the corner of her eye, she caught sight of at least three other young women glancing his way.

Evie fidgeted, dropping her gaze down to her canvas shoes. Wondered if their first thought was "why is he with her?" She was without make-up, her hair pulled back in a limp ponytail. Her shirt hung loose from her shoulders and did nothing for her unremarkable body.

Why *did* he ask her for coffee?

"Evelyn?"

Damn, his voice was like a caress.

"Hmm?"

"What would you like?"

She turned her attention back to the college student standing behind the counter.

"Oh, sorry! Lost in thought. Or something. Just a medium of your Hawaiian blend, please?"

Alec ordered the same, and they both received black cups with the shop's logo on it in white. She turned to the little counter holding various milk products and sugars, doctoring the brew up until it was light and sweet, then joined him at the little table he found next to the window. His long legs curled under his chair, his forearms leaning against the edge of the table, one hand wrapped around the cup of coffee, the book resting under his wrist.

She scooted her chair closer and placed her bag and purse at her feet, squeezing her knees together nervously. "I have to admit, I'm kind of surprised you, you know…" she indicated the shop with her hands. "This."

He raised an eyebrow. "You mean 'asked you out?'"

She frowned. "Yes."

He looked amused. "Why?"

She shrugged. "Well, you know, I look and pretty much feel like I haven't seen the light of day in about six months—which, I might add, is exactly the truth—and I can barely form a coherent sentence. That and on the way over here, I admitted I live with my parents. Why you didn't suddenly have a work emergency I will never know."

The corner of his mouth twitched upward. "Your eclectic taste in books fascinates me," he murmured, his chin dipped down and his gaze turned up to hers. "And I see nothing wrong with you living with your parents."

"You don't know them," she grumbled. "So, my taste in reading material. Is it the fantasy or the mystery?"

"The history and the romance."

"Oh, you saw that." She wrinkled her nose and sank down in the chair.

"Why is it such a terrible thing?" He chuckled.

She waved her hand in the air, refusing to look at him. "You know… it's just embarrassing."

"I don't see how. It shows you're a dreamer. That you are optimistic and adventurous and open-minded."

She narrowed her eyes and turned her gaze back to him. "You get all of that from a book jacket with two mostly-naked adults on it?"

He grinned. "Am I right?"

She shrugged. "Probably not. I am definitely not an optimist, I think I have had my fair share of adventure, and I have completely given up on dreams."

"Ah, but you are open-minded."

When she offered him nothing more than a wan smile, he sat back and took a sip of his coffee. "The accident?" he asked seriously.

"I'm not sure it's really 'first date' material." She then caught herself calling getting coffee a date. "I mean—"

The dimple winked.

"Fine, fine," She sighed. "Short story. My fiancé and I were going on holiday—vacation," she amended. "Calum was yielding at a roundabout when we were hit from behind by a driver who never applied his brakes. We slammed into a lorry."

She tucked a flyaway behind her ear. It sounded so impersonal. Like her whole world hadn't been destroyed. Like it just… was. "The car burst into flames. They were able to get me out but couldn't get to Calum. I was in a coma for a couple of months. They didn't expect me to ever wake up, but, what do you know, Halloween came along and there I was. It had a way of changing my plans. And my outlook on life." She shrugged and pushed away her cup with an unsteady hand.

He gazed at her as if he knew exactly what she meant, exactly how it felt. Others always looked at her with pity, their brows wrinkled, eyes wide as they asked her how she was doing. Or the way her parents tried to conceal a mix of worry and relief. Did they think she would break if she saw it?

But not Alec.

She shifted in her chair and cleared her throat. "So, yeah. My favorite color is purple, I don't like beets, I could eat a trough of popcorn in one sitting, and I think spring is a waste of a season."

The heaviness hovering between them instantly lifted, and he chuckled. "Well, in that case, I have always been partial to blue, beets are delicious, I agree with your stance on popcorn, and give me spring over summer any year."

She grinned, glad they weren't going to pick apart her past. "I would have been persuaded to agree with you about summer, but have you ever spent one in Scotland? It will make you change your mind in a heartbeat."

"Will it now?" he drawled as he lifted the cup back to his lips.

"It's beautiful. I didn't get to spend as much time seeing the countryside as I would have liked, but everything is so green and there is something about the sky that makes it feel like it goes on forever. Scotland doesn't get hot like here, which is part of the appeal, but it gets warm enough. You can lie on the sands and wade into the sea and have picnics on the beach."

"It sounds like you loved it."

She nodded. "Yes. I never would have come back if it weren't for… that."

"Did you grow up here?"

"Ha! No, I grew up all over the place."

"Army brat, then?"

"Absolutely," she said proudly. "I was born in Virginia, but have lived in Washington, Georgia, Germany, Hawaii, Tennessee, New York, Georgia—again—and now here."

"Georgia twice?"

"Yeah. I graduated high school there and then did my undergraduate degree in Atlanta."

He relaxed, falling back against the chair. His face softened. "You're the girl at the door."

She blinked. "Excuse me, what?"

"Yesterday. I almost ran over a dog and I thought it was yours. I came up to the door with the dog. Your house had a college flag flying. That was you, wasn't it?"

Her jaw dropped, but no words came out. She'd been so annoyed at having been dragged from bed; she hadn't paid much attention to the captain on her parents' back doorstep. "No. No, absolutely not. You're thinking of someone else." She shook her head vigorously.

His face split into a grin. "It *was* you."

"You woke me up," she grumbled.

His brows shot up. "It was lunch time."

"I was taking a very important nap."

He chuckled. .

She screwed her mouth to the side. "You know quite a bit about me now, but I know nothing about you. Other than you can't properly read the address on a dog collar.""

He shook his head. "What would you like to know?"

"Well, what do you do, for starters?"

"I'm in the Army."

She rolled her eyes. "So you—"

The vibrations of her phone cut her off. Evie pulled it out of her purse to hit ignore, but saw it was her mother and she had already missed two calls. "Sorry," she muttered. "Do you mind if I get it?"

"Not at all."

"Hello?" she answered as she pressed the screen up to her face.

"Where are you? I told you I needed the car back by—"

Oh, shit. Evie looked down at her watch and saw she was twenty minutes late getting back to her parents', and she still had a thirty minute drive ahead of her.

"I'm on my way." She hit the end-call button before Laena could pile on any more guilt. She stood up then, bent down to retrieve her purse and the bag from the bookstore. "I'm really sorry, I have to go."

He stood, too, the legs of his chair scraping against the fake wood tiles. "Could I have your number?"

She nodded, hiding her pleasure by digging the key fob out of the bottom of her purse. "Of course." She rattled it off and then fled the coffee shop, calling "thanks for the coffee!" over her shoulder.

His dimple appeared as he smiled, raising his hand in farewell.

Lip caught between her teeth and a blush creeping over her cheeks, Evie pushed outside. Could he have been any more perfect?

She released the door as she rushed away and fell down the only step. She yelped, her repaired leg twinging in pain, and tumbled onto the concrete. Her bag tumbled a foot away as she braced herself, her palms scraping across the rough surface.

It had been months since she last fell. How did she manage to end up on the ground twice in one hour?

"You okay?" someone asked from a few feet away.

"Yeah. Mostly just embarrassed." She rubbed at her leg before looking up. "Oh. Hi."

A familiar face from the night before stared down at her. "Iain, right?

His lips pinched together tightly, and he held out both arms to help her up.

"Thanks," she said as she looped her fingers around her bag's handle. "I'm sorry. I feel so stupid."

"It happens. You're okay, though?"

She nodded again. "Yeah. Yes. Thank you."

"Evie?"

She turned as Alec pushed out of the coffee shop. "Are you all right?"

Blood rushed to her face. "You mean more than one person saw that?"

He chuckled, but then his attention moved to Iain

and his face became stony.

"Oh, sorry. Um, Iain, this is my coffee date, Alec. Alec, this is Iain. We met last night at a bar… Wow, that sounds bad," she said more to herself than either of them.

But they ignored her, instead staring each other down. Alec broke his gaze away first and nodded to her in acknowledgement.

"Um, well…" She brushed her burning palms down the thighs of her jeans. "I need to go. But, um, thank you for the coffee, Alec." She smiled up at him. "And thanks for picking me off the ground, Iain."

Brushing past a trio of crows pecking the sidewalk for crumbs, Evie left the pair behind.

Chapter Five

"I think I am going back to school in September."

Laena stopped abruptly and whirled around with an excited gasp.

Evie nearly ran her over with the grocery cart. She swerved, barely managing to control the heavy metal before it clanged into one of the dairy cases.

"That's wonderful. I'm sure Kansas State's program will be lucky to have you—"

Evie let out an exasperated sigh and leaned her forearms on the blue plastic handle of the cart. "No, Mom. I am going back to St Andrews."

Displeasure pulled Laena's lips into a tight, straight line. "Don't be ridiculous, Evelyn." She turned her attention to the display of yogurt and chose an armful of Evie's favorite, a German import topped with lemon custard.

"Why is that ridiculous?" Evie demanded.

"It's on the other side of the world. You won't have anyone to take care of you." She dropped the yogurt into the basket. "And you should never have gone in the first place."

"First of all," Evie began, straightening from her slouch. "I am an adult. I don't need your permission. I was just informing you of my plans. And I am perfectly capable of taking care of myself," she added, under her breath.

Ready to launch into a tirade, Laena turned, lips pursed, the lines deepening around her mouth with age more pronounced. She opened her mouth but stopped short. She adjusted her purse on her shoulder and turned back to the dairy case. "We'll discuss this later."

"Why? There isn't anything to discuss." *Is this really happening?*

"We'll wait until your father gets home."

"Oh, for fuck's sake," Evie threw up her hands and turned on her heel.

Finishing her degree had been on her mind since her coffee date with Alec, but she came to the decision to return earlier that morning. Evan called to invite her out, again. He apologized for disappearing and promised to make it up to her. She did her best to sound reluctant, but truthfully, getting out of the house became her goal each day.

She hung up with him and realized she needed to do more than go drinking once a week and buy a few used books.

A scowl on her face, Evie stalked down the coffee aisle toward the chocolate. Alec never called her, either. And though she kept her phone on her person at all times for a couple of days, by the third Evie gave up hope of ever seeing him again. Clearly she should have been more conservative in what she shared with strangers. telling a date all about her dead fiancé and the car crash that ruined her life was obviously not the way to go twenty minutes after meeting.

When the disappointment of not hearing from him wore off, there was a thick layer of guilt underneath. It kept her awake at night, and then in bed when the sun rose; more time spent remembering Calum. More time wishing he was still with her. She was ashamed at how eagerly she pushed him from her thoughts, how quickly a handsome face could displace his memory.

She stopped and stared at the shelves of candy. But, she could admit the hour she had spent in his company had done wonders for her outlook on life, it was like talking about it, even just glossing over the details with someone who wasn't being paid to listen, had rekindled her will to *live* rather than just exist.

She was making the right decision in going back to Scotland. A reply from Sarah the night before confirmed that. Her former roommate acted as if it had only been a week, not months, since their last correspondence, and she demanded to know when Evie would be back. Going back felt good.

It felt like living.

Half-heartedly, she grabbed a bag of milk chocolate caramels and turned toward the check-out line. What was her mother's problem? They had always gotten along well, and Laena had always given Evie the space she needed to make her own decisions. She was supportive. Proud.

It wasn't until Evie announced she was going overseas for her graduate degree that her mother's attitude changed. And it had gotten even worse since Evie came to stay with her parents. Laena seemed to have no desire to get Evie out of the house. In fact, it felt like her mother wanted to keep her there for the rest of her life, for her to never have a life outside of her mother's home. Hell, it wasn't even a house she had grown up in!

Evie still seethed as she turned the corner of the aisle, and tripped over a yellow *Caution, wet surface* signs propped over the glistening surface. Her heel slid in something slick, and she fell helplessly through the air, head connecting with floor, bouncing twice.

And then there was darkness.

****

Evie opened her eyes as the glass door slid open. The harsh fluorescent light in the emergency room poured into her cubby hole, and she squinted as pain wrapped around her skull. The ache from the back of her head radiated around her jaw and settled in her teeth. Pulling the blinds shut and closing her eyes had helped, but both were quickly forgotten when her gaze made contact with the intruder.

Standing at the end of her bed in crisp Army uniform jacket and pants, stethoscope draped around his neck, was Alec.

"You never called me." She blurted the accusation before she even realized the words tumbled out of her mouth.

A look of surprise crossed his face and she could have laughed as his jaw dropped, but a stab of pain kept her in check.

He recovered quickly, blinking away the initial shock of seeing her spread out over the white hospital sheets. "Oh, I tried. But I was unable to complete my call because I needed the correct country code."

Correct country code? Evie frowned until she realized what she had done. "Oh, shit. I'm sorry. I must have given you my old mobile number." She'd never given the new one to anyone before. In fact, now that she thought about it, she wasn't even sure she knew what it was.

His expression remained skeptical. "You know,

you don't have to say that. It's really fine if you don't want to see me, again." He looked around the small room. "Well, after this."

She gave an apologetic shrug, but inside her heart leapt around her chest, flopping around in an entirely inappropriate happy dance. "No, I've been waiting. Well, I was waiting. Not too long. Too long would be pathetic." Why was she rambling? "It was a non-pathetic amount of waiting. I promise."

His right eyebrow shot up and the corners of his mouth twitched. He turned abruptly to the computer monitor mounted to the wall and signed into the system.

She swallowed, suddenly self-conscious. "*You* weren't just saying that, were you? Just to be nice because you really didn't want to call *me*? You were just being polite, weren't you?"

He shook his head and his shoulders bounced in laughter. When he swiveled to her, he was grinning. He crossed his arms over his chest and leaned back against the wall. "I promise. I tried to call."

She slumped into the foamy hospital pillow. "Oh. That's good."

The screen changed on the computer and his attention flicked back to it, reading over what she figured must have been her triage reports.

She shifted in the uncomfortable silence. "You didn't tell me you were a doctor. Actually, come to think of it, I don't think you told me much of anything about yourself."

"You did cut our coffee date a little short." He kept his eyes trained on the report.

"Mm, yeah, sorry about that. I had my dad's car, but he needed it for some work thing. My mom wanted me back with it because she had a very important appointment to keep with the movie theater."

He looked up. "Movie theater?"

She nodded, then winced and wished she hadn't. "Yup. She had a hot date with a bag of popcorn and a diet soda." And her favorite actor, but there was no reason to tell him that, even if Evie did find the whole thing ridiculous.

They grinned at each other and her heart fluttered. She broke her gaze away. She didn't want him to catch her staring at his mouth or see the red heat rising to her cheeks.

"Well, tell me what happened."

"I got home, she took the keys, and that was that. She didn't even ask if I wanted to come." Evie wrinkled her nose. "Maybe I wanted to watch the smut, too," she muttered to herself.

Alec chuckled. "No, I meant how you got here. What happened?"

"Oh!" she smacked herself in the forehead, but then wished she hadn't. The pain reverberated off the backs of her eyes and she sucked in a breath.

"Sorry. I, uh, I slipped in the commissary. I ran right over the stupid sign they placed over a wet spot to warn idiots like me, and, you know, feet in the air, head on the concrete." She clapped her hands together. "Pow."

"And did you lose consciousness?"

Ah. She deflated. It was all business, now.

"Yes."

He made a sort of humming noise in the back of his throat, and then straightened. "Protocol is to order a head CT, and considering your history, that's exactly what we're going to do. I'll order it, and then someone will be in to wheel you to radiology in a few minutes. Anything else bothering you?"

She smirked. "Just my pride."

His lips tightened, but they jerked upward, and he reached for the door, sliding it open and disappearing down the corridor. Evie suddenly felt a little abandoned.

She didn't know how long she waited for someone to come retrieve her for the head scan, but it didn't seem like much time at all. She only had a few moments to replay the last five minutes in her head, mentally wincing at her own awkwardness.

A stout woman pushed the sliding door all the way open, smiling politely and announcing she would be the one taking Evie to radiology. She spun a wheelchair into the small space, and then held out her hands to help Evie sit down, adjusting the footrests as soon as Evie was situated.

Evie clasped her temples between her hands. Sitting up caused a near-vomit-inducing spinning to join the ache squeezing her battered skull.

The scans were over quickly, and they were done in a dim room, which she appreciated more than she could express. As she was wheeled back into her little slice of the emergency room, she regretted the whole thing hadn't taken longer because, sitting in the chair next to the bed, was her mother.

"I thought you were going home." Evie's eyes narrowed.

"Only to put away the groceries." Laena folded her book shut and uncrossed her legs. "You were brought here in an ambulance. You *really* thought I would just go home, watch a soap opera, and wait for you to call for a ride?"

"Well, I would never accuse you of watching soap operas, but *yeah*," Evie answered. "I'm fine. There is no reason for you to be here. I could probably walk back. It's only what? A mile?"

"Really, Evelyn, this is ridiculous even for you."

"And what's that supposed to mean?" Evie demanded.

"It means you're acting ridiculous."

Evie leaned her head back on the pillow and groaned. This really couldn't be happening.

As if on cue—because, obviously her life was some sort of sick comedy—Alec came back through the door, stopping short when he caught sight of Laena. He blinked a couple of times before offering her his hand.

"Hello, I'm Dr. Carlisle," he murmured as Laena slipped her hand in his.

Carlisle. Interesting, Evie thought. They had never gotten around to the whole full names thing. She supposed he was privy to hers since it was written all over his fancy little computer screen. At least now they were on equal footing

"Laena Blair," her mother answered politely.

Alec turned his attention back to Evie. "Is it all right to…" His gaze flicked to her mother briefly before turning back to her.

She knew what he was asking, and though she would *love* to see her mother's face if he told her she needed to leave, she just couldn't do it. Evie nodded, instead.

"Great. We're still waiting for the results, but they should be done in a few minutes. I just wanted to keep you updated. They brought you something for the pain?"

She shook her head.

"I'll order it and a prescription for you to take home. You'll be able to pick it up in the pharmacy on your way out."

"Does that mean you aren't going to keep her?" Laena asked.

He turned his attention back to the older woman. "We'll need to see the results of the CT first, but as long as everything is clear there, no, you'll be able to take her home."

Evie sighed away her disappointment.

She was alone when he returned. It was easy to persuade her mother to go pick up the prescription at the pharmacy while she waited for the discharge papers, and once Laena left the glass-enclosed cubicle, Evie hopped off the thin mattress. Avoiding hospital beds was her long-term goal in life, and she carefully folded herself into the arm chair Laena previously occupied.

Alec found her with her legs curled up on the fake leather seat and feet tucked under her knees. The space between his brows was creased thoughtfully as he stared down at a print out, and Evie instantly went on alert. She sat up straighter and dropped her feet to the floor as she prepared for bad news.

"You said you were in a coma."

Her brows shot up toward her hairline. "That's right. For three and a half months."

She failed to be more specific: three months, thirteen days, thirteen hours, and three minutes. She had always found threes fascinating, and thirteen more so, and those would forever be burned into her brain.

He ran his tongue over his teeth. "I pulled up your medical records." His gaze remained glued on the paper. Was he avoiding looking at her?

"Okay."

She swallowed. Was he looking for more information? Something was behind his interest and clearly and it had nothing to do with her lovable sense of humor and roguish good looks.

"There seems to be quite a bit of information missing. If your condition today had been any worse, I—well, anyone here—would need that information to best treat you."

Evie frowned. "I don't know what could possibly be missing. All of my records were sent here when my parents had me transferred. My mother even hand-carried hard copies."

He flipped the paper over quickly before turning it back over. "Not one of the scans shows any sort of traumatic brain injury. There is no information about your rating on the Glasgow scale. Your arm injury, broken femur, burns, those are all well-recorded, but the head injury…"

"Are you telling me I *wasn't* in a coma all that time?" she asked through gritted teeth.

"No, that isn't what I'm saying at all."

He hesitated. There was something in his tone. Something she couldn't place.

"I'm asking you if they ever gave you a reason *why*. There's no explanation here. Nothing."

"And I take it you believe that means something?" She folded her arms over her chest and squirmed as his gaze finally met hers. They stared at each other as the seconds ticked away, neither blinking.

"I think that means you are in danger, Evelyn," he murmured. His expression darkened, his mouth falling into a grim line and his eyes hooding beneath slashing brows.

A chill shimmied down her spine and she tightened her hold on herself. Something was wrong. Something was very wrong. She was suddenly aware of how much larger he was than she. How much stronger. And he stood between her and the only escape route.

"What... what do you mean?"

"Be careful who you trust."

His guarded expression lightened instantly, and his lips turned up into a pleasant smile. Had she imagined the darkness radiating from him but a moment before?

"If any of these symptoms appear, you need to come back immediately." He handed her copies of her discharge papers, and in a few steps, was gone.

Evie swallowed, fell back in the chair, and crumpled the stack of papers in her hand.

Chapter Six

"Evie."

She glanced over her shoulder and blinked twice when she recognized the long face standing beside her. "Iain, right?"

"Good memory." He shifted his weight to one foot.

"Here, why don't you sit?" She indicated the leather armchair next to her.

She originally went to the Exchange in search of shampoo. But that expedition didn't take as long as she expected. With nothing else to do with her afternoon, she stopped for a coffee in the café outside the food court and nestled down into a large armchair with a book.

As Iain settled onto the other chair, she shoved her receipt in-between the pages of the paperback and dropped it into her lap.

Iain relaxed against the back and crossed his feet at the ankles in front of him. "We missed you the other night."

Evie winced. "Yeah, sorry about that. I wanted to go, but I tried to give myself a concussion, instead. I ended up on the sofa popping ibuprofen and watching a movie."

"You might have ended up having the better night."

She blinked. Did Iain just crack a joke? After their

encounter last week, she hadn't been sure he knew how.

"Is your head okay?" he asked, pointing to his own temple.

"Yeah, it's fine." She waved it off. "I just had a killer headache for a couple of days. At least if I had been drunk, I would have gotten to have some fun first."

A fleeting smile pulled at his cheeks. "Any chance you'll be coming this week?"

She canted her head. Well, he certainly got straight to the point, didn't he? "I-I don't know. I haven't really heard from Evan, so I don't know if I'm invited…"

"Consider this me inviting you."

Evie stared at him. Was he asking her out? Or was he just being polite? She would have gone with the latter if it hadn't been for the way he was looking at her: intently, but without nervousness. Only expectation. It was seductive.

She couldn't help herself. "Are you asking me out?" she asked cheekily. And then to save a little face, she quickly added, "Or are you just trying to be nice?"

His eyes narrowed, and his lips twitched to one side. "Um. A little of both?"

"Huh. Oh, well, thanks." She brightened up instantly. "I'll be there." She lifted her shoulders up and smiled, an anxious flutter settling into her belly.

"Great," he said and stood up.

"Are you going already?" She tried not to pout and failed.

"Yeah, I was just getting lunch with some buddies." He motioned to a couple of guys standing at the counter, inserting straws into their frozen coffee drinks.

Only then did she realize he was in his own uniform, tanned boots scuffed around the toes, and patrol cap folded in one hand. Her gaze swung to his name tape. "Hier" in black block letters. Iain Hier. It sounded ridiculously made-up.

"Oh, okay," she said. "Well, I guess I'll see you on Friday."

"I look forward to it." He held up a hand and turned away, following the other two men out the doors.

Evie stared after them until they disappeared completely from view and then stared down at her book. There was no getting back into it, now. She dropped it into her bag and collected her coffee cup as she stood.

The heat from the summer sun smacked her like a wall as she stepped outside. The humidity was thick and heavy, the wet air clinging to her skin. It quickly formed a sheen of perspiration. When she opened the driver's door to her mother's sedan, a blast of even hotter air greeted her like the belching of an oven, and she leaned in, turning on the car without baking herself in the process. After hitting the fan until it was on full blast, she plunked herself down on the seat and waited for the car to cool enough she could shut the door.

The blast ruffled a sheaf of papers stuffed between the center console and passenger side seat, rattling them like a playing card on the spokes of a bike. Evie extracted the packet, immediately recognizing the sterile block print of her discharge papers. She'd never looked at them.

Her first instinct was to ball them up and toss them out, but her fingers brushed against a raised spot on the outside sheet. She turned it over, catching sight of a black ink bleed. The third and final piece was mostly blank, only the contact information for the hospital printed across the top.

But beneath it, in an oddly ornate scrawl were the words…

Beware the crows.

Chapter Seven

The moon already hung beside the stars by the time Evie pulled the car into a spot outside the bar. Only half of the back parking lot was full, but summer was in full swing. St Andrews was the same way during the warmer months. Quiet. Empty. Students all gone home on holiday, only research assistants and professors keeping odd hours. She slung her brown leather bag over one shoulder, pushed the car door closed, and skirted the front bumper to step onto the well-lit sidewalk.

She rounded the corner and turned toward the glass doors of the bar.

"Over here!"

Evie dropped her hand and turned quickly, nearly losing her balance. She scanned the other side of the street and found Iain leaning against the stucco of another small building, face cast in shadow and lanky legs crossed at the ankle. He straightened and held up a hand.

She scanned the street in both directions and crossed between parked cars.

He joined her, his hands shoved in his pockets and his chin pointed toward his chest. "We're over here, tonight."

She took in the building's face, the harp beside the logo. "Great." He looked like he wanted to say more, his head slightly canted to the side. Instead, he leaned away, allowing her to move past him, only coming close as he reached around her to pull open the door.

Inside was a reproduction of places she frequented in Scotland. Exposed wood beams, cream colored walls, and a dark, smoky interior. The bar was long and thick, tables peppered around the exterior mismatched, the chairs and stools in varying shapes and designs.

It was exactly the kind of place she preferred, casual, shadowed, a bit mysterious with a hint of history. But Calum liked the posher establishments, taking her to the haunts of golfers and wealthy tourists. Those places were always sleek and modern with glass-topped tables, vibrantly colored stools, and mirrors. So many mirrors.

Was this the first time since the accident she thought of him without tears? She smiled softly to herself and breathed in, the air heavy with hot fish and chips, beer, and smoke. Even if he didn't prefer it, the atmosphere reminded her of him.

A hand brushed her shoulder blade, and she turned toward Iain.

"The others are back there," he murmured close to her ear, his breath warm as it ruffled her hair.

A shiver ran up her spine, and she followed him into a small alcove. She recognized the others seated along the long tables. They shoved in closer to each other to make room for the two of them, and she slid down the back bench shoved into a corner.

Iain took the seat beside her, his denim-clad leg pressed against the thin fabric of her green dress. His heat seeped through the layers between them, and she gulped. He was so close she could smell the laundry detergent still clinging to his shirt, the spice of his cologne, and a sweet hint of smoke.

"I hope it's all right that Iain invited me," she said to no one in particular.

Those that could hear made noises of welcome, and the young female lieutenant next to her, Mandy, wrapped an arm around Evie's shoulders, giving her a squeeze.

"Any time!" she said with a grin that belied one too many drinks.

Evie blushed and sat back in the booth, the tension she held in her shoulders dissipating.

A young blond with a black apron slung low over her hips approached, a pitcher of beer in each hand. She slid them onto the scarred table in front of Iain, catching his gaze. "I'll bring some more glasses," she yelled over the music.

Evie dutifully passed one of the pitchers into Mandy's eager hands.

"Where's Evan?" she asked Iain.

She hadn't heard from him since before her trip to the emergency room, but expected him to be there with his coworkers. But his bald head and bulging arms were absent.

"Why?"

Evie screwed her mouth to one side. "He isn't here."

Iain's expression remained bland. "Were you planning to exact your revenge tonight? Or have you realized that your dislike of the boy is actually lust?"

"Boy?" She raised an eyebrow. "He's what? Three, four years younger than you?"

"Young man, then. If you prefer."

"Oh, I don't care one way or the other. I merely find it amusing that you see yourself as being so much older. Looking into retirement already? Got your eye on that social security?"

He gave her a withering look.

"I'm just wondering where he is. No need to get jealous."

"Jealous?"

She grinned but didn't have time to say anymore. The waitress returned and plunked two stacks of chilled glasses on the table. Evie took two before passing the rest to the other end of the table. She caught the pitcher before it could disappear with them, pouring beer into both glasses and passing one to Iain. She then settled back, cradling hers in both hands.

"Questioning my feelings for Evan?"

She took a sip and scrunched up her nose as the bitter hops bubbled over her tongue. She should have known better; she'd never found light beer particularly appealing. Resisting the urge to rub her tongue on a paper napkin, she set the glass down and shoved it away from the edge of the table. "Classic sign of jealousy."

Iain gave a short huff of a laugh and brought his own beer to his lips, drinking heavily and then sucking in his lips as he swallowed. He leaned forward, placing his left forearm on the table and turning himself slightly toward her on the bench.

"Is that so?"

"Absolutely." She considered taking another sip of the beer, but then thought better of it. Instead, she spun the glass in her hand, condensation heavy on her fingertips. "But don't worry, you have no reason to be jealous," she whispered conspiratorially, the corners of her mouth quirking.

He leaned toward her, bracing his arm on the back of the bench. "Glad to hear it."

Evie gulped. Was he going to kiss her? He was close enough she could smell the beer on his breath and count the flecks of brown surrounding his pupils. She dropped her gaze to his mouth and swayed toward him, but quickly jerked away and cocked her head to the side. She lifted her eyebrow in question. "You know, if I'm going to make out with you, I'm going to need to know you better."

Both of his eyebrows shot up. "If I had known that was an option, I would have forwarded you a full autobiography."

"It's never too late."

Had she really just said that? Was she actually flirting? The corners of Iain's lips twitched. Sure, he was nice to look at, but he was also not her type, at all. And what did she know about him? Nothing. Absolutely nothing.

But there was something about him. Something that made her want to impress him, to have him run his gaze over her. His eyes shifted, his stare skipping down her only to flick back up and meet hers head-on. She found a challenge in the dark depths. As if he knew she always met a challenge. Refusing to back down.

His lips pursed.

Yes, he was definitely challenging her. He was challenging her as if he couldn't wait.

She narrowed her own eyes and turned her body toward him, leaning forward a bit so that the dress tightened against her chest. She knew her body wasn't anything to envy, especially since it was riddled with scars. She'd always been on the high side of her target weight, her thighs touching, her hips rounded, her stomach a hair away from being flat, no matter how hard she worked at it. Which wasn't much, lately. But her breasts had always been one of her best assets. They were large without being too large, round, and full.

The move she made had the desired effect. His gaze drifted down and hovered for a fleeting second. He quickly looked back up and she smirked.

"So, Captain…" she murmured sweetly. "Tell me about yourself."

Evie giggled as Iain lined her up in front of the dart board.

When Evan finally showed up an hour after she had, the dark-haired beauty from the other night in tow, she passed off her warm beer to him and ordered herself a gin and tonic, heavy on the lime. She and Iain spent the evening with heads bent close as they traded likes and dislikes, travel stories, and sarcastic comebacks.

He seemed mildly amused through it all, a hardness reflecting in his eyes, but a slight upturn of his lips. She couldn't shake the feeling he knew something he wasn't saying, but she hadn't had that much fun in over a year, and her face hurt from laughing. She nursed that lone gin and tonic for close to two hours, the glass sweating and the ice melting.

Iain stood close, a hand on each of her hips, bent over slightly, his cheek resting against her temple. "Lift your elbow," he said next to her ear. "A little higher. Parallel to the ground."

She did as he instructed, and squared her feet for better balance, but her heart pumped on double time.

He was so close, the heat of him seeping through his shirt into the skin exposed by the low straps of her dress. It took just as much focus to keep from leaning into him as she needed to concentrate on the dart board.

"You're going to throw on a curve," he murmured. "Not straight forward."

"Okay, okay." She shushed him and took a breath before letting the dart fly. "Ha!" she cried in triumph when the needle embedded itself in the cork. "I did it!"

"If you mean you hit the board, then yes. You did."

She twisted around and stuck her tongue out at him. "You're just afraid I'll beat you."

"Precisely," he said dryly.

She ignored him and threw her remaining darts. Both hit the board, sticking soundly, and she raised her hands in victory. "Score!" She grinned at him and patted him on the shoulder. "Your turn."

Evie expected him to hit the board. Of course she did, he coached *her* through it. What she didn't expect was all three darts to land squarely in the center of the bull's eye, all in quick succession, as if he didn't even have to think about it.

"Holy shit. Did you even blink between throws?"

He shrugged and his face softened around the otherwise sharp edges. His humility was endearing. Sexy. The lust building all evening finally came to a head and she leaned forward, reaching up and cupping his cheeks between her palms, and pulled his mouth down to hers.

If he was surprised, he didn't show it. Instead, his hand snaked around the small of her back and pressed her into him. He opened to her, caressing her bottom lip with his. Even his kiss was steely. But it drove away all other thoughts and worries only he remained, wrapped around her if they weren't standing in the middle of a crowded room.

Just as quickly as it began, it was over and he pulled away, staring down at her with an unspoken question. The niggling ache of the last year threatened to creep in, the pain and heartbreak slithering back. But she didn't want it. And he had been able to chase it away, if only for a moment. She lifted her lips to him again, and they clashed together, the other people, the noise, everything falling away just as she hoped it would.

"Want to get out of here?" she murmured, not even second-guessing the question.

She had never done anything like that before. She held her breath, waiting for his answer. But she wanted it, if only for a few moments. She needed it. The distraction. It kept the darkness away. And after the year she'd been having, she was going to take it. She wanted to feel good for a change, and she wanted him make her feel that way.

Iain didn't answer her, just turned away as he reached into his back pocket. He extracted his wallet, opened it, and threw down enough to cover both of their tabs and tips. Leaning over, he said something to one of the other captains. In less than a minute, her hand was folded into his, and he escorted her out into the warm, summer night. They didn't make it two steps out of the front door before Iain whirled around, his mouth closing over hers once again.

Evie took a step back and hit the brick façade. She grabbed his shoulders, steadying herself, and pressed into him, her breasts flattening against his hard chest.

Her fingers tightened on his polo, the fabric bunching into her palm, as she greedily kissed him back.

He tasted like beer and the Scotch he'd been sipping, a smoky malt that burned with the acidic tones of peat. She hummed with desire, wanting nothing more than to strip his clothes off and run her hands over his lean, muscles.

A wolf-whistle sang out behind Iain. She started and he stepped back, offering her only a mischievous smirk. She bit her lip and reached for his hand. She fumbled for it, wrapping her fingers around his long, calloused palm, and pulled him along the sidewalk toward the parking lot, stopping only at the crosswalk for a quick, stolen kiss.

She should have felt guilty for pulling a man into the back seat of her father's car. But as she opened the back door on the driver's side, all she could muster was anticipation. Turning back to Iain, she threaded her arms around his neck, and their mouths met once more with renewed ferocity. His lips plucked at hers and then trailed away, brushing her cheek and the soft skin just below her ear. His stubble scratched her tender flesh and a shiver ran over her. She moaned softly.

His hands traveled up from her hips until they cupped her breasts through the thin cotton dress and she arched her back further, allowing him greater access to her neck as he nipped at it. Her legs wobbled and she sank down onto the back seat, fisting her hand in his shirt as he followed. She inched across the bench seat as he clicked the door shut. Hand running up her thigh, his fingers grazing the edges of her long, thin white scar, he settled over her, his lips fingers hers, again. Did he not notice the uneven, puckered skin? Or did he not care?

She shifted and he lifted his hand from her thigh. It skimmed her waist and then his fingers hooked into the strap of her dress. He drew it over her shoulder, and she shrugged the other down as well, exposing her breasts to him. A warm, rough hand cupped her naked breast, his thumb rasping over her distended nipple.

She moaned and hooked her ankle around his calf, pressing her hips up into his. His erection was hard and straining against the denim of his jeans, pressing up against the warm, wet juncture of her legs.

He kissed her hungrily and she drew his shirt up just enough his hot skin slid against hers. Her fingers raced back down the smooth muscles until she found the buttons of his fly, and she flicked the buttons through the holes, then dove in, grasping him in her hand. His flesh was hot, and she gripped him gently, running her palm across the head of his erection before pulling back up with more pressure.

In response, he pinched her nipple between his thumb and index finger, rolling it between them. She sucked in a breath, and arched up into him, breaking the hold he had on her mouth.

"Just do it," she gasped, into his ear as she pushed at his waistband, her breath coming in pants.

He hiked her dress up over her hips and yanked her panties to the side before wrestling them down her thighs and over her knees. She kicked them free the rest of the way, one hole still hooked around her ankle.

Shifting his weight to his knees, he dug into a pocket and produced a small, plastic packet.

Evie plucked it from his fingers, then ripped it until the serrated edge gave way. She fumbled with the condom in the dark and tossed the plastic square to the floor.

"Which side is up?" she muttered, turning it from one side to the other, unable to see it clearly in the dark.

Iain hastily grabbed it back and made quick work of slipping it on.

"Finally. Do it now," she demanded.

He thrust inside her.

She hummed her approval and closed her eyes, shifting her hips until each stroke brought her closer.

His hands traveled up and down her hot skin as their flesh slapped in turn with her pants and his groans. He captured her mouth once more and quickly brought them both to satisfaction.

Evie relaxed into the leather and took a deep breath. Her pulse still pounded in her ears.

Iain sat up, nudging her legs aside as he pulled his jeans back over his hips, and his fingers deftly pushed the buttons of his fly back into place.

Evie pulled the strap of her dress back over her shoulder and shimmied the hem down. She pulled her panties off her ankle but wadded them up in her fist. She didn't want to put them back on while he could see her.

Once they were both covered, he opened the door and stepped out. She scooted to the edge of the seat so she sat with her legs hanging through the doorway.

He started to turn away, leaned an arm on the door frame instead. "Can I see you tomorrow?" he asked almost guiltily.

Evie shrugged, but didn't say anything. She hadn't expected he would want to leave her so quickly, but she was also awash in awkwardness. She wasn't ashamed to have had sex with someone she barely knew, and in a potentially very public place. But she was a little surprised by it.

"Meet me at Moon Lake? Around seven?"

She nodded again, and thought he might say something more, but he gazed off into the tree line. She followed the direction in which he stared but saw nothing, only the swaying of the trees in the warm summer wind.

Whatever had caught his attention must have been something of no consequence. He dropped his arm away from the car and raised his hand in farewell, treading backwards for a few steps before turning away.

With the windows rolled down, Evie drove back to her parents' house. The wind whipped at her dark hair, sending it flying around her face no matter how many times she tucked it behind her ears, and she turned the satellite radio up until the vibrations of the music reverberated all the way to her toes. In the low-growing trees surrounding the criss-crossing rivers, cicadas screeched, almost loud enough to drown out the devastated wails of the newest alternative rock princess.

Arm resting on the sill, Evie swam her hand through the air as she hit the back roads of the base, but she worried her lip between her teeth. She should be feeling guilty, right? She should be cursing herself for being such a bad person, one who would jump into the backseat of a car—literally—with another man without a second thought to her dead fiancé. She wanted to let the guilt gnaw at her, she really did, but then... she couldn't. She was too busy *feeling*. Alive and free and sexy and a bit savage.

It was something the therapists, the doctors, the

nurses, her parents had all been trying to drill into her head for months; she was alive, and she needed to start taking advantage of it.

But would Calum's mother see it that way?

Evie groaned. Why even think that? Mrs. Baird had always been a kind, motherly soul, and as far as Evie could tell, had no ill will toward anyone. She hadn't known the woman well, having only spent a handful of Sunday teas at the North Street Bed and Breakfast Mrs. Baird owned, her son reluctantly glaring at her, one eye on the clock. The relationship between mother and son was forced, at least on Calum's end, but Mrs. Baird had treated Evie with nothing but kindness.

She once asked him why he wanted to avoid his mother and he gave Evie a long, thoughtful look. "She places a lot of pressure on me," was his only reply, and Evie was left wondering what his mother expected that he was unable to give. He was an only child. All expectations had ridden on him, alone. And if anything about her current experience told her anything, it was that siblings were a necessary evil when dealing with parental expectations.

Contacting Mrs. Baird was not something she had ever contemplated until that moment, her focus having been on herself and on what she had lost. She worried her lip as a frown replaced the relaxed smile she had worn since leaving Iain. Perhaps she had let Calum down in more ways than one.

She gulped past the uncomfortable lump that had formed in her throat. She was starting to have trouble remembering what he looked like. She could no longer conjure up his voice in her mind. And though she remembered he smelled slightly of bayberry and amber scented soap, even a fresh bar of the stuff didn't help her memory.

Evie pulled into her parents' driveway and shut off the engine. But she didn't move from the seat, instead leaning her head back and closing her eyes trying to conjure up a memory of his lips, his laugh, the feel of his hands as they ran over her skin.

Calum had always been gentle and unhurried. When they shared their first kiss, he leaned over tentatively and brushed her lips with his own. It was she who had pulled him roughly to her. She who screamed "harder" the first time they slept together. She who wanted things faster. Deeper. Intense. More. Calum was always perfectly happy taking his time, gently, worshipping her. She was impatient. She who just wanted to *do* it. She wished she had taken more time. Slowed things down. Savored them.

She squeezed her eyes shut, trying to block out even the little light that glowed from the street lamps. What had his hands felt like on her skin? Soft. Feather-light. But the memory was fleeting, giving way to Iain's rough, calloused fingers. It wasn't Calum's twinkling eyes and gentle brushing of lips that penetrated her memory, but Iain's hard, angular planes, the rough scratch of his stubble, the fast pounding of his hips.

The quick coupling in the back of her father's car had replaced the months of tenderness she had shared with the man she loved.

Evie cursed and stepped out of the car. The back of her throat was dry. It ached, a sob tearing through it. She paced, arms wrapped around herself, fighting the tears and the anguish that finally broke over her. Giving up, she allowed the tears to flow freely and gulped at the air.

It felt good, letting go. Of being sad she would never have Calum with her again, her life not what she thought it would be. But guilt at finally moving on? No, she wouldn't feel that. She refused.

She sniffled and took a deep breath. It stuttered through her but calmed her.

What was that?

She was sure she had seen something move. Across the back alley and in the shadow cast by a small copse of hundred-year-old oaks. She searched the silhouettes, but whatever she saw was either gone, hiding, or a figment of her imagination. Deciding she didn't want to find out, Evie pulled her purse from the car and scurried inside, clicking the door quietly shut behind her.

****

Golden light flooded a plain of waving wheat, the ends flicking and falling like the undulating rhythm of the sea. The breeze was cool, a nip ruffling her jacket, bringing along the damp scent of dead leaves and crushed acorns.

She kept her pace even but trailed those ahead of her. They were familiar sights. She knew them, their names on the tip of her tongue, their faces just out of reach of her memory. The riot of coppery red hair tumbling down like autumn fire. The silvery white blond, slight and petite, her green dress raw and homespun. The tall shadow of a hooded figure.

She bounded over the swell of grain, her movements free from her injuries, closing the gap between herself and the hooded shadow. She reached out a hand, the silvery scar marring her wrist absent, fingers a hair from brushing the smooth leather at his arm… when she woke.

Dawn had yet to break the darkness, and through the blinds, she could only make out the brilliant cobalt blue of a coming sun.

Evie tried to dive back into her mind, to recapture the images playing through her dreams as she slept and recreate them with better clarity. She wanted to connect what little she remembered, piece it together. Force it to make sense. It was a jagged bit of a large puzzle she began to live since waking in a hospital bed nine months before, one she was desperate to see unfold. But it never came together, just as it refused to do in the first light of that morning. She groaned and gave up.

Flicking on the small lamp an arm's length away, Evie reached for one of the books sitting atop her bedside table. She had all but abandoned them there after bringing them home from the used bookstore in Manhattan. She came up with the romance; taking in the front cover, she decided she wasn't in the mood. Tossing it none too gently toward the foot of the bed, she reached for the next.

Sylvia Bascomb-Murray's *Women of Culloden: Taking Up The Tartan.*

Evie flipped it open, ignoring the table of contents and acknowledgments, instead diving right into the introduction, which of course promised heavy analysis of nationalism among women, the glorification of Flora MacDonald, and stories of other female warriors who took up the tartan to defend their homeland and raise up Bonnie Prince Charlie during the Jacobite uprisings. Some even succumbing to death for their actions.

Evie always had a particular fascination with Flora MacDonald, the woman who smuggled a defeated

Charles from Scotland dressed as her lady's maid. The woman's portrait, reprinted in just about every book and article about the infamous uprising—this one included—had always impressed with her stoic countenance, a quiet amusement hiding just out of reach. She had a face more handsome than beautiful and a romantic story to boot.

But as Evie continued reading, it wasn't Flora who most fascinated Evie, nor was it Lady Anne Farquharson Macintosh, the beautiful young woman who was the mastermind behind the Rout of Moy and given the nickname Colonel Anne by the prince himself. No, it was the tale of young Lady Elizabeth Carlisle, née Meyner.

One of the daughters of Chief Meyner himself, she stunned her family by marrying the youngest son of the fourth Duke of Carlisle, Lord Alexander. The young man, born some months after his father's death, was robbed of meeting the duke after a particularly infamous duel in Hyde Park. The eldest son, John, inherited the titles and estates, the duchess moving into the dowager house before her youngest child's presence was even confirmed.

Alexander spent his formative years in England, buying a commission into the Royal Army when he came of age. But the unexpected death of elder brother William, who had blighted the family with a rather scandalous love-match, died at the Lanarkshire estate where he had been overseeing the interests of the fifth duke for some years. Alexander gave up his commission to take over where his deceased brother left off.

It was in Edinburgh that he met the modest Elizabeth Meyner. There is little known about the early life of Elizabeth, only that she was the youngest child of the Meyner laird and his second wife, Mary. Lord Alexander only reports that he saw her from afar and was drawn in by a coy smile. Enchanted by her Scottish lilt and "eyes like the ever-changing mood of the lochs," Alexander began a quick and heavy courtship that saw the two married as soon as the bans could be properly read. The young noble kept extensive journals, which included his infatuation with his bride, who was barely eighteen at the time of their nuptials. He referred to her as his darling Ailsa in those early days, and found it fetching when she called him Alistair rather than his Anglicized given name.

Evie flipped to the middle of the book where the thick, glossy photograph pages were, a thin line between the flimsy sheets of text. The third one back had a small miniature of Elizabeth, perhaps the only likeness in existence. Her eyes were large, rimmed by dark lashes, their centers a murky blue-green. They stared straight out, as if she were dressing the painter down. Her hair was pulled back from her face to showcase her pouty pink mouth, straight nose, and strong brow. The portrait was pretty in the way pictures of people long dead were pretty, antique, a little cracked, likely not an accurate rendering.

And below was a portrait of her husband, a man who was painted much the same; with a hint of amusement turning his lips up at the corners. He was posed against a white horse, one leg bent, the other hyper-extended in white breeches, his Army uniform a slash of color across the page. He would have been handsome had he not been painted to look far younger than his years possibly could have been.

The honeymoon period was quickly over, however, and soon Lord Alexander was finding himself more and more exasperated by Elizabeth's zeal for politics and her disinterest in overseeing an estate that belonged to another. Less than a year after the hasty wedding, he wrote "the woman's incessant prattle about naught but 'the proud traditions of the highlands' is enough to send any man to drink."

Nonetheless, the young man saw something in the uprising, and even went as far as to forsake his family's ties to the king of England, and led a small contingent of Carlisle clansmen to battle under the rebel prince's banner. Some scholars theorize he took a gamble, hoping that if Prince Charles won back his throne, the Carlisle Lanarkshire holdings in the lowlands would be bequeathed to Alexander. Others suggest he was more swayed by his wife's "incessant prattle" than he let on.

But the youngest Carlisle did not return from Culloden. His body never recovered, it is rightly assumed he was buried in one of the mass graves with the men he led, all falling where they stood with the Meyner men. Elizabeth lost not only her husband in that fateful hour-long battle on the Drumossie Moor, but also her father and brother.

When Cumberland's men began their march back to England, they were met with a large contingent of women wielding pitchforks, dirks, and clubs, all widows of Culloden. Elizabeth Meyner Carlisle at their head, musket at the ready.

The rebel women were quickly overwhelmed by the professional soldiers, Elizabeth taken into custody. She was sentenced to death a week later and hanged for her crimes. Her last words, reportedly, were "it is at the guarding of thy death that I am; and I shall be."

Evie jumped as a car engine stuttered to life outside her open window. The book fell to the light quilt, its pages fanning out. The night before, she hurried back into the house, completely forgetting to pick up her trash from the backseat. She didn't think she could live down the embarrassment of her father finding a condom wrapper in the floor board of his own car.

Feeling an impending sense of doom, she tiptoed her way down the narrow servants' staircase, and out the back door. A shaking sigh of relief escaped her parted lips. Both cars were still parked beneath the hide of the oak tree. No one else was in sight. The air was already hot and sticky, despite the early hour, the bugs beginning their morning serenades.

Quietly, she opened the back door of the sedan and sank down to run her hand over the carpeted floor. The shadows still kept it in darkness, but her fingers quickly found a crumpled piece of paper. She knew immediately it wasn't the wrapper, but that met the tips of her digits after another sweep.

She shoved the wrapper into the pocket of her gym shorts but kept the piece of paper in hand. She knew her father kept an immaculately clean car, and her mother had taken it to get detailed right before Evie borrowed it for her jaunt to Manhattan. Whatever was in her hand must have been something dropped last night. She unfolded it in a bit of sunlight, revealing five words in scratchy pencil: Flora MacDonald. Thistle and Rose.

She frowned, her forehead creasing. It was a bit of a coincidence considering her current reading material, but it also seemed odd for Iain to have it tucked into his pocket next to his spare condom.

Deciding she would ask him about it later, she shoved it into the pocket with the empty wrapper and went back inside.

Chapter Eight

"So, where are we going, exactly?"

Iain turned off the paved road half a mile back, his sport utility vehicle bouncing down the hillside between low-lying trees and dodging creek beds. All while ignoring the "No Personally Owned Vehicle" signs as he went.

The sun was moments from slipping behind the hills, the sky a pleasant mix of blues, purples, and oranges bleeding into one another. The heat had dissipated, replaced by a pleasant breeze and manageable humidity. Evening was alive with the sounds of summer; the deep calls of frogs, the chorus of insects.

"You'll see," Iain told her over the growl of the engine.

He looked more relaxed than she had ever seen him, lounging back in a sleeveless shirt, a pair of aviator glasses, and cargo shorts. He was more muscular that she had imagined his shoulders well-defined, his arms sculpted. She hadn't thought he was unfit, but he had always seemed to be the more slender type. He had nothing on Evan, that was for sure. But who did? She wasn't one to be impressed by large, ballooning pectorals, anyway.

"That's a non-answer," she yelled as the truck lurched over a tree root.

He turned his gaze to her with a lazy smirk before giving the dirt road his attention, again. Suspecting she wouldn't get any more of an answer, Evie sighed and let her head drop back against the seat rest. Above the roll bars, thick pockets of leaves and knotted branches sped, a parcel of heavy black birds gliding the winds above them. The vehicle bounced over deep ruts, curving to the left, later to the right, the birds somehow always coming back into view.

Eventually the trail ended in a clearing, deep gouges in the mud from tracked vehicles creating a circle where the large, heavy tanks and infantry fighting vehicles had turned around. The sun officially dipped below the horizon, but the sky was still light to the west, and the shadows cast by the trees become darker and more pronounced. Iain pulled the emergency brake, and shut off the engine, hopping out. He reached into the back bed of the old vehicle, pulling out an old, green and brown backpack.

"I haven't seen BDU material in ten years." Evie laughed as she unbuckled her seatbelt. The old green and brown camouflage of the Battle Dress Uniforms was retired when she was a child, the Army replacing it with colors and patterns better suited for more modern wars.

"I just use it for hikes. It came with the truck."

Evie lifted her eyebrows and shook her head. "That's a rather odd thing to throw in with the sale of a vehicle, isn't it?" When he didn't answer, she decided to let it drop. "So, if you won't tell me where we're going, maybe you can tell me what we're doing?"

"Hiking."

"You do remember that I have a bit of a limp,

right?" She gestured to her bad leg as if she were presenting a prize on a game show.

"It won't be far.

"If I fall over and break my nose, I'm blaming you."

"I'll catch you."

Evie put her hands on her hips and screwed her mouth to the side. "You better."

He cracked a grin, something he rarely did, and motioned for her to follow him. She slung the thin strap of her purse over her head so the leather lay across her midsection and fell in step behind him. They trudged over the tall, waving grass, and she cringed inside, uninterested in picking up any six-legged hitchhikers.

"You know, I like trolling for ticks just as much as the next person, I'm sure," she said as they wound around a fallen tree, cracked and dry, grass growing up through its hollow insides. "But wouldn't it be easier to just rub up against a few stray dogs?"

He snorted but didn't say anything.

"Do you come out here often?" she asked after the silence became uncomfortable. She suspected she wouldn't get anything out of him before they arrived wherever it was he was dragging her.

"Almost every evening."

"Really? Why?"

"I like the solitude. And I enjoy the hike. It keeps me in shape."

At that she allowed her gaze to drift down to his butt. Yup, it was working. "How long are you out here?"

"A few hours."

"So, what you're saying is that if I want to keep

hanging out with you, I'm going to have to buck up and get used to this?"

"Something like that."

"Damn it, that sounds terrible," she muttered.

They continued in silence, the screeches of insects growing in volume the darker the sky became. To the east, several stars made their presence known where the sky was darkest, only the brightest winking directly above head. The horizon was still light but fading into a deeper blue. She had to hurry to stay close to Iain, frightened she would get separated from him. She didn't want to find any of the skunks or coyotes that roamed the hills on her own.

Iain suddenly halted and put his arm out to keep her from walking any further. "Here," he murmured.

Evie frowned as he dropped his pack to the ground and dug through it. He extracted some dark colored clothes then shoved some of the cloth into her hands. When he stood, again, he pulled his shirt off, revealing a smooth, sculpted chest. He tossed his shirt on the ground, and looked at her face, lit now only by the moonlight.

"Put that on."

"What?" She tossed the balled up cotton from hand to hand, her lip curling in confusion. *What the hell was this?* "No, I think I'm good."

"Put it on, Eve," he ground out.

No one ever called her Eve. Even when she was young, her parents always used her full name to show their displeasure. But he said it like he had said it a thousand times before. Like she had always been Eve to him. Had he ever called her Evie? Her brow puckered. She wasn't sure.

She gulped and the tiny hairs on the back of her neck rose. She was out in the middle of who-knows-where, alone with a man she didn't know well.

"I think… I think I'd like to leave."

At her words, a murder of crows circled overhead, their caws mixing together until they became one voice. They spread their wings, taking the air under their feathers, spinning faster and faster, like the hand of a clock speeding out of control.

Beware the crows.

The simple line of text flashed across her memory. At the time, it had seemed so harmless and silly. But the flock moving and growing above twisted those three simple words into terror, and the unease slowly washing over her quickly formed into full-fledged panic.

Evie stepped back. Her heel crunched on a brittle stick, snapping it. Iain's hand clamped over her upper arm, yanking her back. She pushed and clawed at him, but his grip remained vice-like, and she kicked out at him.

"Let me go!'

"Well, well, well."

The throaty, feminine purr stopped Evie short.

Her head snapped up as the words emerged from the cawing, and the crows condensed and faded into the most beautiful woman she had ever seen. Hair as black as a raven's feather and skin of alabaster shone in the silvery cast of the moon, red lips twisting into a feline smile.

"Iain, I am impressed. I didn't think you would be able to track this one down. She's been a bit of a problem, hasn't she?"

Evie's mouth fell open and she looked from the woman to Iain and back. Iain stood stoically, shoulders set and mouth a grim line, but said nothing.

The woman cast her gaze to the ground. "And a fairy circle here? How quaint." A wide circle of mushrooms perfectly outlined the small clearing. "I'll have to remember that my faith in you is always so well placed."

Iain nodded once, slowly, almost like a bow.

The woman's attention turned back to Evie, her light eyes glittering in the twilight. She took two steps forward, her feet crunching on old, brittle leaves and the sweeping black fabric of her dress billowing around her. She pursed her lips and canted her head. "And are you ready, my dear?"

Evie swallowed past the lump forming in her throat, and immediately regretted the move. Her stomach rolled and knotted, threatening to be sick. She pulled her arm once more for good measure, but Iain's hand did not loosen.

"Who are you?"

The woman's sneer remained tight-lipped, not reaching her kohled eyes.

"What the *hell* is going on?" Evie demanded.

"Ah, there is the spirited little warrior we all know. Come, child. It's time to return home." The woman motioned toward the fairy circle.

"Child?" Evie snarled, all of her insecurities bubbling up. "Go to hell, lady."

She stomped as hard as she could on the top of Iain's foot. He sucked in his breath in surprise, his grip dropping.

It was all Evie needed.

She took off, ignoring the twinges in her leg and the screaming in her lungs. Pushing through the dense underbrush, she sprinted away. Low-stretching branches scratched her face, snagged her hair, and she sobbed through the pain slicing through her back and hip, and leg.

She glanced over her shoulder to catch Iain's dark form leaping through the forest with the grace of a practiced hunter. She sharply zagged where she should have zigged and tumbled over a downed limb. The breath knocked out of her, and she struggled to pull in another, panicking when nothing happened, crying with relief when air finally hitched into her lungs. She tried to scramble back up—damn it, she didn't even know what she was fleeing—but Iain caught her by the waistband. He hauled her to her feet then wrapped his hands around her upper arms, stilling her.

He jerked her to him. "No more of that, Eve," he growled in her ear. "You have to come with me, now. Please."

He didn't even sound breathless, and her heart pounded in her chest, her breathing loud.

"Where?" she managed to choke out.

"Back." He whirled her around and nudged her back in the direction they came.

She obliged, what fight she had abandoning her. "Why don't you just kill me?"

"It matters not to me," he murmured. "I will get you back there one way or the other. But it would be far easier if you just come willingly. You'll see that. You will. I promise."

"But *where?*" she demanded.

"You really don't know, do you?" His voice held a

hint of awe.

Was he so surprised? She opened her mouth to ask, but his grip fell away and his cry of pain echoed in her ear.

"Run, Evelyn!"

She whirled to stare wide-eyed at her rescuer.

Alec.

Evie couldn't move.

She knew she needed to, but her legs wouldn't respond, her feet wouldn't work. All she could do was stare slack-jawed at them both, her gaze darting from one to the other.

Slammed into dead and decaying leaves from seasons past, Iain groaned, quickly rolling to his feet, a growl of annoyance ripping through his gritted teeth.

"Evelyn. *Go.*"

His yell was all she needed. She took off at a run, her breath sobbing out of her, tears streaming down her face.

How could she have gotten mixed up in-in whatever the hell this was? She had been so sure she got it right. Who was the woman? And what were she and Iain going to do to her? How did Alec fit into all of this?

She didn't care. Let them have their midnight cult meetings under the moonlight but leave her out of it.

Her mind ran through the possibilities of what they wanted her for. The more distance she put between herself and that fairy circle, the more she felt like she needed answers. So many things didn't make sense, starting with the woman just showing up in the middle of nowhere. And the crows. How had Alec known about the crows?

When an arm snagged her around the waist, she let out a scream quickly silenced by a hand.

"Shh, it's Alec," he whispered.

She immediately quieted and whirled on him. "What the fuck is going on?" she demanded.

"Now is not the time nor is it the place."

"The hell it isn't!"

"I'll explain, but we have to get out of here." He held out a hand.

Evie hesitated, but eventually placed her own palm against his, and he hurriedly tugged her after him. They wound through the darkness to a shallow gorge cut by a deep creek gushing through the woods. At its shore, he oriented himself, and pulled her along behind him.

The pain in her leg and hip became more than she could manage any longer. Grimacing, she collapsed on the fallen leaves. She wrested her hand from him and massaged her thigh, gritting her teeth to keep from sobbing.

Alec knelt beside her. "We have to go, Evie."

She nodded and followed him stiffly, her leg screaming with every step until it buckled, dropping her to the dirt.

"I don't think I can keep going," she said. It was almost as much of a challenge to keep her voice from betraying the pain as it had been to sprint through the forest.

He didn't miss a beat. Bending down, and sliding an arm around her waist, he hauled her to her feet. "Lean on me."

They continued like that for what felt like hours, hurriedly hobbling through the forest until white headlights blinked above.

"Here." He hefted her up against his chest, not waiting for her to wrap her arms around his neck before he sprinted toward the beams.

Why was she allowing him to carry her like a sack of potatoes? The irritation lasted less than a second as the pain in her hip and thigh dissipated. Embarrassment that she needed the help at all took its place.

The break in the trees grew near, a gap high above where the shadowed arbors opened for an indigo sky. The road.

Alec followed it, sticking to the cover of the trees, never straying into the open. He approached a dark car pulled off to the side of the road, hidden in an overgrown ivy bush. As they drew nearer, the lights blinked on. He carried her right up to the passenger side door and yanked it open before lowering her to the ground.

She obediently climbed in, fastening her seatbelt as he jogged around the hood. She massaged her leg as the car roared to life and he pulled out onto the nearly-abandoned road.

"Where are we going?"

"Do you have your ID?"

Her hand instinctively went to the small purse still looped around her shoulder. "Yeah, why?"

"Good." He turned left on the next road and hit the gas.

She recognized it as the one running toward the back gate. It was the same gate she used to leave for Manhattan only a few days before.

"Where are we going?" she demanded, again.

He glanced up into the rearview mirror. She turned around and saw nothing but darkness behind them.

"What did they tell you?"

She rolled her eyes and slumped back in the seat. "I don't know. Nothing that made sense."

"*What* did they tell you, Evie?"

"Um, the woman—who is she?" When he didn't answer, she continued, "The woman said something about it being time to go home. She told Iain her faith in him was always well placed, before that. None of it made sense. After I ran, Iain caught me, but all he said was that he was taking me 'back.' Back *where*?"

Alec pushed out a frustrated breath and slowed to go through the gate. Under the bright lights, Evie could make out the uniforms of the gate guards and the military police standing guard with their rifles. Briefly she considered opening the passenger door and rolling out of the car. It would hurt; she'd likely bang herself up pretty badly. He might try to grab her. But she couldn't make herself do it. Too many questions remained, and since none of the answers seemed to end with her immediate death; she intended to try to get them.

"Evelyn, I need you to trust me."

"Trust you? Why the hell would I trust you?"

The car rolled slowly through the rundown little town situated on the north end of the base. It didn't even have a stop light, just a couple of stop signs that kept traffic from entering the main drag. The depressing little bars had full parking lots, those lots housing the only other vehicles in town.

"Because I got you away from the situation in which you unwittingly placed yourself."

"You sound like an over-pretentious prick," she grumbled.

"Are you really more interested in my grammar right now?"

"Well, you aren't answering any of my other questions!"

He shot a glance at her but turned his gaze back to the road. The lights of the regional airport glowed ahead, and the silence between them stretched into uncomfortable. She could feel his annoyance and hoped it matched her own.

But then, as they approached Manhattan, her resolve began to wane. She let go of her anger and murmured, "Look, I've trusted you enough to get into the car, right? That may have been the biggest mistake of my life, but what can I say? I'm young and stupid. But the least you could do is make up some sort of answers to my questions so I can feel a little better."

He sniffed with amusement. "I'm taking you to my place."

Evie wasn't sure why she wasn't uncomfortable with the idea. "Why?"

"Because it will take her longer to find than if I were to take you to your house."

"*But who is she?*"

The shadows shifted in the darkness as he clenched his jaw. "She goes by many names."

"That isn't an answer," she chided.

"I don't really know."

Evie opened her mouth to say something else, but he quickly added, "I have my suspicions, though."

"I'm really not in the mood for guessing games."

"When I knew her, she went by the name Mora," he murmured.

Something akin to regret seeped into his tone, and

Evie couldn't help but wonder what the story was there.

"And now?"

"It's better if you don't know."

Evie threw up her hands and groaned. "Are you always this difficult to talk to?"

She didn't receive an answer.

Alec slowed the car as they entered town, and then made a left turn into one of the residential streets. The street lamps glowed yellow at odd intervals down the street, and she recognized the general area as being close to the campus. When he pulled into the crumbling drive of a little Queen Anne cottage, she couldn't hide her surprise.

"*This* is where you live?" she muttered in disbelief.

Even in the shadows of the large oak trees flanking it, she could make out the tiny details of the gingerbread. It seemed entirely too ornate, too delicate, too cultured for such a large, surly man.

He hopped out of the car then, skirted the hood as he came around to open her door. Her hand was in his and he was pulling her out onto the grass before she even managed to snap her mouth closed. Hand at the small of her back, he escorted her, up three wooden steps to the front porch. Their footsteps sounded heavy on the planks, especially her uneven ones. Alec shot a look over his shoulder, and then one to the darkening sky above before stabbing the lock with his key.

The front parlor was cast in heavy shadow and Alec made no move to remedy it as he pulled he door shut behind him and threw the heavy lock into place. Evie couldn't make out much other than the rows of bookshelves lining the walls and the heavy, leather chesterfield sofa dominating the far wall. It was a masculine room, dark and warm, but sophisticated.

He brushed past her into the hallway, leaving her to stand awkwardly at the door. She considered following him, but remained rooted. Her hand slid around her waist and her thumb massaged the small of her back where the ache spread. The seconds ticked by as her mind bumbled through her options.

Stay or leave.

She needed little time to consider her answer.

Chapter Nine

Alec emerged from the back room with a brown Army towel cradled against his chest. As he approached Evie, he unfolded it, revealing the baseball-sized silver apple wrapped inside. "Here."

Evie lifted an eyebrow but extended her hand for the trinket as he held it out, towel still cupping it from the bottom. As her fingers grasped the delicate stem, he cupped the underside with his free hand.

When he opened his eyes, it was to the gray light of morning and the lapping of the loch over smoothed stones. The setting was familiar, one he came across more than a few times over the years. And though the pebbly beach was simple, it was one of his favorite destinations, the serene lull of the water and sparsely populated shores a comfort. When he could, he hoped to come to this spot, always feeling a bit of comfort with the vast wilderness surrounding it.

He let out a long breath, and, his legs like jelly beneath him, turned to scan for Evelyn.

She was curled up on her side, her head resting on her outstretched arm, her body cradled by long, green grasses.

As he approached, she stirred, stretching slightly before her eyes fluttered open and she took in her surroundings.

She shot up into a sitting position. "Where the hell

are we?"

Alec offered his hand.

Surprisingly, she clapped her palm into his and allowed him to haul her up.

"We need to move. I'll explain what I can along the way."

She rubbed her temples, fingers distorting her smooth brow as she frowned at an invisible spot across the lake. "Yeah, sure, whatever," she mumbled, her thoughts clearly elsewhere.

He pressed her toward the north shore of the loch where he knew they could skirt a small inlet and head into the mountains. He kept his attention on her from the corner of his eye so she wouldn't notice he watched her. The limp in her gait was almost non-existent, but he wanted to be sure he was aware of how difficult moving was for her so he could slow down if needed. She wouldn't appreciate him hovering and he suspected her pride would keep her from saying anything if she experienced any more discomfort.

He also knew he would have to wait for her to ask questions rather than supplying her with answers right away. If he had learned anything after her visit to the emergency room, it was that Evie was too stubborn to listen to anyone's advice but her own. Otherwise, neither of them would be traipsing around the wilderness of that place.

As they approached the tree line, she broke the silence. "I thought you were going to explain."

Exactly as he had expected. "What is it you'd like to know?"

Annoyance bubbled off her. "How about you start with where the hell are we and how did we get here?"

Eyebrow quirked, he turned to look down at her. She mimicked the expression satirically.

"You don't remember, then?" At her blank expression he murmured, "Interesting."

"Are you always this unbelievably obtuse?" she demanded through gritted teeth.

Most of the short hair at the nape of her neck had escaped the ponytail holder meant to keep it secure. It curled under, tickling just above the line of her shoulders, and wisps stuck out, framing her face like a dark halo.

"We're in the Otherworld."

Her expression didn't change.

"On the other side of the veil. We crossed the hedge. Passed through the shade."

She rolled her eyes. "Saying the same non-answer in a different way doesn't make it any clearer."

"Do you know nothing of ancient mythology?"

"Not a lick."

He stopped and spun around to stare her down.

She almost kept walking past him up the shallow incline of the path but took two steps back to stand toe-to-toe with him.

"What do you know of plane geometry?"

She scrunched up her face. "What does geometry have to do with *geography?* Here I thought I should worry that you had drugged me. Clearly, you are the one who is on drugs."

"What do you know of plane geometry?" he repeated.

She clenched her jaw for a moment, holding his gaze without blinking. "I don't know. I majored in history. I was a history PhD candidate. I didn't exactly spend a lot of time in the math lab."

"But you do know what a plane is, don't you?"

"You mean the thing that flies through the air?" When Alec didn't even crack a smile, she let out an exasperated sigh. "Yes, I know what a plane is."

"And you know what a line is?"

"What do I look like, a first grader? Of course I know what a damn line is."

"Imagine that the world that you know is a line. It travels infinitely from one direction to another, time its trajectory."

Evie increased her frown.

"This, where we are, The Otherworld, is a plane. That line runs along that plane. We sort of passed through the invisible barrier that separates the line from the plane known as The Veil. And here we are."

"Yeah, none of that makes a damn bit of sense. What about the universe? All of space? Does that somehow fit onto your imaginary line? Are you saying this whole place is bigger than the biggest thing in… well, ever?"

"No. Just that time is linear and this place… it is not. It just is, and it has been since it was created by the gods." He held out his arms, as if to encompass their surroundings.

"The gods?" She harrumphed and started her ascent back up the path.

"Yes, the gods," he snapped. He quickly closed the distance she put between them and matched his stride to hers. "Like the one you encountered in the middle of those woods."

"I really have no idea what you mean," she said loftily.

"Oh? The murder of crows that turned into a woman didn't send off any internal alarms?"

Evie pursed her lips but didn't say anything for a moment. "You seem to know an awful lot about this woman you know nothing about."

Alec narrowed his eyes. "I didn't say I didn't know *anything* about her," he grumbled.

Evie shrugged and pulled the elastic from her hair, ruffled the dark locks. She then gathered them back up and rewrapped the black tie so only a minimum would escape.

"So, what's the story, then? Are you some sort of demi-god? Sent to the great Line known as Earth to protect us lowly mortals from the clutches of the almighty gods?" she mocked.

"No."

A dozen steps later she badgered him again. "Well, then what are you?"

"I'm the same as you," he answered simply.

"Then how did you know about this place? And all of this? I certainly know nothing about it, so I don't see how that makes us the same."

"Wrong. You *remember* nothing about it."

She barked a single laugh. "Right. I take it you know this because we were what? Friends? Enemies? More?" Her lips curved wickedly at the last.

Alec briefly contemplated answering her but decided against it; the more she figured out on her own, the better. She wasn't exactly taking to the information he had provided, anyway.

She sighed at his silence. "All right, let's say I believe all of this"—she waved her hands around to include their surroundings—"What exactly is the game plan? What are we *doing* here? And you better not say camping, because after my last experience in the woods, I am over that."

"We're looking for a way out."

"But didn't we just get here?"

"Yes."

"So, then why are we leaving?"

Alec looked down at her. "Throwing them off the scent."

"I fail to see how that works."

"Neither of them know that I have been using the Otherworld for quite some time to keep out of Mora's—*her*—grasp. It's possible they've figured it out now. Or at least Iain has, though it's only a matter of time before he tells her. But even if they have, they'll have to guess at best where I have you here or when I have taken you back."

"What do you mean 'when?' Like time travel?"

"Exactly like it."

She stopped dead in her tracks. "Right. Well. As nice as this has been, I'm just going to…" she pointed behind her with her thumb, the rest of her fingers curled into a fist.

Alec's hand shot out, wrapping around her other forearm. "I'll have you back soon," he told her quickly before she could disappear into the forest. If she lost herself in the woods, he wasn't sure he would ever be able to get her back out.

She stared up at him, her lips twisted to one side as she worried her bottom lip between her teeth. "I don't understand. You brought me here only so you could take me back? How does that keep me out of their 'evil clutches?'" She made air quotes with her one free hand.

"I'm not even sure why they… Wait. Why *were* you there?"

Alec let her arm drop from his hand and turned back to the path.

"Hey! Wait up!" She skipped a few steps to catch up. "You can't just avoid me! *You* brought me here, the least you could do is tell me why."

"It's incredibly complicated."

"You don't say," she muttered.

"Look, I'll get you back with enough time that we can come up with a plan to keep you safe."

"And why exactly is it your job to do that?" she asked, with more than a little condescension.

"Because I didn't keep you safe the first time!" He whirled on her, the anger he felt at himself projecting itself on her.

****

A few beats of her heart passed in silence before he whispered, "Is that what you wanted to hear?"

She almost felt sorry for him, for the clear hurt written across his face. Perhaps she shouldn't have pushed him. She'd always had a knack for being difficult, but was she not an unwilling participant in all of this? Shouldn't he at least tell her what was going on?

"I'm sorry," she mumbled, pressing her thumbs to her forehead and shaking her head to clear it. "I just… None of this makes sense. Iain told me that he wanted to take me 'back.' Was that—whatever it is that I clearly can't remember—was that what you think you needed to protect me from?"

His brow smoothed. "No." Back up the path he went.

"Ugh." She groaned. "This is the worst kind of nightmare."

She pinched her arm, hoping it would help her wake up. All she managed to do was irritate the tender skin there. When it was obvious she wasn't going to wake up, she hurried back to his side.

****

Without the warmth of a sun high above, the air grew cold, prickling her skin into gooseflesh. It was only when her teeth began to chatter that Alec halted. He said nothing to her, just lifted his shirt, pulling his white undershirt down when it rode up against the planes of his stomach—something Evie did not look away from—and handed her the light gray Henley.

She didn't resist his offering, instead quickly threading the neck over her head. She kept her arms hugged to her stomach, choosing not to thrust them through the short sleeves, even though they would have likely hung past her elbows. The cotton was soft and warm. And it smelled of him; a mix of tangy citrus and cloves, perhaps from his deodorant, the faintest hint of laundry detergent, and slightly of sweat. She breathed in deeply, catching her lower lip between her teeth and raising her gaze to meet his.

"It isn't much further." He turned, clearly not in the mood to prolong the venture.

Evie hugged herself tighter but followed. "I don't think I can go for much longer," she admitted softly.

The pain from her leg was killing her, shooting up into her hip and affecting the nerves of her lower back. She felt beaten and broken, all from an activity that should have been easy for anyone else. It would have been easier for her, too, only a year before. Bitterness crept in, but she didn't want it. She preferred to stamp it out, but there it was, drawing unwanted tears from the backs of her eyes. She locked her jaw, fighting against them.

"I know."

She almost didn't see the small stone cottage until he was pushing open the door with his shoulder. Nestled among the ferns, a drooping thatched roof slumped over four uneven walls.

The hinges squeaked loudly, ominously, and something in the trees fluttered away through the swaying branches. He disappeared into the shadows, and Evie followed closely into the single, musty room. The air inside was earthy, but it didn't smell stale as if it had been abandoned for some time. And by the relative tidiness she could see once he struck a match and lit the lamps told her she was wrong to have believed the place was abandoned.

"What is this place?" she asked.

A bed piled with woolen blankets and furs huddled in one corner. The opposite side held a sturdy table surrounded by several chairs, just beside a wide stone hearth. A heavy, black cauldron sat empty over charred stones, and dried herbs hung from the rafters.

"I'm sorry there isn't much to eat." He rummaged through some sacks as he said it, coming up with a pair of small apples, their flesh smooth and multicolored. He held one out to her, but she shook her head.

"I don't think I can eat anything."

He regarded her disbelievingly but set the apple down on the table before motioning her to take a seat as he did. His teeth crunched through the flesh of the one he still held. She glanced around the dark cottage, taking in the shuttered windows.

"How did you know about this place?" she asked as she gingerly sat, avoiding putting pressure on the side giving her so many pains.

"I live here," he said matter-of-factly. "Or I did." He bobbed his head from side to side. "Well, do," he amended once more.

"I don't… get it."

He cracked an ironic smirk. "I know. It's a lot to take in. When I'm on this side, this is where I come. I've done a lot of hiding out here, and we should be safe. Until morning light, anyway."

His accent almost seemed to change. It was a slight dropping of syllables she almost wasn't sure she had heard correctly, but she was fairly certain it was there. "And then?"

"And then I get you back to the other side."

"You said that earlier. I go back like a good little time turner. But then what? It isn't like they won't know where to look for me, you know. My parents live in one of the big houses on post." She drew a square in the air with her fingers. "With our last name plastered next to the door. You were there. Remember?"

"We'll figure something out, Evelyn. I promise."

She rolled her eyes. "Forgive me if I don't feel overwhelmingly confident."

"Neither of them is stupid enough to abduct you from your house."

Evie very much doubted that, but he seemed so sure, she decided she didn't want to argue with him. She had far too many questions buzzing around her brain to dwell on any one subject for too long.

"When I came into the hospital…" She trailed off.

"When you examined my records and said there was something off about them..." She frowned, trying to collect her thoughts. "Did this place have something to do with it?"

"You're very perceptive," he answered dryly.

"I want to know what you meant." She pressed her fingertips into her back, massaging her muscles.

"It was only a guess. A shot in the dark. I don't really have any more answers than you do, just some educated guesses."

"Then why don't you share them with me?"

"Because I don't want to give you partial truths, well-intentioned or otherwise." His teeth cut into the apple, again.

"So, you'd just rather leave me in the dark?" Annoyance crept into her tone just as a muscle pulled in her back.

"I'd rather figure it out with you."

She snorted. "That's awfully presumptuous, don't you think?"

The smile she received was tight-lipped and hinted at quiet amusement. Deciding she'd had enough of the circular conversation, she rose, gritting her teeth as the pain shot through her hip. The muscles pulled, keeping her from fully straightening at first, but once she was on her feet, it dissipated some. Alec must have seen the wince as it passed across her face.

"Why didn't you say something?" he demanded, a hand under her elbow in an oddly supportive gesture.

"It's fine. Nothing I don't deal with every day."

His jaw clenched. "Yes. And I pushed you further than I should have." He cut his gaze away in a blink before turning it back to her. "I'm sorry, I should have known better. I wasn't thinking."

She blinked up at him, not expecting his apology, much less the ring of sincerity. She could have said something, she probably should have. But she hadn't, and yet, rather than berating her for not speaking up, he was berating himself for not knowing. It was…

Unexpected.

Her sudden shift in emotion only served to remind her—for whatever reason, she didn't know—he was going out of his way to help her.

She swallowed and stared back. The reflection of flickering flames danced in his eyes, the rest of his face cast in shadow.

His head bent just as she lifted hers up, and just a whisper from her lips, he asked, "May I—"

But she cut him off as she pressed her mouth to his. There was a momentary hesitation, but then his hand was in her hair, cradling the back of her head gently as his lips explored hers. Her arms curved around his neck, drawing him closer. His chest pressed against hers, warm, and solid, their hearts beating out of sync, his fighting to catch up with hers. Her whole body hummed, a jittery mixture of anticipation and fear. In that moment, she wanted nothing more than to lose herself there, in that cottage, with him, perhaps forever.

Never had she felt so consumed by someone, before. Not with Calum. Not with Iain. Not with any number of boys or men, before.

It was scary. Or maybe it was intoxicating.

She lifted herself onto her toes, gasping a little when her hip and knee twinged.

He broke away. "May I see if I can relieve that a little?" he asked gruffly.

Evie stared at his mouth and nodded dumbly, her mind reeling and lips tingling from his kiss.

Before she could step away from him, he swept her legs out from under her, lifting her up as if she didn't weigh anything at all, and cradled her to his chest gently. He carried her to the bed, gently lowering her to the feather-stuffed mattress, and settled on the edge next to her, his body turned to her. With gentle hands, he pressed his thumbs into the muscles of her thigh, massaging gently, watching her face for any sign of pain.

There was nothing sexual about the way he touched her, but it wasn't in a completely professional fashion, either. She watched him, as well, hoping to catch a glimpse of what he was thinking. But as their gazes met and held, he revealed nothing.

"Tell me about yourself," she murmured. She needed to break up the silence, to focus on anything but the lingering taste of him.

"What do you want to know?" His voice was low, not much more than a whisper. Gruff. He was concentrating on her aching limb, his thumbs pressing in, making small circles.

"I don't know. Whatever comes to mind. Where you're from. What you do. Siblings? Pets? I don't know."

"I never knew my father," he said softly. "He died before I was born. I'm the youngest of eight."

"Eight? Wow."

She could hear the smile in his voice when he said, "I know."

"I bet that made for fun holidays."

Her joke was met with only a soft "Mmm."

"What, no slinging potatoes over politics?"

"We were never tight knit. Not like—" he cut himself off.

"Not like what?"

"Not like my wife's family."

Her head jerked up. "You're married?"

His eyes were unfocused, caught somewhere beyond the shadowed stone walls surrounding them. "Not anymore."

Evie dropped her gaze away. "I'm… I'm sorry."

His massaging momentarily ceased, but picked up once more. She winced as his thumb pressed into a tender spot.

"Sorry," he murmured. "She died. It was… a long time ago. But her ghost is something I will always live with."

She swallowed; it was something they had so very much in common, the loss of a partner. She cut her gaze away, concentrating on his hands, turning his words over in her mind, her heart aching. But it was more for him than for herself. "It-it gets better," she murmured, not really sure if she was making a statement of asking a question.

"No," he told her. "It doesn't ever get better. You just learn to live with it."

She sucked in a breath. "How?"

"You find someone else to live for."

Their gazes pulled together, again, and in his eyes she found a longing so raw she had to break away, again. But his hands continued, the ache beginning to leave her muscles. Who had his wife been? What was she like? What happened to her? She decided not to pry.

"I always thought my family was close," she murmured, wanting to give him something in return. "But I never realized how close we were until I saw how strained Calum's relationship was with his mother."

"Was he your…?" He trailed off but his question remained

She nodded. "Fiancé? Yes. Though I think we were engaged less than half an hour when… when he died. So, it probably doesn't count, right?"

He didn't say anything. But his massaging ceased, and he gently squeezed the muscle just above her knee in something akin to sympathy.

"His father died when he was young, too. So, it was just the two of them, him and his mother. He had been accepted to universities all over the world, but I think he was afraid to leave her. Or maybe he was just afraid of her, period. End stop. Not that St Andrews was a bad decision, but Harvard, Oxford, some university in Tokyo, I can't remember which, they had all offered him acceptance. I didn't meet him until years after that, but knowing him, he had no intention of ever leaving St A's. He applied just to show that he could. Or so he told me." Evie snorted a quick little laugh, her lips curling into a smile as she remembered the way Calum's cheeks pulled his mouth into a grin.

She shook herself back. "It was different when I was around, though. She seemed to… really like me, even if he didn't get along with her. And she was-is-possibly the sweetest person I know. We had tea several times at her insistence. She would make us extra cakes and bannocks and send them home with me. My family was always as functional as you can be with deployment after deployment after deployment and move after move after move. There were years where our whole lives revolved around a countdown. A countdown until the next move, a countdown until deployment. A countdown for R&R, a countdown until R&R was over. And then there was always the readjustment. My mother was always trying to keep us together for everything. She didn't want us to go out on Friday night because my dad was home. She didn't want us to go out on Friday night because our dad wasn't at home. She—"

Evie broke off, her forehead creasing.

Alec's warm hands still cupped her bare calf, but he made no move to remove them. And she made no move to pull away. Instead, she relaxed deeper into him and sighed.

"She was always just trying to keep us together," she murmured to herself, her mother's behaviors and intentions suddenly clear. Their relationship became strained when Evie announced she would be going to Scotland, and she'd never understood why. "She didn't want me to leave because someone was always gone. She just wanted her family to be close." She looked up to meet Alec's confused stare.

"Sorry. I've been… angry with her for awhile. She kept pushing me, *keeps* pushing me to stay close. She never supported me studying overseas, and I always resented her for it. I guess I still do. I just didn't realize until now why that was," she mused.

"You never realize how much it hurts those you leave behind."

A prickling of shame swept over her. She had never thought of it that way. Perhaps she had selfishly held a grudge, not seeing things from her mother's prospective. She wouldn't have changed anything, but maybe... It's possible she wouldn't have been quite so angry the last couple of years. "Know a little something of this, do you?"

"Mm. I do. I was often away from my wife. I was all about duty and country and advancement. She would beg me for time and I wouldn't give it to her. And then... Well, it was too late. I didn't realize what I had lost until there was no way to get it—her—back."

His hands hadn't moved in awhile, and he abruptly pulled them away.

Evie considered pushing herself back up into the sitting position, but she felt so relaxed, she couldn't make herself. The mattress enveloped her in its goose down softness, and she melted into it, instead, watching him from beneath heavy lids. "You must have loved her a lot."

He shook his head. "I don't think I loved her enough."

"What do you mean?" She nestled onto her side, drawing her hands up between her cheek and the feather pillow.

"She loved me. She loved me so much, and with more ferocity than I deserved. I didn't realize... I didn't realize how much I meant to her or she to me until it was too late. And when she was gone and I felt like my soul had been ripped apart, that's when I knew. It was a painful lesson."

"What do you mean? What lesson?"

"To cherish every moment."

"Is losing her what made you decide to become a doctor?" she murmured, her lashes sinking toward her cheeks.

"I don't think you'll like my answer."

She couldn't control them anymore. Her eye drifted shut. "It doesn't matter to me."

The seconds ticked by, the welcome darkness closing in over her, tempting her into dreams.

"I became a doctor to protect you."

Chapter Ten

His words reached her as the fog settled in, and she made no indication she heard him. The mattress shifted as he eased himself away, his warmth leaving with him

With his taste still lingering on her lips, she slipped fully into sleep.

****

Evie's breath caught and she startled awake.

She sprawled chest down on the bed, her ear resting on the crooked angle of her elbow. Shoulder stiff from the position, she rolled onto her side, gritting her teeth at the dueling sensation of relief and stinging pain. The last thing she remembered was Alec murmuring that he was there to protect her before she pushed through golden-grassed fields with the travel companions of her dreams.

Looking around the small cottage, she found Alec at the opposite end, standing by one of the small windows, its shutters open. He had rid himself of his shirt though the jeans he wore were still slung against his narrow hips. Silvery moonlight played along the muscles of his back, the curve of his shoulder. She had always had a weakness for broad, straight shoulders, and her mouth suddenly went dry.

The memory of his hands on her skin was still fresh, the firm press of his fingers gently massaging away the aches. So intimate, his skin upon her skin. As he told her things she was willing to bet he hadn't told many other people. As she recounted things to him she knew she had never told another living soul.

It was an intimacy she'd never felt before. Not with Calum, not in those moments she spent in the back seat of a car with Iain. This was different. Consuming. Longing and desperation sweeping over her, blotting out the rest. The pain, the fear, the confusion all fell away, and all she felt was need.

For him.

Her bare feet met the cold stone floor as she slipped from the bed without murmur or pause. No longer did pain shoot up her hip from her scar-crossed thigh, though the ghost of an ache remained, and she padded across the uneven cobbles until she stood a breath away.

He knew she hovered behind him. He had to. He became too still, too focused not to know. He didn't tense, but his breathing hitched slightly, quickening, and then holding. She appreciated his silence, allowing her to take pleasure in brushing her gaze over him, committing the lines and ridges of him to her memory.

Pressing close, she brushed her lips over his shoulder blade. He tensed and she slid further into him, the thin layer of her cotton shirt only a flimsy barrier at best, and her breasts flattened. Alec stiffened immediately and started to turn.

Evie stopped him with a hand to his hip, her fingers curling around his front, skimming her fingers over the muscle of his hip flexor, her palm pressing forward over his waistband. Her breath whispered over his skin, the rippling muscle of his back, her lips barely rasping over him.

"How do you make me feel this way?" Her eyes drifted closed.

All feeling pooled in her center, her skin pricking and begging to be touched. She pressed her lips against his back, again, trailing her lower lip over his spine as her hands gripped his arms just above the elbows. Evie rested her forehead between his shoulder blades, breath stuttering out of her, her grip tightening and eyes closing.

"I don't feel like myself around you," she admitted, caressing the curve of his muscle with her cheek. "And just when I think I have you figured out, something changes." She ran her palm down his arm, her fingertips blazing the trail over the hard muscle.

He moved, but she fitted her fingers between his, curled them up, stilling him.

"With you, I feel it all."

She turned her lips back into him, her tongue darting out over her own to capture the saltiness of his skin. She pressed a kiss to the center of his spine, and a tremor ran through him.

"You make me angry. And excited. And young. Old. Innocent. Stupid. Brilliant. Lost. And hot." She tightened her hold on his hands. "I've never felt less like myself. Or more like myself."

She dropped his hands, slipping her own around his chest, her fingers carding through the soft hair.

"And I don't know why. Her voice broke, her muscles slackening.

He whirled on her, crushing his mouth to hers as his fingers dove into her hair, getting caught in the tangles. She stumbled back, steadying herself by clapping both hands on his shoulders, her nails digging into the hard muscle.

A sweetness of apple still clung to his lips, and it mingled with the sharp tang of whisky. Their teeth scraped as she pushed closer, demanding more with her mouth, plucking and sucking, his stubble scraping her soft skin.

He walked her backwards until the edge of the wooden table bit into the soft skin around her hips. In one swift motion, his hands trailed down her back, her waist, the tops of her thighs, and he lifted her up just above the knee, settling her on the top of the wood. He stepped between her spread legs, bracing one hand behind her, and leaning in until his hips were cradled against her. He braced one hand on the table behind her, pushing his chest into her, quickening his kisses, and then breaking again, his hot mouth trailing down the curve of her neck.

His fingers dipped into the waistband of her yoga pants, looping into her plain, cotton panties, and edging them both over her hips. She bicycled her legs, pulling and pushing the fabric down as she clung to him, mouth parting, breath heavy and quick, blood pounding in her ears. The spandex capris awkwardly bunched around her ankles, and a hint of embarrassment crept up her chest when he dropped to his knees before her.

She gulped anxiously as he pulled black fabrics over her ankle, dropping them to the floor. And then, before she even realized what he intended, he buried his face between her legs.

She gasped, leaning back, immediately trying to disconnect her flesh from his seeking lips, but his hand shot out, steadying her, and pressed her more closely to him. As his tongue connected with her most intimate parts, her hands began to shake. No one had ever touched her like that, before. Her knees trembled, her arms shook, and she dropped her head back between her shoulders as her center muscles contracted and relaxed.

Tensing as his tongue flicked over the little bundle of nerves, her whole body vibrated as he worshiped her. She nearly melted into the table, one hand bracing against his shoulder, her short fingernails digging into his taut flesh. His hand ran up the trembling muscles of her thigh, over her scars, his thumb rubbing in a soft circular motion. Comforting. Quieting. She willed herself to relax with each gentle reminder.

And then he lifted up her thigh, hoisting it over his shoulder, forcing her to tip back. Her free hand, the one not kneading the muscle just above his collar bone, was forced back onto the wood to keep her from falling flat on her back.

She didn't recognize the mewls echoing in her ears as her own, but when his hand slipped beneath her shirt, slid into her bra, and plucked at her nipple, the sound slipped out again. She moaned, her hips rocking, pushing into him, and he encouraged her, the hand not at her breast cupping her buttocks, pressing her closer.

Evie's breath hitched as she came closer to finding the ultimate pleasure in him. She was close, but wanted so much more before she let herself go. She wanted him, all of him, and she'd only been given a small taste. She pulled at him, bending her knees and dislodging him. He stood standing between her thighs, and brought his mouth down on hers. She thought nothing of the taste of herself on his lips; the only thing she wanted was his kiss. They met hungrily against each other, her hands fumbling with his jeans, both of his hands now under her shirt, pushing it up into her underarms.

She popped each button from the loops of his jeans, but that was as far as she got. The stiff denim rasped and rubbed against her naked flesh, and she shuddered. So close to coming undone. But she wanted more. Needed more. Needed him closer. Needed him inside her.

He stepped away, drawing a condom out of his back pocket, and she leaned back, chest heaving as he stepped out of his jeans and boxer briefs, the cold air cooling some of her ardor. She pulled her shirt over her head with just enough time to welcome him back between her spread knees.

But rather than taking her fast and hard as she expected, he nuzzled her neck, laying gentle kisses just above her shoulder as his fingers pinched the bra clasp open. He drew the straps down her arms, dropping the plain, blue garment to the floor. Her head rolled back, giving him more access, and slowly, he trailed his lips down her collarbone and between her breasts. When his mouth found her nipple, he licked at it leisurely, eliciting a purr of satisfaction from her.

She didn't know how long they remained wrapped in each other like that; it could have been hours, or only seconds. She fell into a trance of softness and pleasure where time didn't exist, didn't matter. Where she didn't care.

When he finally slid between her thighs, it was slow, agonizing, and she stretched to accommodate him, humming with pleasure. He kissed her, then, slowly, savoring her and allowing her to do the same. Slowly he moved like the lapping of low tide on quiet shores. She demanded more, fingernails digging, mouth working faster. The flesh of her backside rubbed against the smoothed wood of the table, and though they started frustratingly slow, Alec brought their lovemaking to a crescendo.

****

Evie nestled closer to him, her head on his shoulder, one hand resting on his chest, her finger tangling with his chest hair as she tried to figure out how she had jumped into bed with this man as if it were the most natural thing in the world.

Upon serious reflection—okay, maybe not serious, but reflection nonetheless—she had been making some questionable decisions as of late. Before the accident, never in a million years would she have participated in any of the activities she had in the last month. She wondered if she needed to be concerned about her complete lack of caution. Perhaps her traumatic brain injury had resulted in some sort of bruising to the part controlling impulses. Or maybe she had a tumor.

Yes. A tumor. That was probably it. This whole thing was probably just a side effect of a tumor, as well. She had watched enough medical soap operas since being confined to the house to know exactly how these things worked.

Logically, however, she knew that they probably would have found some signs of a tumor during all of her head scans and blood work over the last year.

"What are you thinking?"

His voice rumbled through his flesh and bone, echoing in her ear. She shifted, nestled in closer.

"Just wondering if this is all the by-product of a brain tumor."

118

"It's not."

She shifted, propping her chin on her hand to look up into his eyes. "How do you know?"

"For starters, I've seen your medical records. And it's highly unlikely we would both have identical brain tumors causing identical hallucinations."

"And how do I know you aren't a hallucination?" She quirked an eyebrow.

There was a long pause. "I guess you'll just have to trust me."

"That's what I'm afraid of," she grumbled. "Trusting a tumor."

Only her stomach answered back.

"Hungry?" he asked with amusement.

She blushed, and bit down on her lower lip as she shifted her gaze away from his. "Maybe."

He extracted himself out from underneath her, rolling away and standing in one move. Rays of sunlight ran along his naked form, a play of light and shadows, as he strode to long table at the other end of the room. A blush warmed her cheeks as she took him in. Every thick muscle and broad bone. Every towering inch.

She shifted uncomfortably, pushing herself up until she sat with her back pressed against the headboard. She pulled the blankets with her, ensuring her extra plumpness and scars were covered, rearranging them under her arms and over her legs, suddenly self-conscious of her softness. She swallowed. Surely he was used to perfect bikini bodies, and here she was pale and untoned, her skin splotchy and uneven, and the slight roundness of her belly, the jiggle in her thighs.

She drew her knees up to her chest and lowered her

gaze to the blankets, her eyebrows drawing together. He caught her off guard, dipping down to kiss her on the lips before placing an apple in the hand that wasn't clutching cloth to bosom. He stood back up as she blinked in surprise and picked his clothes up off the floor. Stepping into his jeans first, he left them slung low and unbuttoned on his hips as he pulled on his shirt.

"I'll be back."

****

When Alec returned, it was with a fish the size of Evie's torso in one hand and a basket of grubby looking vegetables in the other. Evie didn't move from where she was sprawled across the bed, her head leaning over the foot so everything was upside down. Just like her life. The basket thumped down on the table, the fish next.

Evie wrinkled her nose. "Isn't that unsanitary?"

He ignored her question and rummaged through the pack he'd brought with him, producing a small blade which was unceremoniously stabbed into the gullet of the fish. "You dressed."

Evie made a face as he removed fish guts onto the table and flipped around onto her belly, spots momentarily prickling at the backs of her eyes as the blood rushed out of her head. "What, did you expect? Me to wait here for you, ready and naked?"

He didn't look up, but she caught the smile playing along the corners of his mouth. "The thought did cross my mind."

She rolled her eyes. "Even if I had been, you would have ruined it with your fish fingers."

His gaze snapped up. "You don't like fish?"

"Oh, no, I love fish. I just don't want to *see* the

poor thing get murdered right before my eyes, and then gutted on the table upon which I assume I will be eating it."

"It was already dead when I got here."

"I'm glad to see we are arguing the semantics."

"Anytime, love."

The endearment, so casually tossed out, slapped her like a bucket of cold water. Her expression stiffened and she immediately tried to soften it, but her heart was already beating at twice the speed and it threatened to jump up into her throat. Only one other person had called her that. She swallowed and stood, rubbing her palms against the thighs of her pants before awkwardly crossing her arms over her chest. She moved to the opposite side of the table.

He drew the knife through the fish along the spine and ribs, and though she protested before, she couldn't keep her eyes off it. Perhaps as a way to from staring at him.

"You must bring all the girls here." She tried to joke, to offset the pet name he had given her, how uncomfortable she suddenly felt. But she was sure her tone was a note off, her face a little too strained to be convincing. "Cook for them. Feed them wine."

"If you're asking if there's alcohol, the answer is yes." He nodded at a handful of small casks in a corner but kept his attention on the fish as he removed the first tender strip of flesh. "But it'll be whisky, not wine." He flipped the fish over, and gently slid the blade through scales. "And you're the first."

Evie shifted from one foot to the other and then groaned. "Why did you have to go and make it awkward?" she demanded.

"Was I the one who made it awkward?" He flipped the fillet skin-side-down onto the table next to the other half and then wiped his hands on a rag.

"Yes!" She threw up her hands. "I've only known you"—she frowned as she tried to work out how long he had known him—"for like ten minutes and you're already acting like… like…"

"Like we're involved?"

"Yes!"

"Well, aren't we?"

She made a face and shook her head minutely back and forth. "No!" Part of her was just deeply annoyed that he was so nonchalant about the whole conversation. "I didn't just jump into bed with you for the hell of it," he said evenly.

He moved around the cooking space efficiently and she wasn't really tracking what he was doing. Only that it was distracting from the fight she was trying to pick with him. The fight she so desperately needed.

"We're in this for the long haul, Evelyn."

"And I don't get a say in it? Maybe *I* just jumped into bed with you for the hell of it!"

"Then I suppose that's something we will have to work on."

"I slept with Iain! Like, not even"—how long *had* she been in this stupid little cottage?—"a week ago." She clenched and unclenched her fists, moving her weight from one leg to the other, ignoring the muscle twinges.

"All right."

"All right?" she yelled. "All right!" Her voice rose an octave. Why wasn't he at least a little upset with her? She felt like she was on a violently rocking boat, ready to be thrown into a furiously churning ocean, and he was so *calm.*

"Look, Evelyn, I'm not entirely sure why you are trying to talk me out of you, but it's not going to work."

"The hell it isn't!"

She knew it sounded stupid the minute she uttered it, but when he laughed, *actually laughed*, she stormed straight out of the cottage. The wooden door stuttered against the jamb as she slammed it shut.

Twilight fell over the forest and the shadowed trees swayed in the gentle breeze, their branches creaking and leaves fluttering. She took a deep breath, marveling at how it just smelled so *clean,* like the untouched reaches of the Cairngorms. Free of pollution, of people. Thinking of Scotland always calmed her; it was the most magical place she had ever been; it spoke to her soul in a way no other place had. It was old and wild and full of an energy she couldn't explain. This place reminded her of that.

And as if her surroundings meant to remind her, something whizzed past her ear, a high-pitched, tinkling hum. She stepped back, searching the darkness for a glimpse, but she only caught a faint glimmer as something flitted into the leaves above, leaving a blue-green trail in its wake. A firefly, she decided. Perhaps a little larger than any she had seen before, but what else made sense? She turned her face toward the sky and caught sight of more stars than she had ever seen in her life. It was stunning, and not something she thought that even light pollution could cover up. This was…

She wasn't in Kansas, anymore. Literally.

"It's quite beautiful, isn't it?"

She didn't turn, but instead let Alec's warm voice

wrap around her. "Quite." The corner of her mouth twitched upward.

She suspected he wanted to touch her. The need vibrated off him, but he kept his hands to himself. But did she really need the space he was giving her? Did she want it? This was all too confusing.

Evie turned to him. "Sorry for getting a little crazy."

"It's all right. I can back off."

"No, I...I like you. I'm just..."

"Scared."

"However did you know?" She grinned.

"I may have felt the same way once or twice in my life."

"Pfft, I doubt it." She changed the subject quickly, feeling she needed to say more. "And I'm sorry for having sex with Iain."

"Are you?"

She lifted her shoulders. "Kinda?" After their encounter the other night, maybe she should be more sure of herself.

"Well, you don't need to apologize to me for that. It's none of my business."

She resisted the urge to scratch her head. "Huh? Isn't that like Guy One-oh-one?"

He chuckled. "You don't see me apologizing for the other women I've slept with, do you?"

"Well, no, but—"

"None of my business."

She frowned. "But aren't you worried you're just another notch in the bedpost?"

"No."

"Why not?"

"Because I know I'm not." Before she could groan her frustration, he asked "Hungry?"

"Kind of. But I'm a little worried about getting food poisoning and dying."

"Are you calling me a bad cook?"

"I'm saying that you got salmonella all over that table."

He leaned in close, conspiratorially. "What if I were to tell you that in this place, salmonella doesn't exist?"

Evie looked up at him through narrowed eyes. He wiggled his eyebrows comically.

"I would say…" she paused. "Tell me more over dinner."

He grinned and she slid her arm into his, allowing him to lead her back into the cottage, the sounds of the night playing a symphony around them.

Inside, she slid into a chair, rested her elbows on the table, and cradled her cheeks in her hands as she watched Alec work. He quartered a few potatoes, dumped them into a small cauldron, and placed the black pot on the small fire he must have built before coming outside after her. Liberally, he salted and peppered the fish before sprinkling sprigs of a bright green herb over the white flesh.

As the potatoes began to boil, he sliced a small white onion and broke it into rings. They were arranged along the bottom of an iron skillet and the filets were placed on top. He then poured milk over the whole lot of it.

"Where did you get the milk?"

"From a cow."

"It was just wandering around the forest?"

"We're situated not far from the shores of the loch. There is a farmer there with a small herd of cattle. He allows me milk when I need it."

"How generous of him."

Alec ignored her jab and put the pan on a grate over the fire, just to the right of the pot of boiling potatoes.

A strange sense of déjà-vu settled over her as the lick of fire caught her attention. The orange flames danced wildly in the wide hearth. She'd never been here before, of that she was certain. But could it be the millions of flames bouncing sinisterly against soot-covered stone? Or the billions of stars above the landscape? The scent of the simmering fish? The hair on the back of her neck rose and her arms prickled into goose bumps.

Alec slid something toward her on the table and the feeling was gone. She looked down at the stone cup before her.

"Whisky." He held a similar cup in one hand and poured the contents over the fish.

She briefly considered accusing him of trying to get her liquored up, but instead sipped at the amber liquid. It was smooth. Silky. She sipped on it until a full plate was placed before her.

The food was amazing, if simple, reminding her of the traditional Scottish meals that Mrs. Baird fed Calum and her those few Sunday evenings. She couldn't shovel the fish into her face fast enough and was disappointed when there was none left. Between bites of potato, she sipped at the whisky, not complaining when Alec refilled the stone cup again, and then once more. When she could eat no more, she pushed the plate away and threw back the rest of the alcohol.

The whisky warmed her all the way down to her core, every cell in her body vibrating with warmth.

"Why do you like me?" she blurted, the words a surprise even to herself.

"What kind of question is that?"

"Why are you helping me, then?"

"Perhaps because I like you?"

She pushed away from the table. The legs of her chair scraped against the scarred floor and Alec watched her with curiosity as she rounded the table. She straddled his lap and stole his mouth with hers. His hands landed on her waist as his lips opened for her, the scratch of his stubble around her cheeks igniting a fire within her. His hands adjusted her hips, moving her a scant few centimeters until she was situated over his growing erection. She rocked forward, and then again, and again, the pressure and friction eliciting moans from them both.

"If you knew me better, you wouldn't like me at all," she murmured, her breath heavy with whisky.

His fingers tightened. "You can't talk me out of you, Evie." He nipped at her ear lobe.

She shuddered, the shiver running down her spine. She rocked into him, her breasts pressed against the hard planes of his chest. She wanted his hands on them, again.

"At least let me try," she insisted breathlessly.

His rumble of laughter had her gasping around her grin.

"You're the best of all of us." He claimed her mouth with his and her thoughts along with it. "You just need to believe it, yourself." His hands traveled up her hips to the warm skin beneath her shirt, and his thumbs hooked into the bottom of her bra.

Who else could he mean?

He pulled the cups over the swell of her breasts, and cupped them, filling his palms. His lips trailed along her jaw to her ear.

It didn't matter anymore.

Chapter Eleven

"Do we have to go?" Evie pouted as she regarded the outside of the little cottage wistfully.

Behind her, Alec sniffed in amusement. "No."

She whirled around to meet his gaze. "Really?"

He shrugged. "Sure. If that's what you want. We can hide out here forever for all I care."

She twisted her mouth to one side and narrowed her eyes. "I feel a 'but' coming on."

He shoved his hands in the front pockets of his jeans and rocked back on his heels. "But I thought you wanted some answers."

She groaned. He was right, damn him. She wasn't going to learn anything about the strange woman from the forest, why she wanted Evie, or how Iain worked into the equation if she stayed there with Alec, no matter how tempting the idea was. She shot one final, hungry look at the cottage, the memories of her time there like warm honey pooling around her heart. "All right. Fine. Let's go then," she grumbled.

Alec held out his hand, and she slipped her palm against his, allowing him to lead her down the narrow, dirt path.

The morning air was crisp and damp. She shivered and hugged his arm to her, cradling it to her chest. Her breath puffed out in front of her and her nose burned from the cold.

The weather there made even less sense than the sun cycles. Summer had been ripe and heavy in Kansas, the temperatures similar when she awoke on the shore of a loch. But no matter how hard she tried to determine the passage of time, the arc of the sun, or when the moon might appear, everything just became muddled and her confusion multiplied exponentially. At times she was certain they had been in that cabin for only a matter of hours, but others she was sure they had savored each other for weeks. She recalled the ways they explored one another, how well he knew her body. Hell, how well she knew his. Could it have been a month? No, none of it made any sense.

Alec tugged on her hand. "We're almost there."

"There." She didn't say it as a question.

He'd rattled on about leaving since they woke up, but little of what he said truly sank in.

"Down there." He pointed through the trees, down the slope of the gentle swell of mountain where the shimmering gray water of the loch lapped a rocky shore. In the center of the inlet, a small island rested, large standing stones set in a circle around it. "The gateway that will take us back."

"Doesn't going home kind of defeat the point? I mean, don't get me wrong, I enjoyed the interlude, but how does going back accomplish anything? Won't they still be there?"

"Probably."

"So….?" She released his arm as they began the descent down the slope, but he caught her hand in his.

"We aren't going to the same time."

"What do you mean?"

"I mean, we're going to backtrack."

She shook her head. "I don't think I am ever going to understand any of this. I will just follow you, oh fearless leader."

Alec snorted and led her around a large tree root. As they approached the island, Alec walked right into the water, tugging her along after him. The lapped at her ankles, cold, but not as frigid as she expected. It was far clearer than it had appeared from above, and small fish skittered between smooth, round pebbles.

They waded across the shallows to the island's ruffling green grasses, the ring of large rocks circling its center. The stones lay on their sides, long, smooth rectangles with barely a foot between them and too high for her to step over.

Just outside the ring, Alec dropped his bag onto the grass. He knelt next to it and flipped the flap open to rummage through it. When he stood back up, he held a Christmas ornament, a bright red globe with the previous year plastered across it in bold, block script.

Evie quirked an eyebrow as he stood and slung the pack back over his shoulder in one movement. "What, no silver apples?"

He sniffed and held his hand out.

She eyed it and twisted her mouth around to the side. She kept her arms firmly folded against her chest. "Will this be the same as last time?"

"Essentially."

"Will I… do you always black out?"

He ran his fingers lightly down her cheek before caressing her chin. He trailed them down the line of her scar, a slender white line barely visible after months of healing. She was acutely aware of it. A reminder of how her appearance was forever changed. And her coming out of the blackness only to find her entire world destroyed.

"The first few times, yes," he told her gently. "But I learned to overcome it. Crossing the veil is a lot for the body—and the mind—to handle, I think. It's nothing to be ashamed of." He dropped his hand from the caress.

"How-how do you stay conscious through it?"

"Truthfully?"

"No, I want you to lie to me." She rolled her eyes.

"I hold my breath and focus on something else."

"Like what?"

"Well, this time it will be your breasts, but really anything with do," he said with a sly grin and a knowingly twinkle.

She dropped her head back and made a sound of disgust in the back of her throat. "Yeah, okay," she muttered. "Let's just get this over with."

Alec stepped into the circle and she followed close on his heels. Once at its center, he turned to her and reached for her hand. He pressed her palm over the ornament until it was sandwiched between their palms. Around them, the world dipped and swayed, spun and turned.

Evie caught her breath and held it as her stomach rolled. What could she focus on? She frantically racked her memories, but all she could conjure up was her own breasts. Heat flooded her cheeks. He had done some marvelous things to them...

Her stomach pitched. What little food she ate before they left threatened to evacuate, but then the spinning stopped, leaving her with only a dull headache. Still unsteady, she glanced around to find herself back in Alec's little Queen Anne, the hardwood floors dull and in need of refinishing, the wainscoting thick with many layers of paint.

The electric sconces remained off, but the room was warmly lit by the colored lights shining in through the antique glass of the windows and draped along the plastic boughs of an artificial Christmas tree.

Evie turned to her companion, the question about the tree on the tip of her tongue when the whole room tilted and her stomach clenched right along with it. Lightheadedness slammed into her, and with two stumbling steps, she reached the umbrella stand next to the door. Grasping the edges, she violently lost her meager breakfast.

As her body shuddered, Alec's hand grasped her shoulder. His thumb caressed the back of her neck as she breathed heavily, willing her body to calm. When she was sure the retching had subsided, she fell to her knees and then sat heavily on the floor with her legs curled in front of her.

Alec still sat on his haunches, his elbows resting on his knees, looking down at her with sympathy. "Water?" he murmured as if knowing her skull was hell bent on crushing her brain.

Just the thought of anything passing between her lips had her stomach seizing up once more. She pressed the back of her hand to her mouth to suppress the unladylike belch threatening to erupt and shook her head.

He took her free hand in his and rubbed his thumb across her knuckles. "It'll pass in a few minutes."

"You mean you knew this would happen?"

"You get used to it, figure out how to get past it."

She frowned. "I think this was a one-time deal, thank you very much."

The look he gave her said he didn't think that would be the case. "Let's get you off the floor." He slid his hands under her arms and hauled her to her feet.

"Do… do you think you could take me home?" Her voice rang small and wobbly even to her own ears.

"No."

"No? What do you mean 'No?'" She whirled to face him.

"I can't take you there because you're already there."

"What do you mean I'm already there?" she demanded.

"Where were you last December—*this* December?" he amended.

She screwed up her face. "At my parents' house. But why does that matter? I'm here, and—"

"Yes, you're here. But you're *also* there." He held out his hands, moving them in front of him for emphasis. "If you were to walk into their house right now, there would be two of you, and…" he trailed off, huffing out an exasperated breath. "And I have no idea what would happen, but none of the options are great."

She pursed her lips and refused to meet his gaze. "Then what the hell am I supposed to do?"

"Avoid yourself and anyone who knows you from that time. Otherwise, you're good."

"Really? *Really?*" The good thing about the anger was that it made her forget how much her head hurt and her mouth tasted like the inside of a dumpster. "What the hell am I supposed to do, then? Just hang out in your front room for the next eight months?"

"Look, searching for you right now would be like searching for a needle in a haystack. It's going to take them awhile to find you, and if you play the game right, you might be able to get out of their reach forever. Use it. Find out what you need to know. Make the best of it."

Use it. Use it. How did she use it? She groaned, dropped her head into her hands, and screamed into her clammy palms. "Why is this happening to me?"

"Evie, I—"

"Just leave me alone, Alec," she grumbled and bent at the waist to lean into her knees. Darkness closed around her, the lights finally dimming from the backs of her eyelids.

He didn't move for the longest moment. When he did and his steps echoed down the hall, her shoulders sagged in defeat.

Everything was spinning out of control. From the moment she first saw him standing on her parents' back porch with the neighbor's dog, it just spiraled faster and faster, each moment taking her further from feeling steady.

Her fingertips slid away from her eyes and pressed into her temples. She massaged the sick feeling away until her heart stopped racing and the cramps in the pit of her stomach dissipated.

Once she was sure she wouldn't be sick, again, Evie braced herself against the wall and straightened. The floorboards creaked as she entered the small white kitchen. He waited for her, his gazed fixed on the doorway, his hips resting against the edge of the counter, feet out before him, arms crossed over his chest. On the stop top, a pair of pans popped and sizzled.

She stopped and hung her head, glancing up through her lashes. "I, um…"

"Hungry?"

She nodded, thankful he interrupted her weak apology.

He withdrew a pair of plain white plates and set them down on the counter. As she passed her weight from one leg to the other, he spooned eggs, bacon, and spiced potatoes onto each dish. Without a word, he slid both plates onto a small drop-leaf table. He strode back across the kitchen to withdraw forks from a shallow drawer and paper napkins from a cabinet over the stove. He laid out both next to the plates and held out a hand toward one of the chairs.

She sat down at the closest setting, balancing on the edge of the seat, her legs crossed at the ankles below her. She folded her hands in her lap and waited for him.

"Please," he murmured, waving at her food and moving toward the refrigerator.

Hesitantly, she picked up the fork, rolling it between her fingers.

Plunking down a pair of water bottles between them, he sat down and dug into his pile of eggs.

She took it as a sign and stabbed a small cube of potato with the tines.

"Feeling better about everything?"

She thought about lying. "No."

They ate in silence, but the discomfort was too much for her to bear.

"I, uh, I was thinking about what you said. About using the time travel—whatever, you know what I mean. I just… I don't know how."

He chewed, regarding her lazily, but even after he swallowed, he merely regarded for her a moment. "Well, what is it you hope to discover?"

"How am I supposed to know?" she shot back, instantly defensive. But she knew. Of course, she knew. She took a deep breath and sighed heavily. "What they want with me, and from me."

He nodded and shoved some potato across his plate while he chewed. "And what do you know so far?"

She shrugged. "I don't really know. I met Iain at a bar. I was with a friend." When had Evan become a friend? She decided to mull over that word choice later. "I mean, it wasn't a set up or anything, he was just there with the rest of the officers in his unit and we were introduced. We talked a little, but he didn't ask for my number or anything, he was polite. I ran into him again at the coffee shop in the exchange, he said hi, and asked if I was going out with everyone again that night. I saw him there…" she trailed off, wondering if she should really delve into how she had had sex with the other man. Alec had told her it wasn't any of his business, but…"We got better acquainted—"

He jaw ticked. He was obviously gnashing his teeth, and she pretended not to notice. But her heart skipped a beat and blood rushed through her ears. Her face grew hot and she licked her lips free of salt and spice and grease. She wanted to tell him it was only a hurried, semi-drunken coupling that was more like scratching an itch than an intimate rendezvous. They'd barely lasted a few minutes once the condom was on.

"There was something odd." She furrowed her brow, remembering the condom wrapper she felt compelled to retrieve at the crack of dawn the next morning. "He, um… he dropped a scrap of paper." She paused, trying to remember the words scratched across the crumpled college-ruled lines. "About Flora MacDonald." She brightened. "It said Flora MacDonald, and then underneath it 'Thistle and Rose.' Or maybe it was 'Rose and Thistle.'"

He dropped his fork onto the plate with a clatter, his eyebrows meeting over his nose. He braced his elbows onto the table, folding his hands together as he frowned. "That is odd."

"I thought so, too! She's one of the most famous Jacobite women in history. I've read everything there is to read about her, and I've never come across anything to do with thistles or roses. Prince Charles's father James had a claim to the English throne, sure, but *she* didn't."

"Aye," he murmured absently, his gaze staring off into some unknown space in the scarred wood of the table.

She quirked an eyebrow at his use of such an antiquated term but was too excited about the little piece of the puzzle she may have unearthed from the depths of her own mind.

"What do you think it means?"

She leaned forward, a bubble of excitement curving her lips up into a grin. It was an excitement she felt with the first blooming of a new idea, a new hypothesis, when she was lost in research. A tiny fragment of a theory could blossom into something bigger. Something no one else knew.

He didn't answer but relaxed against the back of his chair and fished his phone out of his pocket. His thumbs tapped rapidly over the screen.

After a moment, he flipped the device around to her. "I think that it means there is a woman by the name of Flora MacDonald who owns a shop called the 'Thistle and Rose.'"

Her gaze jumped from the screen to his face. "Really? You searched it??"

He shrugged and pressed the screen off before laying it face down on the table. "Got the job done, didn't it?"

"So… where is this shop?"

"Outside of Atlanta. Georgia."

"Yeah, yeah. I know where Atlanta is. I went to college there, remember?"

"Know where it is, then? The shop, I mean." He picked the phone back up, flicking the screen on and entering a pass code. He held the screen toward her so she could read the name of the town.

She leaned forward but shook her head. "I mean, I've heard of it, but I've never been there."

"And Flora MacDonald?"

She rolled her eyes. "I'm pretty sure I would remember a woman who had the same name as, well… Flora MacDonald. I'm a Jacobite Rebellion scholar."

Alec was silent for a moment, his stare unfocused, his finger idling tapping on the wood of the table. "What do you have in that purse of yours?" He nodded toward the slender leather strap of the pocket book draped across her middle.

She lifted an eyebrow. "My wallet, some hair ties, a few pain pills—"

"ID?"

"Yeah, I have them all with me."

"All?"

"You know, military, driver's license, student ID, passport—"

"You keep your passport in your purse?"

"Habit. From living overseas."

"That's odd."

"I don't think it is," she said then bit off a piece of bacon.

"Right." Abruptly, he stood, picked up his plate, and dumped it in the sink. Pulling open the blinds with one hand, he looked out into the dark. "I'll be back in an hour. You should be safe here. Don't let anyone in."

All she could do was blink at him. "Wh-what?"

But he was already shoving keys into his pocket and pulling open the back door.

Evie sat there in stunned disbelief for a few minutes. "Well, that was weird." She looked down at her plate of half-eaten food. She contemplated letting it go to waste, but instead picked up her fork and finished it off, a little sad when it was all gone.

With a sigh, she set to the task of cleaning up the dishes, finding soap resting next to the sink, a sponge propped up against it. She left everything drying in one side of the sink, and turned to scan the room. She felt awkward just waiting there, but she also felt like she was covered in a month's worth of grime. Hoping he wouldn't mind, she went poking through the house, looking for a fully-stocked bathroom. She found one tucked between a linen closet and the laundry room near the front of the house.

After turning the water all the way up to scalding, she dropped her summer clothes on the ground, and got to the pleasing task of ridding herself of Otherworld dirt and sweat. She came away smelling of Alec's soap, spicy clove and citrus.

Evie was wrapping herself into an over-large towel she found under the vanity when a knock landed on the door.

"Evelyn?"

She tucked the towel around herself and stuck her head around the jamb.

"I brought you some clothes."

She arched an eyebrow. "Should I even ask?"

"I'll let you get dressed."

She pulled the bag open and looked inside. A pair of jeans and a red sweater were carefully folded there, a little tissue-paper packet on top, and a pair of ballet flats nestled among them. She drew the tissue paper out first, finding a pair of ivory satin panties and matching bra. She sniffed in amusement that he had gotten her anything other than her preferred cotton but wasn't sure how she felt that he managed to find her exact size in either.

Dressed, she met him back in the kitchen. "I could have gone with you to pick out the clothes."

He was putting the dishes she had washed away in the cabinet. "I had to go get my car, too, only have one helmet. And it's cold out," he added as almost an aside.

"Your car?"

"Yeah, it was at the hospital."

She stared at him in confusion.

"I'm on shift this evening. I drove the car in, but I'm going to need that if we're going to Atlanta. I traded myself the bike."

"Bike?" she echoed, but shook her head, not waiting for an answer. "We're going to Atlanta? What?

Now?"

"If you're ready."

She stood there in silence for a moment. There had to be a good reason why she couldn't hop in his car and drive across the country. On the other hand, she had already broken all of the "Don't go with strangers" rules, as it was, and what was her other option? Live on his couch until a better option materialized? "I… I guess…"

He turned off lights, and she followed him to the front of the house. He hefted his pack back over his shoulder and opened the door for her.

"Aren't you going to be confused when you leave work and find your car gone?"

"No." He pulled the door shut behind him and turned to lock it. "This isn't a first."

"Oh."

"Besides, I remember coming out of work one night in December to find the bike in the spot I left the car. I cursed myself a few times, and then slept it off in the on-call room."

Evie shivered and immediately understood why. "So, you do this often?" she asked.

His hand was at the small of her back, leading her off the front porch and to his car. He opened her door for her first, and then the back passenger door, slinging his pack onto the back seat.

"Frequently enough." He shut that door, and quietly clicked hers shut, as well.

"For how long?"

He turned, meeting her gaze in the dark. "Honestly? I can't even remember."

Chapter Twelve

The car purred to life, but instead of immediately backing out, he pushed buttons on the navigation system. She wasn't sure where the address would take them, only that it was close to the Rose and Thistle.

Alec did all thirteen hours of the drive to Atlanta. Evie half-protested once they made it through Kansas City, offering to take the wheel and let him rest, but he only gave her a withering look and possessively tightened his hand on the leather steering wheel.

She stifled a yawn, thankful he didn't take her up on the offer, and leaned her head against the passenger side window. He closed the distance between them, wrapping her hand in his then pulling it toward him to rest their entwined fingers over the gear shift. The gentle hum of the engine vibrated up through it as he lightly ran his thumb over the soft side of her hand, and in moments, she was fast asleep.

Her nap was short-lived, lasting only until he stopped halfway through Missouri to fill up the gas tank. As the dark countryside sped by, she found herself having the conversations she would have had before sleeping with him. Conversations that take place in coffee shops and across a dinner table. Getting to know one another conversations they would have had sooner if her world wasn't quite so inside out.

They arrived sometime around noon, and he

steered them through the tree-lined streets dwarfed by turn-of-the-century mansions, the odd antebellum mixed in. Grand old ladies, they held court with their expansive porches, great gables, and manicured lawns. Many were done up in beautiful, artful Christmas lights, though one had a whole pack of blow-up snowmen and reindeer. She preferred it. The ridiculousness and child-like whimsy interspersed between classic holly and tasteful boughs of pine.

The main street took them right through the town square where the lamp posts were wrapped in garlands and sparkling white lights and an enormous tree shot up toward the sky next to a splashing fountain. The Thistle and Rose was huddled in the center of it all, tucked in between a bakery and a children's boutique.

She pointed it out, but Alec kept going until they reached a sprawling hotel on the other side of town. It was long and white, Georgian in style with thick Grecian columns and a perfectly symmetrical facade. It, too, was festively draped in twinkling white lights and large evergreen boughs. Just inside the glass-fronted doors, an enormous Christmas tree draped in reds and golds stood in the main lobby.

He left her in the car and secured a room, coming back to pull around into a parking spot and escort her to a third-floor suite. Evie fell backwards onto the king-sized bed, sighing as her tired muscles stretched, and then turned to her side, propping her head on her elbow.

"What's the plan?" she asked lazily.

Alec dropped the bag he'd carried up on the wing-backed chair in the corner before falling down beside her.

She bounced up a little as he hit the mattress, the

delicate white fluff of the comforter lapping up at their sides.

"Sleep."

Evie giggled and inched closer, nuzzling her head against his shoulder. "You're not tired, are you?"

"Can't even begin to describe it." He curled his arm around until his hand was on her shoulder. He rubbed it, squeezing gently.

"You sure?" she asked mischievously. But she had no answer; his breathing already slipped into the heavy, even rhythm of sleep.

Despite her own dry, burning eyes, she twisted her head up to regard him. His auburn eyelashes lay fanned out across his cheeks, longer and fuller than was fair, and his features gained some innocence she never would have expected to see there. He appeared younger, the stress he carried with him melting away, and leaving behind a hint of youthfulness.

She shifted, rolling onto her side, her head still nestled on his shoulder, and reached up a hand, caressing his cheek with her fingertips. It was rough with stubble, and she dragged the pad of her thumb down over the cleft in his chin. How easy it was to become enchanted with him. To get lost in him. She dropped her hand to his chest and snuggled closer, breathing in his scent.

She hadn't slept particularly well in the car, but her eyes still refused to close. Naps had never been a particular strength of hers, and mind racing, she counted the possibilities of what they might find at the shop. It was unlikely anything there would be of any consequence, and yet, a niggling remained in the back of her mind: Iain must have had good reason to keep that slip of paper in his pocket.

****

The ring arced before her on a delicate silver chain, swinging back and forth, back and forth. Winking in the dim, orange glow of the fire, the center stone was only a breath away from hitting the tip of her nose. It was so familiar. How did she know it? The memory played on the outskirts of her mind, just beyond reach. She almost grasped it when—

"Evelyn."

Her eyes opened with a jerk.

Alec stood over her, his short hair wet. Face dewy and smooth, the stubble she admired before was completely gone. A white hotel towel rested low over his hips, and he was bare-chested, droplets still clinging to his chest hair. She blushed and quickly turned her gaze away to stare over his shoulder, hoping he didn't catch her admiring him.

"Evelyn," he repeated, a bit of amusement in his voice.

He canted his head to the side and when their gazes met, the heat of her cheeks was so severe, it seared.

"S-sorry," she stuttered. "I didn't realize I had fallen asleep. How long have you been awake?" She cleared her throat, refusing to look him in the eye, again.

"Not long. Hungry?"

She sat up and assessed. "Starving."

He turned to his pack and rifled through it, pulling out some clothes. He dragged a plain white undershirt over his head. "There's a restaurant downstairs if—"

She wrinkled her nose. "Maybe we can find something a little more casual? We could walk down to where all the shops and restaurants are? My roommate in college was from somewhere around here, I think, and she always talked about an Irish pub. I would die for a beer and some fish and chips right now."

No sooner had the words left her mouth than her stomach grumbled. And though that same roommate had raved about a Cajun restaurant and a restaurant where rum punch was served in buckets, she craved the deep-fried seafood and potatoes. Nothing else was going to be an acceptable substitute.

"Well, I see no need for that. Fish and chips it is, then." He buttoned his jeans over his hips, and then sank down beside her to pull socks over his feet.

She bounced off the bed, grabbed up her purse from the side table, and slipped the strap over her head. "Can we find an ATM, first? I need to get some cash."

"No, I've got it covered. Besides, you can't be making withdrawals in Georgia while you're holed up in Kansas, remember?"

She pursed her lips and made a face. "I can't let you do that."

He pulled a gray shirt over his head. "And why not?"

"Well, because…. Because." She stopped while she thought about it. "Because it makes me feel weird."

He rolled his eyes and stuffed his wallet into his back pocket. "Well, stop."

Outside, the air was crisp, and there was a bite to the wind. She slid her arm through his, curling elbow around to tuck her fingers between his bicep and her chest. His warmth pressed into her side. Did they look like a real couple strolling down the street, arm-in-arm? It was a silly thought.

She tilted her head back and took in the set of his jaw, the curve of his lips, and the warmth inside her chased the cold away.

****

"What?" he asked, perplexed as she beamed up at him.

They waited for the walk signal to flash, and she tucked her bottom lip between her teeth, glancing up at him through the dark fringe of her lashes. She had never looked at him like that before. Sure, there had been some moments, like that first time they had met in the bookstore, when she saw him with fresh, curious eyes. Or when she was drunk on desire and a hair too much whisky. But never had she gazed up at him like he was the only other person in the world.

An ache formed in his chest, one he hadn't felt in a very long time. He forced a smile of his own, and was saved by the walk signal flashing at them.

They crossed to one of the shop-lined sidewalks. The Thistle and Rose stood dark at their backs, and though Alec was curious about what link the location held to Iain and Mora, he could wait to find out until the next day. Something about it didn't sit well with him, and he preferred to get lost in her than pulled toward whatever was inside Flora MacDonald's shop.

She bumped into him as they strolled by a boutique, a magic shop, a little cafe, a dance studio, and a few antique stores, her head whipping around to take in the wares displayed in windows, her eyes sparkling and unburdened. All were closed but the dance studio, a light shining through white plantation shutters, offering only a cursory view of dancing silhouettes, piano music muffled by the glass and glossy wood.

Across the next intersection rose the pub, housed inside an old firehouse, the front brick façade three stories tall. Customers spilled out onto the sidewalk, young, college-aged students intermingling with the middle-aged and retired, a rainbow of people and experiences.

He pressed Evie in ahead of him, keeping one hand on her waist as she wove through the crowd. A harried-looking waitress met them as they came around the corner into the bar. "There might be a table or two in the back," she called over the dull roar of conversation and the tuning of instruments in the opposite corner.

Evie turned to beam up at him, and other than her angry rants, it might have been the most animated he had ever seen her. Her skin was flushed with pleasure, eyes bright.

"They have my favorite beer from Scotland!!" she called excitedly over her shoulder as they passed the chalkboard advertising the pub's alcoholic offerings.

The back room, down a narrow hallway and to the left, was nearly empty. Two men stood near a rear entrance, lowball glasses filled with warm amber liquid in hand as they smoked thick cigars, but otherwise, Alec and Evie were alone.

Evie chose a small table standing on spindly legs against the long outer wall, plopping down in one of the mismatched chairs. A pool of light flickered across the center of the scarred wood, the flame atop a drooping candle dancing within its old, brown hurricane. Alec drew his gaze across the bookshelves lined with old, dusty tomes along the shorter back wall, board games shoved into the bottom cupboards, and a set of ragged bagpipes tacked to a post.

"I am so excited," she stage-whispered as she tapped her fingers on the table. She hummed with energy, nearly vibrating in her seat as she swung her head from one side to the other, candlelight dancing in her eyes. "I haven't had a real beer—a *good* beer—in ages. And it *smells* like a pub! Did you ever go to that one in Aggieville? Not the obnoxious shamrocky place, but the one across the street? It was close but didn't smell right. And the beer selection was piss. What?" she asked when she noticed him smirking at her.

"Nothing. It's just… I never thought that it would take beer to get you this excited. If I had known, I would be done things *much* differently."

"Oh, what? Differently than fish on the table and whisky straight from the barrel? Didn't you know that's the fastest way to most girls' hearts?" She fluttered her lashes at him. "I simply dare to be different." She executed an overdramatic hair-toss over one shoulder.

If she only knew.

She leaned back a little to look around as another couple, much older than they, took one of the remaining two tables. "I almost feel like I am home here."

"Home being…?"

"Scotland. Definitely Scotland. Although, I did like living here. I did tell you I lived here, right? Well, not here," she stabbed the table with both index fingers and laughed nervously. "But here," she waved her hands around her head in circles. "My dad was at Benning for a few years. I finished high school there and went to college in Atlanta. I loved that, but wow—nothing compared to St Andrews." She grinned. "I loved— *love*—St Andrews. I went sight unseen. I knew nothing about modern day Scotland. Or the UK for that matter.

The last British history class I took before I applied was Britain from 1790 until the present, but I don't think we even made it through the First World War It was all Disraeli and William Gladstone and Tories and Whigs and Labor movements. My professor had that 'Oxford' accent. You know, the sort of puffy, self-important one?

"Anyway, I think I might have had half a class that talked about the Jacobite Rebellion in 1745 my sophomore year, and that was only sort of in passing, but wow. I was in love. It was like the American Revolution but better, you know? The end of my junior year, there was a visiting professor who was there to help set up some study abroad program. I was heartbroken when he said that the program wouldn't be ready in time for me to do an exchange. I even asked about taking off a year just so I could do it." She grinned to herself and caught her lower lip between her teeth. "I think he thought I was joking when I told him I would do that. But he suggested looking into a post-graduate program, instead. I'm pretty sure it was the next week that my mom started sending me Kansas State brochures. I made up my mind then and there—I was going to Scotland, mother be damned." She chuckled a little. "Have you ever been? To the UK, that is?"

"Yes. A long time ago." It wasn't a time he particularly liked to dwell on.

"Were you in Scotland?"

He didn't want to answer, but, yet, he didn't want her to shut down. She was talking about a place she loved. And she hadn't mentioned Calum's name once. She hadn't shut down, losing herself in the thing she had had with another man. But he couldn't answer her without digging up his own ghosts.

He cleared his throat and stared down at his hands where they rested on the table. "My wife was from Scotland."

"Oh, really? Where was she from?" she asked excitedly.

And then his words dawned on her and she deflated a little as she remembered that he had said he was a widower.

"Oh, no, I'm sorry, I didn't mean to bring up—"

"It's all right. Her family was from Glen Lyon. Near Loch Tay."

"Oh."

She fidgeted with her fingers, shifting her legs under her chair only to shift them back, and then relief flooded her features, her shoulders relaxing and her frown disappearing. The waitress who had directed them to the back room came to stand to the side of the table.

"What can I get for ya'll?" she asked in a heavy southern accent. She popped her black-trousered hip to the side, resting the empty round tray on the apron tied around her mid-section.

"I'll take a bottle of the Scotch ale, please. And fish and chips?" Evie asked, as if she wanted to be sure they were on the menu.

The girl nodded and turned her attention to Alec.

"I'll have the same. And—" he pulled his wallet out, flipped it open, and extracted a card. "Just start a tab."

The girl took it without a word, slapped it down on the tray, and disappeared back around the corner into the louder dining room.

Evie shifted uncomfortably, her gaze darting around the room. She refused to look at him. She clearly wanted to press him for more details, wanted a glimpse into the life he had guiltily left in the past. But he desperately wanted to keep it there. He had little time for his mistakes, and instead needed to look toward the future, instead.

After the pause because too much to bear, she asked, "Is Riley your first duty station?"

"Uh, no."

"But it is the worst?" She leaned forward conspiratorially, her grin mischievous.

"That's the truth." He relaxed, leaning back into the ladder-backed chair. "No, it's my second. I started up at JBLM."

She looked at him blankly.

"In Washington."

She blinked. "Oh, Fort Lewis! We were there when I was a kid! But it was just Lewis then. Well, Fort Lewis and McChord Air Force base. They were two separate entities." She pushed her hands together and then drew them quickly apart to demonstrate. "Did you like it any better?"

"Yes, I quite liked my time there."

"Quite?" She lifted a mocking eyebrow. "I don't remember a whole lot about it. I was pretty young, but I know it drove my mom crazy. She hated how dark it was all the time. And she has always been a big one for seasons. I think she felt very cheated out of a few while we were there."

"It *was* dark and cold a lot of the year."

"And wet."

"Very."

She canted her head to the side. "Are we really talking about the weather?"

"I think we are."

She giggled at his answer, a small tinkling that bubbled up between her even white teeth and bare lips. Had she ever laughed like that with him before? He didn't think so, but definitely wanted more.

The laughter fizzled out and she fiddled with one of the paper coasters left on the table. Green and red lettering wrapped around the circle, advertising a domestic beer's holiday edition. She turned it over, sliding her fingers around the curved edges, flipping it over.

"I thought about going into meteorology briefly."

Nothing would have surprised him more. "Really?"

"Yup. How weird is that? I mean, it was maybe for half of a semester. I had to take an earth and atmospheric science class for my general education requirement, and I kind of got sucked in. Meteorology sounded cool, so did volcanology."

"Volcanology?"

"Yeah, the study of volcanoes," she said as if she had had to explain it a few times before.

"So, why didn't you make the switch?"

"Fear of volcanoes?" She chuckled. "History has always been my first love… and I can't do conversion math to save my life." She shook her head and rolled her eyes heavenward. Her smile stiffened but she held it as the waitress arrived with their beer.

Evie dropped the coaster, and a sweating glass was slid in front of each of them. Evie eyed the near-black brew, her hungry gaze all but willing the server away.

"Fish and chips might take a bit," the girl said in an almost apologetic tone. "Kitchen's real backed up. Can I get you anything else?"

Alec looked to Evie who didn't seem to have even heard the question, and then shook his head.

As soon as she was gone, Evie had the glass in hand and took a long sip.

"It's even better than I remember." She sighed. "Have you ever experienced that? Remembering something being so amazing, and then, in reality, it's even better?"

He stared across the table, taking in the curve of her cheek and set of her chin. The spark of mischief in her eye. Lifting his own glass, he took a long sip of smooth, nutty malt and considered her question.

Yes. Yes, he had.

Chapter Thirteen

Evie pushed away the basket, knowing if it stayed too close, she would continue to eat. The fare had been even better than she could have imagined, just like the beer. She'd always had a soft spot for fried foods paired with heavy beer, and the pub did not disappoint her. She had laid ruin to the fried halibut and left only a few of the gloriously thick, salty chips on the paper. She wanted to devour the rest, but she was afraid if she did, she might never be able to move again. The second beer sent her into an acutely happy state, her mouth rising into a relaxed smile.

Their waitress becoming scarce, Alec took himself off to pay for the rest of the tab as the back room became more crowded. In the front of the house, the bands switched out, a lone banjo player and his two fiddlers giving way to a larger piece band out of North Carolina.

Part of Evie wanted to stay, but she feared she might fall asleep at the table, her eyes heavy from a combination of their long drive and the heavy alcohol hitting her stomach like a sedative.

The first song of the band's set was lively. It was a catchy combination of bluegrass and rock, something that just made her want to get up and move, and she was not the type to dance in public. Or in front of other people. Or in rooms with mirrors. But she tapped her foot to the beat and wished she could make out the words the singers belted. She leaned back, scanning the crowd for Alec, but he was nowhere to be seen.

Instead, as the first song came to a close, a couple stumbled back from the front of the pub, their arms intertwined and gazes turned to each other. The woman smiled giddily and clung to her companion, both arms wrapped around one of his as if she were afraid he might slip away. But the bounce in her step was a happy one and her mop of red curls bounced around her flushed face.

Evie stared wistfully as they stopped just shy of the back door. The route was a popular one all night, patrons taking their drinks to go sit by the wood-burning fire pit. The woman held her face up to his, melting into his chest as he lowered his mouth to hers.

Clearing her throat, Evie pulled her gaze away. She didn't want to appear a voyeur, but she found them again. Wistfully, she sighed. She wanted a connection like theirs. One so easy, no words needed to be spoken to draw them together.

She glanced over her shoulder, seeking Alec once more.

Maybe she already had it.

Smiling softly to herself, she peered back at the couple. They ended their embrace but didn't pull away immediately.

Evie startled as Alec's hand landed on her shoulder.

"Ready?" he murmured.

She turned her face up to him and her heart slammed into her chest. Once. Twice. Again. Speeding away in a wild gallop. And the world melted away around them.

Evie stood, sliding her arms around his neck, and pressed herself into him as she pulled his lips down to hers. They met with a spark of electricity and she swallowed a gasp as a shiver ran through her.

He pulled away first. "That was unexpected."

A blush crept over her cheeks and she blinked her gaze down. "Sorry, I—"

"No, don't be sorry." He pecked another kiss on her lips.

She tried to recapture his, but wasn't quick enough. And then his mouth was nipping back at hers, a little game of cat and mouse until they were pulled together like magnets. The music crescendoed as they came together, her hands dragging his face to hers.

She had never been one for displays of public affection, but now she didn't care. If not now, when? When she no longer felt a connection with him? When it became forced? When their time ran out? She wanted to be with him *now*. And if she had learned anything in the past year, it was to seize the moment.

He dragged his mouth from hers, his breath ragged. "Somehow, I don't think here is the place."

"Are you sure?"

"No, but I think the locals might feel differently."

She snorted. "Oh, but darling, surely they would love something to talk about?" she drawled in her best southern accent.

"They and perhaps the local media. 'Couple copulates on pub table in public while baby boomers sit nearby.'"

"Has a nice ring to it."

"Yes, until your parents see your mugshot on the

nightly news while you're supposed to be snugly tucked in bed. In Kansas."

She rolled her eyes and threaded her arm through his. "You make me sound like a wild teenager."

Evie wasn't sure he heard her as he cut a path through the throng of people waiting for an empty table in the front room where the air hung thick and heavy with smoke from cigarettes, cigars, and what she was sure was a pipe.

They spilled out onto the cracked sidewalk, and he disentangled his fingers from hers to drape his arm across her shoulders instead. She sank into the warmth and matched his strides, ignoring the slight twinge in her leg.

"I imagine you *were* a wild teenager," he mused after they had crossed the street.

It took Evie a moment to realize he was picking the conversation back up. And that he had, in fact, heard what she said.

"Then you, good sir, would be very, very wrong. I was every parent's dream as a teenager. I was respectful, a good worker. I never got in trouble. I was an academic overachiever. I told my parents what my plans were and I never drove fast or had sex with strangers." She paused. "Well, not as a teenager, anyway," she amended.

"I'm not sure how I am supposed to take that."

"However you would like." She lifted her right hand, grasping his fingers where they idly stroked her shoulder. She couldn't seem to keep her hands off him. "It wasn't until I had finished college that I became the rebellious hellion you know and love now."

He tensed.

Evie glanced up at him, but he stared forward, his lips pressed into a firm line. She tightened her hand around his. He tangled his fingers with hers and dropped a kiss to the top of her head.

The walk back to the hotel seemed to be both an eternity and a blip in Evie's memory. All she could think of was getting him naked, of getting herself naked. Of all of the amazing things he was going to do to her body. That she was going to let him. They barely made it into the elevator before she pressed herself into him again, sliding her hands up under his shirt, her fingers gliding over his warm skin, the heat of him burning her cold flesh. They felt their way blindly out of the mirrored car and bumped down the hall to their room. He inserted the key card and no sooner had the lock clicked open than she dragged his shirt over his head.

Clothes created a breadcrumb trail to the bedroom until Evie stood before him wearing nothing more than the lovely pair of satin panties he bought her, yanking at the stupid button fly of his jeans, sure a masochist had designed them. Alec reached down between them and stilled her fingers, bringing her hands up to his lips. He placed a kiss to the knuckles of her fingers and looked into her eyes with longing and an emotion she was almost certain he would find in her own. An emotion she was scared to put a word to, herself. And one she wanted to keep buried.

"Evie I—"

"No."

He was momentarily taken aback. "Evelyn, I need you to know I—"

"No," she repeated. She jerked her hands away and

slid them around the back of his neck, pulling his mouth back to hers. "Not now. Just… be with me for now."

She could tell that he was prepared to argue, but it never came. He gave her exactly what she wanted, pulling her firmly to him. He breasts crushed against the hair on his chest, and all of the tingling feelings that overtook her body turned to raging molten pools of arousal. She wildly attacked his mouth, pressing her hips into his, desperate for the hot, quick release she had been dreaming of since before they had left the pub. She was already on the edge, and all she needed was for him to push her over it.

And then she was falling back, caught by the softness of comforter and mattress, his jeans were unceremoniously kicked to the side. And she was given exactly what she had craved. It was all she needed; a promise he was hers.

****

Evie resurfaced slowly, her body weightless, full and sated and tingly everywhere. And, as her mind cleared suddenly very, very embarrassed.

Alec ran his lips over the pink, puckered scar running from hip to knee, the place where her femur shattered and the doctors had to use screws and bolts, stitches and staples to put her back together. Tenderly, he moved down, his fingers light as a whisper as he traced the jagged line before pressing his soft kisses along the same path.

Her scar. The worst part of her. The most broken, the most repulsive part of her. The part of her she wished she could make disappear, the part of her that caused her the most shame and insecurity. She did everything in her power not to look at it and to cover it from the view of others. The night they had spent in the cottage was different, only the light of a single candle casting shadows through the already pitch interior. It had been bad enough he'd felt it as he administered the massage as a medical professional, but this…

She closed her eyes, shifting away, letting him know she was awake. But, he didn't stop.

"Alec," she begged, urging him to look away.

She pulled her leg up, trying to cover herself with her hand, but he only nudged it away. And he continued to worship the worst part of her. She tried to sit up, to dislodge him as she adjusted, but he placed a hand on her opposite hip, pressing her gently into the soft cocoon of the bed. His thumb kneaded the smooth flesh just above her hipbone. And he kissed the scar, again.

"Stop, Alec, please." She buried her face in the crook of her elbow. "I don't want you to see me like this. It's so ugly, and terrible, and I don't even want to—"

"Don't ever say that about yourself," he admonished gruffly. "This is the best of you. This is the mark of a survivor, the proof that you went to battle and you came out alive. This is the part of you that tells your story. This is the most beautiful part of you."

Her eyes stung, filled, and he swam out of focus. She clamped her teeth together to force the tears back in, to keep them from spilling over. She refused to blink knowing they would fall the moment she did.

He slid up her body, his flesh warm on hers. A sob tore through her when she couldn't hold it in any longer, and the tears slipped down her cheeks.

But he was there to kiss them away. Slowly. One

before the other. His lips brushed hers lightly, bringing them nose to nose, and he plucked at her lower lip, a quick capture and release. The salt of her tears found her tongue through trembling lips, and another sob rushed forward. He cradled her cheeks in his big hands, his thumbs wiping away the drying tracks of her tears.

"You are more than your body, Evelyn." He pressed another soft kiss to the corner of her lips. "You are more than your past." Another kiss. "You are all of you, and there isn't an inch of you I don't—"

Was it embarrassment or pleasure burning across her skin? She couldn't be sure. With a jerk, she broke his palms from her cheeks.

"Has anyone ever told you talk too much?" She pressed her mouth to his, silencing him.

He nipped her lower lip. "Has anyone ever told you you're exasperating?"

"All the time," she murmured.

And then she slithered down and showed him just how exasperating she could be.

Chapter Fourteen

Evie snuggled into his side, breathing him in. Gray light crept through the windows; the clouds hung thick and heavy with unspent rain. The curtains had never been drawn, and they framed the large picture windows overlooking rolling green parkland.

She pulled the blankets tighter around her shoulders and wiggled further into Alec's arms; the room was cold, matching the gray sky, and she craved his warmth. They were wrapped around each other, one of his strong thighs nestled between both of hers, her toes tickling at his calf. She found herself thinking about Christmas, of waking up like this to snow flurries and carols and twinkling Christmas lights.

She imagined bringing him home to her parents. Her father would be pleased. He would offer Alec a beer while she went to help her mom in the kitchen with the hors d'oeuvres. She knew the look that would be on her mother's face: concern mixed with curiosity and a little bit of pleasure. The straight set line of her lips when she learned he was in the military. The twinkle when she heard he was a doctor.

Or would they see his family? He had a lot of siblings, that she knew. And his mother, was she still alive?

"What was Christmas like in your family?"

"Nothing like you are probably imagining," he

murmured sleepily.

"Oh, and what am I imagining?" She closed her eyes and nuzzled closer.

"Something full of family and celebration. Gifts. The like."

"And it wasn't?"

"Perhaps a little. We would gather for a feast, but the New Year saw more celebration. We would exchange a gift, give to the servants, listen to my sisters sing carols—"

"Servants? You grew up with servants," she muttered with disbelief.

She had always considered herself privileged. At least as far as a middle class military kid could be. She had seen from her time at St Andrews that there was a whole world of wealth that existed in a bubble she would never be able to penetrate, but it was foreign. A fairy tale. Something that didn't happen to people she knew.

He cleared his throat. "My upbringing is not terribly interesting."

"Oh, I beg to differ."

He sniffed in amusement. "My family and I are no longer on speaking terms, so to speak."

"Why? Is it because you joined the Army?"

"It probably has more to do with marrying my wife."

"Oh." Well, that put a damper on things.

"Tell me about Christmas with your family."

"Hmm, well. When I was young, we always tried to go back to my grandparents'. My mom's family. Her grandparents were still alive when I was very young, and so she and her parents and cousins always gathered together at their house. We would have Christmas Eve together and then spend the evening with everyone on Christmas day, too. My family always takes advantage of the season. We go looking at lights, drink too much eggnog, watch sappy made-for-TV movies. It's all very rooted in tradition.

"After my great-grandparents passed, we still would go back when we could, but more frequently my grandparents would come to us. Last Christmas... hmm, I guess it's this Christmas?" She paused trying to work out the weird time thing, and then giving up. "Anyway, they came to us in Kansas so that they could coo over me and make me feel like I was the luckiest person alive. Well, my grandmother did. My grandfather got really heartfelt for a second and then told me I should rethink my hairstyle." She smiled, loving the teasing she always got from him.

"It sounds nice."

"It is. Next year, will you come?"

The words were out of her mouth before she realized what she had done. Making plans with him for quite some time in the future. She could easily imagine him there with all of them; she wanted him there with all of them. With her. She was fairly certain she wanted him there always.

"I think I would like that," he said gruffly and pressed a kiss to her hair.

Not knowing how to act, she pushed herself up. "We should probably get going before the shops get busy."

****

Alec grabbed the handle before Evie could reach it, and pulled the door open wide so the strap of bells hanging from the inside danced merrily. The silver orbs rang like sleigh bells, and their pleasant jingle was the perfect touch for the cozy little shop. A choir singing old Christmas carols played softly in the background and every empty surface was draped with faux holly and pine boughs.

Evie stepped in, taking in the high ceilings and not-quite-cluttered displays of imported fig pudding, silver crackers, and tins of Scottish shortbread.

"Did you remember the sugar this time?" someone with a thick, Scottish accent called out from the back of the shop somewhere, her consonants dropped at the end of each word. "Because if you didn't, you can march yourself right back out and—oh, hello."

A slender woman only a couple of years older than Evie appeared from behind a circular rack housing a large display of women's tartan skirts. The pencil skirt she wore was of the finest wool, dyed in the red and green plaid of the MacDonald clan, and a gray shawl was draped across her front, pinned with a silver brooch.

It took her a moment, but Evie recognized her as the woman who had caught her attention at the pub the night before.

The redhead came forward, a polite smile pulling her lips across model-perfect teeth, but it quickly fell and she came to an abrupt stop. She blinked, her lips parting as her jaw dropped, and for a split-second she looked as if she had seen a ghost.

The shocked expression was quickly wiped away, and she rushed forward, beaming, to wrap her arms around Evie in a hug meant for relatives and long-lost sorority sisters.

"Eve! I had no idea what happened to you! I never thought in my wildest dreams—well, perhaps my wildest dreams, considering—but I didn't know what happened to you. I thought I'd never see you, again."

Her kinky, copper hair bushed out from the loose ponytail at the nape of her neck and tickled at Evie's chin. Evie blew at it awkwardly as she tried to pull away.

"I, um… Are you Flora? Flora MacDonald?"

The woman stepped back, her brow creased in confusion and disappointment. "You don't remember me." She said it like a statement, not a question. As though she weren't confused at all, but merely sad. She sighed deeply through her nose and her lips quirked in a pitying sort of smile. She turned her attention to just above Evie's shoulder.

She shook her head. "I apologize, I am. Flora, that is." She held out her hand.

Alec took a step forward and shook it, but his gaze remained on Evie.

"Why did you call me Eve? And how do you know who I am?" Her heart played a quick tattoo on her ribs and a pit formed somewhere in the depths of her stomach. The only other person who had called her "Eve" was Iain.

"When I knew you, that's what everyone called you. It's how you introduced yourself." Flora held out her hands helplessly, her eyebrows coming together and pushing toward her hairline.

"And when did you know me?" Evie's eyes narrowed.

The last time someone had claimed to know her and she shared no recollection of them, the cicadas had shrieked in the Kansas heat, a woman appeared from a cloud of crows, and a madman tried to cajole her into standing in a circle of mushrooms.

Flora let out a breath, ruffling a lock of hair flopping across her forehead to skim her cheek. "You were always suspicious of me," she murmured forlornly. "I never thought you liked me much. I probably didn't like you much, either." At Evie's lifted eyebrow she gave a knowing little laugh. "I think it's more *whe*re did I know you than when."

Evie shot a glance to Alec, but he wasn't paying her any attention. Instead, he gazed at the shop owner suspiciously, his arms folded across his chest and his feet spread apart. Evie shifted closer to him.

"You've been there."

Flora canted her head to the side as she considered Alec and his softly spoken observation. "As have you."

Flora sniffed suddenly and pushed past them to the door. She held the handle with one hand and flipped the little sign in the window from Open to Closed. Turning back to them as she let out a heavy breath, she ran the palms of her hands down her thighs as she collected herself. After a beat, a, serene, wistful smile pulled her lips wide.

"I only opened the shop a little over a month ago," she began. "It was an odd bit of a whim, but my life had just imploded and I needed something just for me. A few days before opening, the weather was foul, and a man came in with a large box he claimed was left out in the rain." She cleared her throat and moved forward, suddenly, swiftly, skirting the glass display cases holding a plethora of brooches and kilt pins. "I had many shipments coming in at the time. Antiques and the like for the shop, so I didn't think anything of it."

She turned to a shelf and began pulling things down. Old books, for the most part, and a little box. Flora splayed her hands over the leather covers and looked up at Evie.

"I simply assumed they were from a lot I had won during an estate sale auction. But then the man... my friend... well, anyway, he and I got close. And then he vanished."

"Vanished? What do you mean, 'vanished?'"

Flora's brows knit and she gathered the heaviest of the books up into her arms, pressing it to her chest. "I haven't worked out how all of this comes into play. He told me his sister owned the shop next door, and when he stopped coming 'round, I went to her. She told me he had been killed in a training accident." At Evie's blank stare Flora added, "He's a pilot. With the army."

Oh, goodie, another one. Evie chanced a glance at Alec from the corner of her eye, but he continued to stare at the other woman.

"I was in shock. I had no idea what to think, and when I returned back to my shop, it was to a woman. She was beautiful and tall, regal—"

"We know who she is." Alec's, his tone harsher than Evie had ever heard it.

"So you know her, too?"

He swallowed, his Adam's apple bobbing and his lips parting. Evie thought he would answer, but instead he dropped his gaze to the books.

"Where did you get that?" He nodded to the smallest, a leather-bound notebook, a thin strap of the same tanned hide looped around the cover.

"From her. They were all from her. I believe,

anyway. But she never confessed, so I can't know for sure."

"She had it?"

Flora shrugged, noncommittal. "I can only assume," she murmured.

Evie looked from Alec to the book and back. "What is it?"

When he didn't answer, Flora did. "The journal of Lord A. Carlisle."

Evie lifted a brow. "Carlisle, eh?" She shot a smirk at Alec and bumped his arm with her elbow. "Any relation?"

Alec's jaw ticked and his eyes met her, but he remained tight-lipped.

Evie's gut twisted. "Oh."

Flora looked back and forth between them, the little crease forming between her eyebrows growing deeper with each passing moment. "Are—?"

"Please continue," Alec said, his voice unusually harsh.

Flora stared at him quizzically for a beat too long and pulled the little book a little closer to herself. "The woman told me he was being held captive, and that if I chose to, I could rescue him. It was odd, I hadn't known him that long, but his loss… It was a blow. She told me to choose my weapons wisely. I contemplated that for quite awhile, and the next morning, I woke up on a forest floor. I wandered until I came to the summer kingdom, and that's where I met you, Eve. Evie," she amended.

"And what was I doing there?" Evie asked with some amusement. It was all a bit much to take seriously.

171

"You were a soldier. You mistook me for the emissary of Arianrhod because of my necklace. I was taken to your king and you were eventually assigned to take me into the winter kingdom as a spy. It was all very… archaic. Another, Iain, was to—"

"Iain!" Evie leaned into the glass countertop. "He's the one who tried to kill me!"

"Kill you?" Flora blinked rapidly and gave a soft, wistful smile. "I always thought Iain was in love with you. I can't imagine him trying to hurt you." Her head tilted sympathetically to the side.

"In love? With me? Well, he sure has a funny way of showing it."

An involuntary shiver ran through her, and Evie wrapped her arms around herself. She chanced a glance at Alec, but he remained just as grim as he had been a moment before, his face an unreadable mask. Before they left the hotel, he seemed just as eager to get to the shop as she had been, but standing there, he looked more like a man being tortured.

She turned her attention back to Flora. "Anyway…"

Flora looked from Alec to Evie. "You didn't like me very much. I knew that from the beginning. Everyone assumed I was some sort of witch, and that made you… suspicious. Or perhaps you knew all along I wasn't who I let you believe I was. My only focus was to get to Owen and get him home. But I didn't know if he was alive or dead, and I didn't know what would happen if he tried to cross back with me, but—"

"Wait. What do you mean alive or dead?" Evie cut in.

But the bell hanging from the door jingled,

breaking through the tenseness hanging between them. Flora gazed beyond Evie, her face brightening with a smile as her cheeks flushed with delight. "Did you remember the sugar this time?"

Evie turned just as a man approached, two paper cups in hand. She recognized him from the night before, though she'd only caught glimpses of his features are he passed through the shadows. He was classically good looking, his hair golden and shoulders broad, with light eyes only for Flora. They came alive as his gaze landed on her. He might not have been as tall as Alec, but he made up for it in presence. He placed the cups on the counter before turning to look at Evie and Alec.

Flora came around the display case, tucking herself into his side. "Owen, this is… I'm sorry, I don't think we exchanged…"

"Alec." He draped an arm across Evie's shoulders. "And this is Evelyn."

Evie made a face. "Just Evie is fine." She held her hand up in an awkward wave as Alec and Owen shook hands.

"Evie was with me in the Otherworld," Flora murmured.

Owen frowned, but turned his gaze to Evie. "Was your hair different?" he asked after a careful perusal.

Her hand instinctively went to the dark length where it skimmed her shoulders. "I-I don't remember."

His eyebrows quirked just as the edge of his mouth did the same. "I don't remember much, either. What memories I do have only came through dreams."

"I don't remember anything," she muttered bitterly, almost accusingly. "Wait. You said you thought he was dead?" She snapped her gaze back up to Flora.

She nodded. "The best anyone can tell is that he was knocked into unconsciousness. They found him washed up on shore a couple of days later."

"I was in a coma," Evie murmured softly to herself. But… was she really? Alec had not seemed convinced when she'd shown up in his emergency room.

Flora gave her a sad look, but then it quickly vanished. "How-how did you find me if you don't remember me? Us?"

Evie's mouth formed a little "o." She didn't even know how to answer the question. Even thinking about the events leading up to learning Flora's name brought a fresh blush to her cheeks. Best to not bring that up. Where to start, then? And what would Flora do with the information? She turned to look up at Alec for help.

"Your name and the name of your shop were the only clues Iain left behind," he said.

Her eyebrows shot up in surprise. "He knows about the shop? How would he?"

"How do you think? He does her bidding," Alec said through clenched teeth.

Flora quickly shook her head. "No, that can't be right. She visited the court, but he gave no sign of knowing her. They never spoke. He…" She trailed off at Alec's cocked brow.

Alec tossed a look at the small, leather bound book on the counter, and. Evie glanced back to Flora just as Flora's own gaze fell on it, her eyes narrowing. "I-I never thought to question why, all of it."

She looked back to Evie, to Alec. "I don't know. I don't know why me or why Owen. Or why you, Evie. But the last time I saw the woman, she said nothing more than other women's names. Anne Macintosh and Elizabeth Carlisle."

Chapter Fifteen

The square was quiet, few people strolling the worn concrete sidewalks. But most of the parking spots were full and across the green from Flora's shop a steady stream of visitors entered the county courthouse, an imposing, modern brick building standing sentinel over the turn-of-the-century storefronts. A few young mothers gathered with their small children along the edges of a small playground, and an elderly couple sat feeding pigeons from a wrought iron bench.

Flora promised to meet them back at the pub for lunch. A new shipment of teas and specialty biscuits arrived not long after Owen, and she explained she wanted to get them inventoried and sorted before Mrs. Dunkirk made her weekly visit later that afternoon. Evie and Alec bowed out, but Evie was left with more questions than she had come with. And by his silence, Evie had a feeling Alec knew more than he was telling her.

"What did she mean about 'dead or alive?'"

"The Otherworld… it has a varied history."

She lifted an eyebrow. "And here I thought it existed on a plane that was outside of the laws of time and space." She wiggled her fingers near her face.

He let out a harried sigh. "What do you know of the ancient mythologies?"

"Nothing. Remember? Not really my specialty.

Maybe the bare bones?"

They crossed the street and slowly strolled along the brick path outlining the square.

"The Kingdom or Annwn dwells in the center of the Otherworld, ruled by Arawn, King of the Harvests and Snows. Across the great Ford, a shallow river splits down the center of the Solstice Kingdoms, separating Annwn from the spring and summer lands. Those who pass from living to death must walk through the summer kingdom, fight at the ford for their summer ruler, cross over to the autumn kingdom, and die for Arawn to be reborn. The battles happen twice a year at the equinoxes. Hafgan's Army takes the spring battle, Arawn's the autumn."

Silence settled between them as Evie tried to wrap her head around what he told her. Her heart beat faster with every step of her feet, echoing in her ears as a knot formed in her throat.

"What you're saying is the Otherworld is the afterlife?"

She knew the answer, but she needed him to tell her. No, she *wanted* him to deny it.

Alec stopped and reached out a hand, halting her, as well. He gripped her arm just below her shoulder, his thumb rubbing softly over the red sweater. Worry glinted in his eyes, in the slight inward pull of his brows, but the rest of his face was a mask, his lips pressed into a straight line. She knew she wasn't going to get what she wanted.

"No." He gave his head a slow shake, and she held her breath. "No, but the afterlife… It is nestled within the Otherworld."

"I don't understand," she whispered. But she did.

She understood all too well.

He swallowed audibly, his Adam's apple bobbing. "When the gods of the old world were no longer needed… As the Romans and the Christians wrested the old Kingdoms from the Celts and the Picts, the Cornish and Welsh peoples, the old gods retreated. They gathered the true believers, the other peoples, and they left this world to the humans who had given up on them. They settled their remaining followers in the land of their births, in the Otherworld where they have always dwelled."

"How do you know this?"

"I was a member of her court. For many seasons."

"And you knew where we were. How far?" Her shock wore of and festered into anger.

His frown deepened and he withdrew his hand. She didn't want it there, anyway. The crack of betrayal left a wound on her heart, enough to see it shatter.

"How far?" she repeated.

"Time doesn't work the same way there—"

"How. Far."

"Hafgan's kingdom lies on the other side of the mountain range from my cottage. "

Her heart broke before he even finished, a strange feeling, like falling from a great height. The anger, the hurt of it rose in her throat, threatening to sob out. He had known the dead were there, just over those mountains, not far from the cottage, just a breath away. Calum was there, just within reach. If only she had known.

"And you've been there? You knew. All this time, you knew." He had betrayed her. He knew she and Calum could be reunited and he had said nothing.

"Evie, it's not that simple."

She took two steps back, putting space between them so that he couldn't reach out, so that he couldn't touch her.

Her eyes welled up and she cursed herself. She didn't want him to see her tears, only her fury.

"It *is* that simple, Alec." Her voice remained even until she said his name, and then it cracked, high and reedy. "It *is* that easy. He was *right there.*" Her voice wasn't hers, pitching between a too high cry and a whisper.

"Evelyn…"

He reached out, but she backed away, her feet shuffling against the concrete. She caught a glimpse of the pain on his face before he swept it away, steeling himself. But the anguished look in his eyes mirrored her own.

"I need some time," she said with surprising calm. She straightened her shoulders and took a deep breath, the cold air stinging her dry throat. "I'll-I'll see you at lunch." She turned on her heel and went back the way they had come, back toward the shop.

"Evie," he called desperately behind her.

But she didn't turn. And he didn't follow.

****

Flora watched as her guests departed and let out a shaky breath. Owen's hand was instantly at the small of her back, just under her shawl, his thumb brushing back and forth against the silk of her blouse. The heat of him was comforting even through the fabric.

The time they had together here on this side of the veil had been brief, and he remembered their time in the Otherworld as if it were no more than a dream. Pieces were missing. Different events melted into one another, not making much sense at all. She was able to connect them, tell him where one thing stopped and the next began, but to him, it ran together like oil in water, swirling and mixing without logic.

When he walked back into her life, he remembered enough to come looking for her, but not much else. He knew her the moment he saw her, yet with a skepticism she couldn't hold against him. But their connection was still strong, and here he was, weeks later, still at her side. Those days were numbered, however, and he would be going back to his unit; his convalescent leave was almost up.

With desperation, she soaked up each moment with him, hoping he didn't notice. She was just coming to terms with the fact that her entire life wasn't a dream, that she really had spent an extended period of time in another time and place, one where the rules of her world didn't apply. She was still gaining her footing after her short, doomed marriage, and the invisible thread connecting her to Owen was almost the only thing making any sense. The thought of having him leave, if only a few hours away, made her feel unbalanced.

She sighed and slipped around the glass counter, opening up an old apothecary cabinet she picked up at an antique market shortly before opening the shop Scarred dark and rough edges meant it was desperately in need of refinishing, and she had every intention of restoring it, but the flaws and rough edges spoke to her.

Upon returning from Annwn, she cleared away the novelty items she originally stored in the cubbies and drawers, packing them instead with her growing collection of herbs. Most she ordered or bought through a local herb shop run by a practicing hedge witch, one who asked no questions, though she saw the suspicion in the older woman's eyes.

Flora removed a swath of linen, laid it over the counter and then placed a simple mortar and pestle over it. She withdrew a few of the herbs, sprinkling them into the bowl before fervently mashing them.

Owen stood across the counter, leaning his elbows on the glass.

"Spelling?" he joked.

In the Otherworld, they labeled her a witch, a term she originally took great offense to, but soon learned it was a great honor. Whenever she took to plying the trade she took up in Arawn's court, Owen teased her.

She shot him a pointed look. "I have a headache."

"I thought you hated her."

"I do. I did." Her movements stopped and her shoulders sank. "I didn't really hate her. Not really. She hated me, I think." She let out a sigh. "But did you see her, Owen? She looked so young and lost. The woman I knew was… hard. Very sure of herself. She was a force waiting to break free. The girl who was just in my shop? Frightened and confused."

"You've said I was different, as well."

"You were. But only a little."

She went back to her herbs and scooped them into a little silver ball. The shadow of Owen she met on this side of the veil was charming and full of energy. He joked, was playful, he danced. The Owen of the Otherworld was serious, dedicated. He was loyal to a fault, driven, purposeful in everything he did. This Owen—the *real* Owen was both. He was all of those things and more.

"I need water," she muttered and skirted the counter for the back room where she kept an electric kettle.

Flora stalked back in a few moments later with a steaming mug. She set it down and dunked the little silver ball into the water. He said nothing, just regarded her.

"What?" she demanded.

"There is something you aren't saying."

She pursed her lips. "I thought it was done. I did what I needed to do. I got you out and things went right again. But... what if it was only the beginning?"

The bell on the door jangled and Mrs. Dunkirk, her favorite customer, shuffled in.

Flora smiled brightly and moved to greet her, pushing away the fear curling inside.

****

Evie didn't have anywhere else to go, and she knew she needed answers, even if her questions had changed. She walked back toward the shop only to turn and pace down the block, her nerves on edge, not sure what to do or what to say.

Alec consumed all of the space in her head. His smile, his touch, his taste, his *lies*. Lie upon lie, over and over and over. He had listened to her talk about Calum, and he had done nothing. She told him how her life lay in pieces, destroyed, and he strung her along, let her feel safe, let her care...

Alec was selfish. He made her feel things for him. *How dare he?*

She knew she promised Flora that she would see her at lunch, let her get through her work day, but it couldn't wait. She needed answers immediately, and so back to Flora's shop she went. By the time she stood in front of the large windows, Thistle and Rose etched in a gold arch across them, her leg ached painfully, but the shake plaguing her hand calmed.

The little bells jangled as she entered through the shop door, happy and light. Flora looked up in welcome from where she stood, chatting with an elderly woman in a pillbox hat dotted with flowers and a purple wool coat. The old woman's knee-high stocking sagged down one leg, revealing mottled skin over her orthopedic shoes. Flora's smile faltered and a crease appeared between her brows but Evie waved her off and went to mill through the goods she hadn't taken the time to see when she arrived the first time.

The Thistle and Rose was cozy and reminded her of some of the small shops near the Old Course in St Andrews. Dark, lots of wood, and the smell of wool. She picked her way around the shelves and racks as Flora and the woman chatted quietly. Many of the pantry items she recognized, some she had kept stocked in her kitchen cabinets once upon a time.

She fingered a heavy, cable knit sweater when Flora approached, stopping just on the other side of the stand.

"How does it work?" Evie asked.

"I don't really know. I only passed through the veil the once. I remember sitting down to read, and I looked up and something was out of place. I can't remember what it was. I went to move it, and then I was waking up in a summer forest."

Evie dropped the arm of the sweater. "For me it was a silver apple." The corner of her mouth quirked at the memory of Alec unfolding it from a brown Army towel. She quickly pushed it away with a shake of her head. "Okay, never mind." Evie rubbed her temples, hoping the movement would release some of the tension building. "New question. What do you know about Lord Carlisle?"

"Only what was in the journal. He was desperate to get away and back to... someone. But the entries stopped when he figured out how to use the focus points."

"Focus points?"

"The stone circles. Standing stones."

Evie nodded, picturing the stone circle on the little island in the loch. "And what do you know of the dead?"

Flora's eyes grew round and she drew a sharp breath. "Eve, I don't think—"

"Please."

"They know they are dead, Evie. They know and they... they don't regret it." She gave her a sad look then reached out and took one of Evie's hands in both of hers. "You were there, Evie. In both courts. All knew you. If whoever you are looking for was there... everyone knew who I was and that you went with me."

Evie knew what she was saying. If Calum had wanted to be found, if he had wanted to be with her, he would have had every opportunity. She finally owned the feeling that gripped her chest and tightened around her like a vice.

Guilt.

She replayed every moment she spent with Alec, the two of them in the cottage, sharing their lives with one another on that fourteen-hour car ride from Kansas.

She thought about the words she knew hung between them, how she had stifled him from saying them because she knew when he did, she would say them back. She'd been planning her life with him, could see him at the dinner table across from her father, see him offering a hug to her mother. She had envisioned herself in his house, helping him cook dinners then sitting across from him at his drop leaf table. And she had wanted it. Craved it.

But Calum could still be out there.

He could still be out there and he came first. Even though the future she envisioned with him had flickered to nothing more than a wish made long ago. A fading dream.

But he could still be out there.

And she had allowed herself to move on.

She had allowed herself to feel again.

She'd promised to be his future once, and then she moved on without him. If he were out there… she owed him that promise. Didn't she?

But what of herself? What did she owe to herself? She couldn't help the question as it bubbled up. If she were to go back there, back to that place, she needed to know why she was wanted there, first. How did she fit into all of this? And what did Alec know he wasn't telling her? She had a feeling the answers to Alec lay in that journal.

She bit her lip and pleaded with Flora. "The journal?"

"It's yours," Flora murmured. She collected it from the shelf behind the counter and gave it to Evie.

"Thank you. For everything. And… I'm sorry for however I treated you before… you know?" She gave a watery sniff. "Could I ask one more favor?"

Flora offered a slight tip of her chin.

"Give me a head start?"

****

Alec waited outside the pub, watching the minutes tick by on his watch. He had allowed Evie her space as his own conscience warred with itself. Had he not told her enough? In protecting her, had he pushed her away?

As the minute hand descended lower and lower across the clock face, he knew it was the latter. When neither she nor Flora arrived, he made his way back through the cold, desperately hoping they were waiting for him at the Thistle and Rose, instead.

When he entered the shop, Flora was still there. Alone but for a paperback spread open across the glass countertop of her display case.

"What are you doing here?" He looked around the shop, his frown increasing. "Did Evie come back here?"

She straightened and inserted a bookmark between the splayed pages. "She did. Right after you both left. She wanted to borrow the journal and asked if we could all meet here…" Flora turned and looked at the mantel clock ticking behind her on a shelf. "…About fifteen minutes ago." She shrugged. "I assumed you were running late."

His heart slammed into his ribs and then leapt into his throat. Had they been found?

"I haven't seen her," he said, panic rising.

He checked his watch, again; how long had it been? Two hours? No, almost three. He pushed out of the shop and scanned the square, as if he would see her or Mora or Iain.

But the world passed by him just as it always had.

Chapter Sixteen

Fife, Scotland

The gray landscape puttered by, cold and unmoving. Evie rested her forehead against the glass of the taxi's back passenger side window, purse tucked under her arm, and fingers rubbing absently over the soft leather of the journal.

She read it through. Twice. And then a third time to make mental notes. There wasn't much there; the accounts were short, just for him, not meant to ever be read by an audience. But there was enough there. She knew she held a personal account belonging to the husband of Elizabeth Menzie Carlisle, one of those women of Culloden Sylvia Bascomb-Murray wrote about.

Two things were certain when she left that small, suburban town in Georgia: She was relatively clueless about the Otherworld. She had a guess as to how she would get there, but no real knowledge. And once she was there, she would be lost and alone. She knew nothing of the geography, the history, the people, the animal species. All she knew was that to arrive, she had to go willingly. Or be dead. Without a game plan, without a basic knowledge of the terrain, of the people, or the culture, it would be suicide or worse.

Two: Elizabeth Meyner and Anne Macintosh were

of great importance. She was sure Flora MacDonald's name was no coincidence either, and she would find out why. Fortunately, she knew someone who was an expert.

Because she was finally home in Scotland.

She thought she would… feel more. But everything seemed as empty as the fields lying between the final stretch of road leading out to St Andrews. Scotland had lost some of its magic. Perhaps it was because Calum was gone and he had taken some of it with him. Or perhaps it was because Alec had lied, and everything she thought was good in the world wasn't.

Perhaps it was because she was not the same Evelyn Blair she once was. Before.

Maybe it was stupid to go back. The path had seemed so clear up until the moment she stood in the airport, passport in one hand and father's credit card in the other. Alec had insisted she leave no traceable evidence of her time-travel, but a distinct memory of her father disputing a charge days after Christmas—a day yet to happen, now—was enough to set her conscience at ease. Nothing ever came of it but a lot of head scratching. Then again, maybe it wasn't stupid at all. Maybe it was just brilliant enough to keep them all off her trail.

Hope Street, where she spent a year of her life living in splendid student squalor, was one of the first turns after arriving in town. It was just beyond the lane down to the North Sands, up the hill from the Old Course. In the shadow of old Chattan Hall, cloistered between North and Market Streets. It skirted a pretty little rose garden that bloomed beautifully in the summer, and the Victorian townhouses stood stately and clean among some of the oldest buildings in one of the oldest universities in the world.

Her driver turned onto Hope Street quickly, pulling up to a halt outside the light gray townhouse her old flat was carved into. She recognized Sarah's little red car a few parking spots down next to the rose gardens. Their flat was in the cellar, and she limped down the stone steps to the cold, dark doorstep, knocking thrice and waiting.

A few moments passed before a string of muffled curses neared and the door was hauled open.

"Do you know what bloody—*Evie!*"

Sarah launched herself at her roommate, nearly pushing them both off balance. She wrapped her arms around Evie's neck, rocking them back and forth before yelping something about cold feet and jumping back over the threshold. She held the door open and motioned Evie in, executing a little bouncing jig before she slammed the door shut behind her.

"What are you doing here?" she cried.

Oh, where to start? "Can't I just want to see you?"

"Too right you can! But I am not daft enough to think that would be your only reason for flying halfway 'round the world and right before Christmas!"

Sarah spoke at a mile-a-minute in a thick Glaswegian accent not unlike Flora MacDonald's. However, where Flora's was posh and upper middle class, Sarah's was decidedly not. She dropped half of her consonants, and when she spoke too fast, her voice growing in volume, she sounded a bit like a sheep. Her thick riot of black curls flew out from her head in a round puff of a ponytail, and ratty pajamas covered her light brown skin. She flopped down onto the overstuffed sofa in the living space and drew her slender feet up under her.

"No luggage?"

Evie shook her head and took the small armchair that had always been her favorite. White with a riot of little flowers, it looked like something belonging in a little old lady's drawing room, but had always served her well when she drank wine out of a mug while watching the small television in the corner.

"I came on a whim."

"A whim?" Sarah repeated, one of her thin eyebrows shooting up. She gave Evie a look that was meant to convey concern for her friend's mental state and depths of her pockets.

Evie let out a sigh. "I need to do some soul-searching. I think I got in a fight with... I don't even know what he is... And—"

"There's a he?" Sarah raised her hands into the air. "It's about bloody time! I thought you would never find anyone, you would just be off by yourself in a library for the rest of your life while the world passed you by."

Dumbfounded, Evie stared at her. "What are you talking about?" Did she not remember Calum, the permanent fixture in her life?

"Oh, come on, Evie," Sarah threw back her head in mock exasperation. "I was always trying to get you out, to meet someone—*anyone*—who might flick your fancy, if you know what I mean, and you were always off on your own making photocopies and ringing up archives for Professor Bacon-Munchkins."

"Bascomb-Murray," Evie corrected reflexively, her mind still whirring.

Had Sarah been completely oblivious? She was out

with Calum or at his flat as often as she was here. Sure, they hadn't spent much time here, but he didn't have a roommate.

Sarah waved her hand dismissively. "Ach, but look at you! You're looking so fit! How is that even possible? When you left last month, you looked positively dreadful."

"Thanks, Sar."

"I mean it. You were being wheeled onto a plane with half your hair shaved off and now…" She trailed off.

Evie's eyes grew wide, but she managed to school her features before Sarah caught her looking like a deer in the headlights. Her accident and her current timeline's proximity was something she failed to take into account, wasn't it? If her calculations were correct, she had gotten onto that airplane six weeks before. Her mother had indeed pushed her up in a wheelchair, her leg still in a brace, stuck out in front of her because she wasn't supposed to bear weight on it. She'd still been wobbling around on crutches at Christmas. And here she was with a fairly normal looking face, a mostly full head of hair, and a gait still a bit wonky, but not a far cry off from undetectable.

"I, um, they're very pleased with my recovery," she explained lamely.

"I would think so. Now tell me about this man. He has to be bloody brilliant to get your head out of a book." She leaned forward, her dark eyes twinkling teasingly.

Alec's image reared up in the back of her mind, and the sick feeling she carried around since she left that shop in Georgia steamrolled through her with renewed ferocity. Despite the hurt he caused her, he was never far from her mind. But then all she had to do was think about the last time she saw him and the anger resurfaced.

He betrayed you, he lied became her mantra.

"He's an army doctor. He's tall. He's a good cook, likes travel, and, um... history." She shrugged.

"Ooh, at least something good came out of you going to the middle of nowhere, right? A doctor." She grinned. "Does he have any doctor friends in uniform?"

"I'm sure he does," Evie answered wryly, aware she had never met any of his friends. Did he even have friends? She really hadn't known him long enough to find out, had she?

"Must have been some fight to have you fly all the way here." Sarah tilted her head knowingly.

Evie couldn't tell her she really didn't have any other place to go. It wasn't like she could have just gone back to Kansas to share a room with herself. Besides, she needed Professor Bascomb-Murray's expertise to connect the dots not in her book. How were Flora, Anne, and Elizabeth linked?

And why the hell was Sarah acting like Calum hadn't existed?

"Ah, shite. I have to be at class in twenty minutes!" She jumped up. "I'm done at one. Meet me for fish and chips at lunch?" And then she ran off into her room, feet slapping against the old wood floors.

Evie got up slowly, the jet lag pulling at her. She wanted nothing more than to go crawl into her bed, but she knew that was the worst thing she could possibly do for herself. Besides, she had so much to do.

She peeked into Sarah's room. Sarah was in the

process of pulling off her pajamas with one hand and spraying herself with hefty amounts of body spray with the other.

"Do you mind if I shower?"

"What? No! Why would I mind? I think your mum left some of your clothes in the wardrobe in your room, too!" She pulled a jumper over her head. "I am going to be so late," she muttered.

Evie retreated, wondering what the hell was going on.

Laena had left about half of her wardrobe, all of the things Evie loved and her mother abhorred. Old jeans soft as butter, sweatshirts so worn the cuffs were fraying, a pair of panties she bought her sophomore year of high school that made her ass look amazing. Evie left the pretty sweater and jeans Alec bought for her in a pile on the bed and pulled some of those old favorites on.

Despite the softness of her curves, the jeans still hung low on her hips, threatening to fall off if she moved too swiftly, and the hooded sweatshirt hung down to her mid-thighs. She borrowed a pair of boots from Sarah's closet and a heavy coat before exiting into the cold mist.

Her eyes still drooped with exhaustion, but she needed to get through the day if she wanted to get acclimated to the time change.

Mrs. Baird's Bed and Breakfast was located halfway down North Street across the road from St Salvatore's Chapel. It was one of many in a long line of stone townhouses much older, much less ornate, than the Victorian ones on Hope Street. She pulled her coat tightly around herself as she brushed past a gaggle of students, their black robes still worn despite the harsh temperatures and biting wind. She turned up the stone stairs to huddle under the little overhang and knocked gently on the door.

There was no answer.

She tried again with more force, her knuckles smarting against the old wood. Silence. Shifting back off the porch, she stepped into the mist and looked up at the paned windows. Every one of them was dark.

"House's been empty for years," a graveled voice called out from the next door down.

Her heart dropped as she turned to the middle-aged woman standing on the doorstep. She was dressed smartly in tailored trousers and a cashmere sweater, pearls hanging from both her neck and ears. Her coat hung open and she clutched an umbrella in one arm, shaking it out toward the street. She carried a reusable bag with the local grocery's label plastered across it and a fine leather purse in the crook of her arm.

"Y-Years?" Evie repeated dumbly.

The woman's head tilted to the side, much like a dog's does when it doesn't quite understand the command given.

"Do you know where I could find Mrs. Baird?" she asked, her voice roaring in her own ears.

"Oh, dear, I don't believe I've known any Bairds to live in this part of town for some fifteen years. The last owner was Alan Kirk and his wife Mags. He retired from the biology college some time ago after poor Mags passed."

Evie blinked and looked back to the bright blue door. The paint was duller than she remembered it, more worn.

"Thank you," she called, likely not loud enough for the woman to hear her over the turning of tires through puddles. "I must be mistaken."

She had come to this door at least once a week for months. She'd entered through it, walked down the cheerily papered halls to sit at the small kitchen table overlooking the garden the row of houses shared to the back. She'd hugged the woman who owned it. She had kissed her son. Was going to marry him.

And it was like neither of them existed.

She stood in the mist as it grew to a steady rain, collecting in her hair, seeping into her clothes and down her borrowed boots, staring up at those dark windows. And wondered what had happened to her life.

****

It hadn't taken Alec long to know that Evie was gone.

In fact, he knew it the moment he had entered that little shop to find Flora McDonald casually reading a paperback, the leather journal gone.

He ran back to the hotel, his footsteps pounding in tune with the muscles of his heart, only to find the room exactly as they left it. She hadn't returned.

And there was no telling where she was heading.

He tore apart the room, looking for anything that didn't belong there, knowing he would find an apple or a slender branch or even a ball of yarn. They were everywhere, small keys to the Otherworld gateways. In the back of the small closet he found one, a single branch with an apple bloom in pure silver. He held his breath as he was shot across the veil, landing in a clearing he recognized as one of the Otherworld's favorite gates.

195

It was located along the far eastern edge of the summer kingdom ruled by Hafgan, just along the southern edge of the peninsula shooting into the ocean separating Scathag's Island from the Solstice Kingdoms.

The challenge was to remain unseen, and so he traveled under cover of darkness, up through the mountains and into the forest where his cottage sat nestled in the trees. But it was just as untouched as the hotel room.

If she was in the Otherworld, he may never find her. But if she wasn't, where would she have gone?

Home.

Chapter Seventeen

Evie found herself nursing a hot tea for the rest of the morning as she waited for it to be time to meet Sarah. She'd scrounged a bit of paper off the printer, eventually found a pen lodged between two sofa cushions, and began taking notes of each memory she still possessed.

How had she met Calum? Outside a bakery near the castle. She hadn't intended to go inside but stopped to pet a dog standing at the door. The smell of freshly baked meat pies was enough to drag her inside, and she ended up leaving with a take-away order and cup of fresh coffee. Calum was the first person in line standing behind her.

"Your accent. It's beautiful. Where are you from?" he asked after she stepped away from the counter after placing the order.

"I, uh, what? Th-thank you. No one has ever said, I mean... Where I'm from, it's boring," she amended, flustered.

The memory still made her warm with pleasure. He'd escorted her to St. Katharine's from there, and she'd nearly been late for her first meeting with Sylvia Bascomb-Murray. But the professor didn't see them together that afternoon; he left her at the outside door and continued on his way.

Their first date had been a film at the theater over

by the library. Also alone. She had not gotten popcorn even though it had smelled glorious and she could have easily eaten a whole bag on her own.

She absently tapped the pen against her cheek, going over the fine details of her life at St Andrews for almost a year. Second date? Dinner. Third date, she'd cooked for him while Sarah was gone for her brother's birthday weekend. Fourth date? Sex at his flat.

She blushed. He hadn't had a roommate and what was planned as a guided tour of the most haunted spots around town ended up being a sweet, breathless coupling on his sofa. He was so eager to please, so focused on her, she couldn't help but feel a little guilty it hadn't been the best romp of her life.

And then she tried to recount all of the times they went out with others. She remembered trying to convince him to come to a dinner party at her flat; he'd had a prior engagement. Meet up with her friends at Sarah's favorite bar on The Scores? He had an exam to study for. Last minute trip to Monaco? He thought maybe he was getting sick.

The more she wrote down, the more she realized he had avoided meeting her friends. And the only person in his life she had met was his mother. Looking at it on paper, she realized how ridiculous it seemed, but how had she never noticed? How had it never bothered her that he didn't want to meet her roommate? That he had never made mention of meeting her parents?

And her parents. She was angry at them for months for never mentioning him. She had been grieving and felt abandoned because no one would even utter his name, and... and had he existed at all?

How could she have been so stupid? The anger and

embarrassment warred in the pit of her stomach and she dropped the pen to press the heels of her hands into her eye sockets. She ran from Alec when there was no reason to, chasing after, what? A ghost? A hallucination?

She was a jerk, pure and simple. It stung, but she had no way to reconcile it now. And… well, maybe she was still a *little* mad at him. After all, he hadn't known Calum was a figment of her imagination, either. He should have said something. Warned her. Let her down gently. Anything but keep it a secret.

She threw back the remainders of her tea, the last dregs gone cold, and dropped her notes in the kitchen rubbish bin. She hadn't bothered to change into dry clothes when she had arrived back at the flat, and she saw no reason to when she was just going to trudge back into the rain-soaked outdoors again, anyway.

Her favorite fish and chip shop sat on the western edge of the old town, near the cathedral and the pier, on the last narrow sidewalk on of Market Street. The location had been under construction when she first arrived in St Andrews. The previous owners had owned the small strip of real estate for nigh on forty years, selling beer battered fish, thick cut chips, and deep fried chocolate bars over a metal counter. The stone shop had been dark and cold according to those who had been there prior to the turn over, but the new owners brightened it up, bringing in little tables with checked table clothes, and ice cream parlor chairs. She and Sarah ate there at least twice a week before the accident.

The walk from Hope Street took her almost twenty minutes. By the time she stepped into the small dining room, it as crowded with hungry students and her leg twinged angrily at the prospect of waiting for a table.

"Evie!" Sarah waved her over to one of the little tables.

Evie let out a sigh of relief before pushing through the throng of waiting people and sliding into the chair opposite her former roommate.

"Hope you don't mind," Sarah said around a bit of vinegar-soaked chip. She motioned to the plate at Evie's spot, filled with the same fare Sarah munched on. "I wasn't sure how long you'd be, but I've only an hour."

"This is great. Cheers," Evie murmured before breaking off a piece of fluffy, battered fish.

It steamed deliciously into the air and she dropped it to allow it to cool. Time to test her theory.

"Sarah, have you heard from Mrs. Baird?"

"Who?" Sarah asked around her food.

"Calum's mum."

It was so easy to slip back into the local slang. But as right as it felt, her heart still pounded and she waited for Sarah's answer, hoping it proved she wasn't crazy. She had a sinking feeling disappointment was in her grasp.

Sarah regarded her with a slender eyebrow quirked. "Who is Calum?"

"The bloke I was seeing. He was driving the car when I had my… accident."

Sarah's eyes narrowed and she canted her head to the side. "Are you all right?"

Evie waited.

"You were alone, Evie. You were driving a rent-a-car. And there wasn't anyone in it with you."

Evie's breath caught and a dry sob reared up, ready to break free. She stamped it down, the effort sending prickles to the backs of her eyes, and they began to water. It was just as bad as she'd feared. Were all her memories wrong? She told Alec she must have a brain tumor for the world to make sense. Maybe she wasn't wrong. Maybe the trauma—that coma—had done more damage than she thought. What if everything she thought she remembered was… incorrect?

"But I remember you mentioning a Calum. Three or four times, perhaps."

Evie's attention snapped back to Sarah. "I did?" She sounded surprised even to her own ears.

"Yeah. I told you should bring him 'round, but you never did. I figured it wasn't that serious or you scratched that itch and found it… lacking," she purred mischievously before taking a long sip of diet orange soda.

Hungry, Evie, bit into the fish and chewed automatically, but it lost some of its taste as she focused on what Sarah said. She couldn't enjoy it knowing everything was incredibly, decidedly not right.

"Evie," Sarah murmured softly, leaning forward. Her forehead puckered as if she suddenly realized something about Evie was different than she remembered. "Why are you really here?"

****

Evie pushed through one of the traditional blue doors and took the stairs up to her advising professor's office. Most of the history faculty had their offices in an old—by American standards, anyway—building overlooking the North Sea. The little street on which the building was situated was the northernmost lane, a large stone wall separating the street from the shore. At one end, St Andrews Castle crumbled into the sea, at the other, the Old Course rolled off into the distance.

The door stood slightly ajar, her office hours having begun fifteen minutes prior. Evie knocked quietly before poking her head in.

Evie assumed Sylvia Bascomb-Murray was somewhere in her mid-forties. Her dark hair was strung through with bits of silver, and the straight-as-straw curtain hung down to her shoulders. Stylish reading glasses perched on her nose, and she moved them to the crown of her head as she studied the face of the guest at her door. A slow smile spread across her bright red lips and she leaned back in her desk chair.

"Well, aren't you looking well," she crooned with warmth as she stood, her arms open.

Evie had known the older woman would not be greeting her with the kind of reaction she had received from Sarah, but the embrace she received was just as welcoming.

"I was unaware I should be expecting you back so soon," she said as she turned back to her chair, motioning to the wooden one on the other side of the desk.

Her office was cluttered, bookcases taking up any available space and filled to overflowing. Books lay on their backs, stacked six and seven high, teetering on the edges of the dark wood, one good dusting away from falling to the ground. It smelled faintly of must and old wood, dark from the dreary outside. The window offered little light even on the sunniest of days.

"It was… unplanned." Evie glanced at her watch; the afternoon was growing old and soon, the sun would be dipping from behind the heavy cloud cover to leave the streets dark. "With my extensive free time, until I am back full-time, that is," she hastily added. "I was reading *Women of Culloden,* and I, um, I couldn't help but wonder why you chose those women."

The professor raised her eyebrows. "You flew back from America just to ask me that? You have my email address. And my mobile number," she reminded Evie dryly.

"I was thinking I might like to do some research of my own in the field."

"In the field?"

Evie's palms went sweaty and she cleared her throat. Why did it feel like she was being grilled by the high school principal for skipping a class? "I have a particular interest in Elizabeth Carlisle."

"Mmm. There is precious little about her other than what her husband wrote. There are some accounts kept by the British Army and locals about the uprising of clan women she incited, but most are gossip at best. There aren't even records of who her mother was or when her father inherited. We knew she had a brother, but only because of her husband's writings. We know where the family holdings were but have no idea where she was even born." She held up a hand and gave a slight shrug to her shoulders. "Usually there are baptism records, but there is nothing for her entire family. It's as if they were born of nothing, just arriving on the scene for the uprising, and then disappeared just as fast by giving their lives to the cause."

Evie leaned forward, ignoring the twinge in her hip. "But why her? Flora MacDonald's contribution speaks for itself. As does Anne's. But Elizabeth Carlisle didn't smuggle a prince to safety or lead a company of men. She... protested."

The professor's lids fell heavy in thought as she contemplated her student's question, her lips slightly pursed toward the fingers she held steepled in front of her face. "You ask an important question. Perhaps one I didn't explore to its fullest potential. Her contribution was at the back of my mind, but I could never seem to make what she did fit into the historical context. She was... ahead of her time. This was a young woman who mobilized other women in a way the world didn't see again for at least a hundred years. More."

"But in France—"

"Instigated by men."

"Couldn't we say the same about Elizabeth?"

"Perhaps. But she—none of them—intended to march. Not then, not ever. They were alone in their march; no men stood at their sides. She mobilized an all-female force, and quickly. Nor was it to the tune of being the exception, but that the fight belonged to all of them."

"So why include her?"

"Why not include her?" The older woman's eyebrows puckered together. "Someone else posed that question to me when I was first beginning my research. I had traveled to Culloden's historical center to speak with one of the curators, and she was the one who suggested I include her."

"Would she still be there? This curator?"

Evie was already making mental notes on the map of Scotland. She would start at the Carlisle estate in Lanarkshire, make her way to the Meyner family seat at Loch Tay—if it even still existed—and then to the

North to the moor if she still had questions. After that…
well, she had no idea. Perhaps she would figure out
exactly how she could use the Otherworld to her
advantage.

"It's possible. This was a few years ago, however,
and she was not a young woman then."

Evie uncapped her pen and reached for the paper
she had folded up and shoved into her bag. "Do you
remember her name?"

"I believe it's in my notes."

She turned away from Evie to click through the
documents on her computer. The only noise was the
gentle tap of new rain on the old window panes, the
gentle tick of the analog clock on the wall, and the
occasional click as the professor dug through the files.
The minutes stretched uncomfortably.

"Ah, here it is. Mary Baird."

Chapter Eighteen

Evie spent the duration of the evening poring over the peer-reviewed journal databases for any information about the *other* Alexander Carlisle and his bride, Elizabeth Meyner. He was a source of very little academic inquiry, his name appearing more in passing than in any sort of subject matter. She found herself feeling almost a bit sorry for the youngest son of the duke; great detail was put into the study of his father, and yet his life was relegated to two or three lines in any given text. Even his wife received a few more passing nods, though the only primary sources of her life were the journals of her husband. Evie half-wondered if he had made her up, some sort of mid-eighteenth century pre-internet trolling.

The journals were a part of the university's rare books collection. She requested access to them, knowing the appointment would include hours down in the dark basement rooms, her hands covered in white cloth gloves, likely learning nothing she didn't already know.

The great hulking palace that had once been the family seat of the Carlisles was torn down in the early twentieth century, so she wouldn't be visiting it for any additional digging. One of the crown jewels of Europe, and all that was left were the sprawling parklands. She sat scowling at the screen as she realized the first act of her plan was shot to hell.

"Are you going to growl at that thing all day?" Sarah lounged on the sofa, her socked feet rocking to the beat of the music playing from her phone.

"No. Yes." Evie tapped her fingers on the mouse pad. "Can I borrow your car?"

"Are you going to drive it into the side of a lorry?"

Evie rolled her eyes toward her friend and pursed her lips. "The thought did cross my mind," she mused wryly. "But no, I need to take a trip to Loch Tay and I like my consciousness, thank you very much."

"Why would you go all the way out there?" Sarah wrinkled her nose as her lips pulled back into a disgusted grimace.

She had made her preference for the city life very well known during their time living together. While Evie was ready to give up her creature comforts for short bursts of time, Sarah wouldn't even consider visiting the country. "What for?" she had muttered once when Evie had invited her to see Dunnottar Castle near Aberdeen. "I can see pictures on the web any time."

"I don't know," Evie grumbled. "Chasing ghosts."

"Ooh, well, in that case, you are more than welcome to it. It desperately needs petrol, though, so don't get any ideas about not filling it up."

The car was more for show than anything else, Evie suspected. It was used biweekly for clubbing in Dundee, but little else.

Evie rolled her eyes. "Want to come with me?"

"To Tay? Not on your life."

"There's supposed to be some snow. I'll buy lunch?"

Sarah snorted. "I fully intend to be hung over all

weekend. Especially if there is snow."

"You're the worst."

"Why don't you just wait a week? Go later."

"Because the money in my Bank of Scotland account is already dwindling."

"And you can't ask Mummy and Daddy for an advance?"

Evie faked a dramatic eye-roll. "They don't exactly know I'm here."

Sarah shot up, her wild curls bouncing around her like a dark cloud. "Where do they think you are?"

"Asleep in my bed?" Evie muttered to herself, but then said more clearly, "Visiting my sister?"

"And your sister won't let that slip?" She made a face that told Evie Sarah thought she wasn't terribly bright.

Evie shrugged. "I'll deal with it later."

Sarah rolled her eyes and flopped back onto the pillows. "Wanna hit up the pub tonight?"

Evie shook her head and suppressed a yawn. "I'm surprised I made it this late."

She shot a glance at the clock on the computer screen. It was just past six. Dark outside for hours, already, the winter nights were long on the shores of Scotland. And the last time she slept had been for a few hours on the plane, cramped up in a window seat near the lavatories, her head resting on her curled arms atop the tray table. Just the thought of it had her rubbing her eyes, which were dry and burning ever so slightly.

"Could you make sure I am up when you get up?"

"Sure," Sarah said, the frown entering her tone of voice.

Evie waved goodnight to Sarah and yawned, her

bare feet slapping on the wood as she slunk into her room. It was much the same as she had left it, minus many of her personal items. The bed was unmade, her sheets and quilt folded neatly on the foot of the mattress; courtesy of Laena, probably.

Rather than making the bed, she kicked off her jeans, pulled her bra off through one sleeve, and threw open the quilt, wrapping it around herself as she fell onto the bed. She didn't even bother hunting down a pillow, the absence of one only entering her mind moments before she had drifted off to sleep.

****

She dreamed of golden fields. Of tall grasses skimming her hips, waving like the sea, autumn winds flirting with the heads as they bowed and danced. A heavy sun hung low in a clear sky, casting shadow and flaxen light across the vastness of the lands. Twenty yards ahead was the man in the hood; he moved with the fluid grace and ease of a stag. Between them was a soft female figure, her hair like fire in the sunlight, a riot of curls falling wild over her shoulders.

Sweat dripped down Evie's back, a trickle worming its way from somewhere between her shoulder blades all the way down to the waistband of her breeches. She itched to wipe it away, to splash the dirt and sweat and grime from her flesh. To soothe away the ache of her feet.

But the breeze felt lovely, cooling the glistening tracks framing her sun-kissed face, running over her jaw, dipping into the collar of her tunic.

She ran a gloved hand over the swaying grasses, her fingertips scattering tufts of fuzz into the air. She looked down at her hand, at the leather vambrace

209

crisscrossing her wrists and forearm, noting the intricate details there. Three twisting circles, a triangle between them.

And when she glanced back up, the woman between her and their leader had vanished, and instead, there was another there. At first she thought Alec had joined them, but his silhouette was all wrong. He was tall, but with the shape of a gymnast, not Alec's lithe swimmer's body. His arms were left bare, toned with muscle, well-sculpted, shoulders straight. A tattoo ran down his biceps, under the leather jerkin covering his back. The blue ink stood in sharp contrast to his sun-kissed skin. He turned, as if to make sure she was there, a mischievous smile splitting his bronzed face, and black hair flopping across his brow.

Calum.

****

Evie shuddered awake, dragging in air as if she had stopped breathing, filling her lungs.

She hadn't dreamed of Calum since before Evan showed up at her parents' with a bottle of mustard. And then, they were nothing more than snippets, usually the memory of him at St. Rule's tower, looking up at her, the sun shining in his face.

He had looked so happy, as if the joy he felt would consume him. As if he would never be happier. As if she had given him the greatest gift in the world.

She snuggled back down into the quilt and wondered if he would still feel that way now. After knowing how easily she had given herself to someone else.

Chapter Nineteen

Alec approached the caravan circle on silent feet, keeping to the darkness just beyond the campfire's light. He leaned against one of the brightly-colored wagons and waited. The notes played by the lone fiddler were haunting, low, the song of returning to a homeland where you no longer belonged. He had heard it many a time, a guest at just such a bonfire.

Few knew the Ellyll were the unseen eyes and ears of the Otherworld. They were the silent, the few. The forgotten. They existed on the fringes, wanderers, their caravans dotting the landscape between.

They were of the ancient race, the one there before time, before the gods created and entered the Earth realm. As their deities slipped across the veil, to the wilds unknown, it had been that ancient race of Ellyl who joined them. They who lived among the humans, worshipping their gods and plying their magic in a world only just born. When the gods retreated, the Ellyll, now a race that looked nothing like the humans and, yet, nothing like their ancient homeland ancestors, followed, but to find a much-changed Otherworld.

Their home was nothing more than a distant memory, their magic diluted by Earth and the humans with whom they had mingled. The faeries they had once resembled were strange and no longer welcomed them into their towns and cities. They belonged not with the faeries, nor with the humans, and so they wandered, keeping to themselves, stoking the fires of fear and distrust. Many called them elves for their pointed ears and their slender builds, their lack of magic. It was a reminder that even with their immortality in the Otherworld, they were no more magical than the horses pulling their wagons.

"Your hair is much changed, pet. I almost did not recognize you."

She was a slight thing, like her people, with silvery hair and moon-white skin. She was dressed in a simple green tunic over a calf-length brown skirt that showed off the intricately stitched stockings under the laces of her gilles. He gazed down his nose at her, not straightening his stance, his eyes sharpening at the jab.

"And you are just as you've always been."

She lifted a shoulder, not looking at him but at her people gathered together around the fiddler. "It's been some time since last you joined us."

"Has it?"

They both knew he referenced the fact that time stood still here. Events played out, one falling after another, but otherwise, they dwelled in a place where time stood still. Nothing changed in the Otherworld.

But in terms of events, many had passed since he saw her last. It was with these people he had finally come to terms with the fact that his life would never be as he imagined it. He had come back to the Otherworld and been lost, without direction. In those days, he and Delyth had become friends of sorts, and it was she who had first instructed him in the ways of the healers. With her he found he enjoyed the mending of bones, the stitching of flesh. He far preferred it to the hunt. To killing. He owed her for much of the peace he eventually found.

"What brings you to us?" she murmured.

He had known those soft lips, once. When he was broken and thought he would never be able to piece himself back together. She had helped with that, too.

A lump formed in his throat. "I found her," he whispered, his voice threatening to break. "And I think she has slipped back here. Have you, do you know anything?"

She raised her nearly-invisible eyebrows and turned to him for the first time. "You ask me to track down your dead once more?"

He repressed a shudder at the thought. "No, no. She would have passed through the veil alive. She is looking for someone in one of the solstice courts."

"You wouldn't need to be asking your questions here if a mortal were sniffing around the kings. Especially the way things are."

He narrowed his eyes in a question he didn't need to ask.

"An emissary of Arianrhod, a witch of the Archives, tricked Arawn out of his general. She dragged him from the battlefields before the great battle of the Ford and disappeared with him, likely back to the Archives. His fury rings through every corner of the kingdom."

The Archives were Arianrhod's domain, where she had retreated with her magic-wielders when the gods abandoned his world. But Alec knew Arawn's general wasn't cloistered in the Archives to the North, and by the amused look in her eye and curve of her lip, he had a feeling Delyth knew it as well.

"If you hear whispering of the names Evie or Calum—"

"I know," she murmured. "Will you be at the cabin?"

He shook his head. "If she isn't here, there's one other place she would go. If she's not there, I'll send word of where you can find me."

"May Debrenua grant you speed."

"Thank you, Delyth."

She nodded and Alec slipped back into the night. Delyth turned back to the campfire, her gaze on the four crows watching from a tree branch at the edge of the clearing.

****

Stone circles dotted the landscapes of the Otherworld. Some were less powerful than others, though no physical characteristics told of their strength. Alec always used the whisperings of the winds within their diameter to determine how best to use them.

Alec squinted at the symbols on a small piece of paper. The closest stone circle to the Ellyll's camp was a few kilometers away, in the middle of a farmer's field. With each trip across the veil, he marked the location of the stone circle on a crude map he drew on the back of a title page he tore from a poetry book. He kept it rolled up in his pack, always within reach when he needed it for unexpected trips. It was usually tucked up against a raggedy leather-bound notebook used to record each jump. In the beginning, he allowed his own timeline to get so jumbled; he was seen by his professor and fellow students two places at once. Delyth was the one to suggest he keep notes for himself. Or, rather, she threatened to beat him over the head with his own shoe if he didn't get his act together.

He rolled up the map and shoved it between the journal and the other artifacts he could ever need this side of the veil or the other. Each little knickknack connected with a time and place, ensuring he returned to the correct year and location. They were especially important when the stones lacked a powerful connection to the mortal world. Finding himself on the wrong continent only happened once, and he never wanted to repeat the experience.

The journey across the gently rolling fields was lit only by moonlight and stars. The farmers of these valleys had long plied their trade, this ground a part of their bones. They tilled and tended their crops and the pasture beasts with a loving hand, the bountifulness of the land all they needed. These were not rich people, but they were also not people in need of monies. There was no poverty in the lands of the gods.

Around him, the night creatures played, the sprites giggling in the grasses, their laughs like the chatter of chipmunks, the pixies flitting in the air, their songs the hum of their wings. They glittered prettily, buzzing through the air like brightly colored fireflies, their magic whipping behind them like condensation trails left by aircraft. Pixies were always most plentiful in the valleys of the warm-lands and kept away those who were unfamiliar with their kind. They avoided passing through Hafgan's and Arawn's kingdoms and he rarely saw them up in the mountains near his cottage. Seeing some flit around Evie one evening at the cottage was a rarity, he had lived through many battles of the ford before he had seen his first pixie.

The white standing stones rested on the crest of a

hill, their smooth surfaces surrounded by a sea of waving wheat. As he approached, he swung his pack forward. He dug out a small signet ring and the ornament he used when last he had been in the Otherworld. This particular circle had a stronger bond with where he wished to go, but he wasn't taking any chances. As he swung the pack back over his shoulder, he walked into the circle and listened to the tales it whispered.

And then he thought of the one he once lost. Of her home.

And of Evie.

Chapter Twenty

The bed was entirely too cold and empty when she woke up.

She hurriedly dressed in whatever clothes she could find, many of her ripped up and faded jeans and long-sleeved t-shirts were still stuffed into the drawers of the built-in dresser. She pulled out a sweater that had belonged to one of Sarah's one-night stands. Evie had confiscated it when the offender never came back around, wearing the gray cable knit on wash days.

Her outfit made her look every inch the poor student, the jeans low-slung and tight but the shirt and sweater over-sized. But it was warm enough once she pulled on the boots and jacket. As long as she wasn't stranded anywhere. For more than five minutes. Worrying about her utter lack of acceptable winter clothes kept her from focusing too much of her energy on the trip to come.

Evie left before the sky lightened. The clouds had already moved in, heavy and dark, and she knew there would be no sun that day. She hoped to make it to the shores of Loch Tay and back to St Andrews before the winter weather rolled in. The winds had picked up though there was always a breeze coming off the water. Otherwise, it was quiet but for the faint whine of the seagulls; they never seemed to sleep, and she had always found their presence of some comfort.

Nervous, she slipped into the driver's seat of Sarah's little car, hands shaking. To get out of town, she had to drive the same route that had killed Calum. Despite the fact that she questioned his entire existence, the pain and guilt and loss barreled back to her. Yet, the face she couldn't get out of her mind wasn't his. And the loss she felt was a different kind.

The narrow roads, the opposite direction of traffic, the manual transmission, it was all a little daunting. But she managed to spend the few minutes it took the engine to heat up to talk herself into pulling into the street. And then turn to head toward the stop sign across from Chattan Hall. Pulse beating wildly, she eased the car out onto the road that would take her to the Leuchars roundabout where her whole world had gone topsy-turvy.

As she had lain awake the night before, mentally planning the trip ahead, her thoughts would slip away, going back to a little cottage in the forest. Instead, she would try to dash those visions away with thoughts of Calum. Alec had betrayed any right to her brain space by not telling her Calum could be just across the mountain. It didn't matter if it was true or not. The act of not telling her was the real crime. But the anger was really only a case of strong annoyance. Alec, after all, made her feel alive, again. And he challenged her in a way Calum never had.

She knew she wasn't the easiest person to live with; she held onto grudges for a long time, perhaps longer than any mortal person should. And she knew she was a little sarcastic, hardheaded, skeptical. She always had been. The loss of Calum had perhaps exacerbated some of her worst qualities. And Alec had risen to meet her head on. He never backed down. Never turned away from her. He never talked down to her or promised her fairytales.

It didn't matter. He was remaining on her shit list whether he liked it or not.

Even if she missed him.

Even if a fresh hole was ripped through her heart when she walked away from him.

But he had lied and he had hurt her. And she didn't need to hurt any more than she already did.

Focusing on him made it easier to direct the car west. But the distraction only lasted so long.

To the north of the road, the water sparkled faintly in the early gray light. It wasn't darkness, but it wasn't morning, either. The water lapped at the shores, at the edges of the tall grasses, at the borders of the farms. Her heart thudded as she approached the traffic circle and she turned the radio off despite the already low volume and inaudible thrum.

Breathe. In. Out. Watch the cars. You can do this. You can do this, breathe. Breathe…

And then she was through the circle and heading west. To Loch Tay. Toward Glen Lyon and Elizabeth Menzie Carlisle.

****

Castle Lawers had no real business calling itself a castle, at least in Evie's opinion. The seat of the Tay Meyner Chieftain was little more than a squat rectangle overlooking the loch's waters. Built of unassuming gray stone, the structure was devoid of turrets or towers unless one got very creative and called its four stories a tower. Every inch of it was crumbling, as were most of the outbuildings, the stables, laundry, kitchens, and a barracks. Over time, they had become little more than half-walls and bird perches. All but the visitor's center, which marked the castle as one of the Historic Scotland sites.

The visitor's center was set inside a stone structure likely rebuilt over a pre-existing foundation to appear ancient itself. Some of the stones appeared old and weathered into softness, The top half was lighter in color, less grimy, and still had fresh, sharp edges. The foundation wasn't much smaller than that of the main building and Evie wondered if it had been the stables at one time.

The only other car in the graveled parking area was an old sport utility vehicle and she pulled up near it, scattering a cluster of crows pecking at the pebbles and rubbish left behind. She cut off the engine only after she gathered her purse, an unused notebook, and a handful of black ink pens.

Outside, the winds stung like ice, the scent of the coming snows heavy on the sharp gusts. She pushed through the brightly painted blue door and inside, the air was warm, the temperature bordering on hot. An unassuming wooden desk stood in the far corner, a cash register that should have been replaced a decade before perched on its scuffed surface. A few touristy items were displayed around a postcard dolly.

But the rest of the space was set up like a small museum. The light was terrible despite the building's upgrade, and the displays were shabby. She intended to comb through everything there. But first she had to speak to the matronly woman she surprised when she walked through the door.

"Good morning." The woman bobbed her head in

greeting, not a strand of silver-peppered hair moving from the severe bun perched atop her head. Skin flawless and unadorned of makeup, she could have been anywhere from forty to sixty. Her clothes were plain, a cable knit jumper over a pencil skirt too dull and misshapen to be anything but part of a uniform.

"Good morning," Evie murmured as she warily stepped toward the desk. "I was hoping you could tell me about the Menzie-Carlisle collection. I'm a post-graduate at—"

"If you're here tae see the castle, you'll be wanting tae be quite quick. Weather won't be getting any better."

"It doesn't appear there is much to see," Evie joked dryly.

Not even a lift of an eyebrow.

"Yes, I would love to see the castle," she muttered and dug for her National Trust of Scotland card, which allowed her to see the castle without any additional fees.

The woman looked it over, but averted her eyes away, as if she was bored, once she was done perusing the expiration date. From under the desk she withdrew a crude map of the property, and pointed to the different rectangles representing buildings, offering a brief overview of the significance of each.

"And we hope you will enjoy the rich history found in our castle museum." She pointed the pen toward the small exhibits behind Evie.

"Thanks," Evie muttered as she picked up the map.

There was surprisingly less than she had originally anticipated. One case displayed some rusted tools, nails, and some other artifacts excavated from the foundation of the current museum building. Originally a workshop of some sort, it had contained findings that were far older than the foundation itself, some of the artifacts dating back to the Picts.

The castle itself was originally built in the eleventh century but the records of who had inhabited it were lost. Mention of a brief occupation by British forces during the English occupation of the thirteenth century had been uncovered at the closest monastery. But otherwise, the castle was thought to have been unoccupied until 1745.

Evie frowned. That couldn't possibly be right. The castle, the Meyner chieftain, had only come to the area the same year as the second Jacobite rebellion?

She turned back to the woman. "Was there another castle?"

The woman looked at her like she had two heads. "This says the Meyners didn't occupy the castle until 1745. Where were they before that?"

The woman just pointed to a plaque on the other side of the display.

After Lady Elizabeth's capture and subsequent hanging, the castle was looted and sacked. All records of the small Meyner clan were lost but for the few personal journals of her husband, Lord Alexander Carlisle of Lanarkshire. Lord Alexander was either unaware of his wife's family's history or he did not feel it important enough to record. Most of the Meyner clan died at Culloden, and the remaining members, mostly women and children, disappeared, many likely fleeing to the Americas as indentured servants.

Evie flipped open her notebook and jotted down a few notes, then turned to the northern wall. The whole of it was a display about Elizabeth Meyner, though Evie guessed the entire site was dedicated to her, minor player in the rebellion though she was.

A slightly enlarged version of the miniature found in Sylvia Bascomb-Murray's book was displayed next to the wall of text. It was all information Evie knew, almost a synopsis of the historian's first chapter about the young Scottish woman. The next column was about her marriage; how she had fallen in love with the son of the great Duke of Carlisle. That her fervor for the Scottish people was so great that she turned him from the country and king he had once served.

She moved down the wall to where two portraits hung. She looked down at the captions first, which said they had been found in the cellar under some oil cloth in the early nineteenth century and kept in the home of the local vicar.

She glanced up and swore softly as she looked right into Alec's likeness.

But it was the portrait next to his that caught her breath in her throat and threatened to choke her.

Because she was staring into her old face.

Chapter Twenty-One

Evie shivered as she quietly walked across the gravel path toward the entrance of the castle. She wasn't entirely sure how she had managed to steer herself out of the little visitors' center and toward the stone structure a few hundred yards away, but she welcomed the cold whipping through her hair and through the fibers of her clothing. She was just as cold on the inside as she was on the outside.

There was no logical reason why her portrait would be next to Alec's. She and Alec must travel back in time. They could do that, right? It was the closest thing to a logical explanation she could find. But she couldn't explain away the fact that the portrait showed her as she had looked before the accident. The way her chin had been a little longer and had jutted forward just a bit. How her face was slightly lopsided to the right. Her nose a little fuller, especially at the tip. Those fixes were ever so slight, but changed how she saw herself entirely.

It was just the artist's rendering. It had to be. She didn't look *that* much differently than before. It was coincidence. Sheer coincidence.

She huffed out a breath. Snow hung in the air, the scent of it sharp and stinging.

There would be little for her in the castle ruin, but she owed it to Elizabeth—to herself—to see it, anyway.

She stepped through what had once held a large door and looked up.

It truly was a ruin. The roof was gone, ripped away by wind and rain and rot. Part of a second floor, constructed of stone, was visible in a far corner, but the uneven, square stairs had crumbled as well, and whole chunks of them were missing. The first intact step was well over her head.

The castle was as empty and cold as it appeared; no one lingered. Not even ghosts.

"Evelyn."

She whirled, her breath catching as her heart sprinted.

Alec stood in the doorway wearing the same clothes she'd left him in. The first shadow of stubble grew on his chin and his cheeks. His eyes looked tired, but relief slackened his features, the worry smoothing from his forehead and the line between his eyebrows. Part of her wanted to run to him, to fling herself into his arms and his warmth, but she hung back, afraid she would betray herself.

"I don't understand what is happening."

Her voice cracked a little. She tried to control it, to stamp down on the huge lump in her throat threatening to choke her. It burned, bringing tears to her eyes, and she fought to keep from spilling over. She failed.

He took two steps toward her, but it was enough to bring him close without physically touching her.

She just looked at him. "Tell me everything."

****

They sat in the car, the heat turned up to high, a gale force wind of tropical warmth blasting their faces.

"I joined the King's Army when I was barely old

enough to shave. My eldest brother bought my commission, which, if I am to be perfectly honest, was far more generous that I ever would have expected from him. He was twenty-two years my senior and had little to do with me up until that point. Honestly, I think he wanted to save himself having to pay me an allowance commensurate to our brothers'. I was born seven months after my father's death, so there was no mention of me in his last will. I would have been... expensive. So John ensured I would have a way to support myself. It was a good option for a younger son. I liked it.

"And then my older brother, William, died. He had been sent to oversee the estate in Lanarkshire after a particularly embarrassing scandal involving a woman far outside the family's social circle. The duke didn't want to pretend he welcomed the lowborn wife of his younger brother to his great many parties—I was barely allowed in the door and I was his *brother*—and so they were packed off to the great North.

"Our heritage was Scottish, and the title came from a Scottish king, not an English one. But keeping the Scottish estate was more of a symbol than anything else. The family had made London and a hall in the south inherited through my great-grandmother the primary residences, so Carlisle House was the perfect place to leave a spare heir who made a mockery of 'all we hold dear.' Anyway, when William died, John—my eldest brother—offered me the position. I had just made the disastrous decision to offer marriage to the second daughter of a wealthy earl. Her father laughed in my face, she right along with him. All of society knew of my folly and John was furious I had been so bold without even consulting him first. But he needed someone to run Carlisle, and he couldn't be bothered. He hated Scotland. I would have free run of the house, given a monthly stipend, and I would take my own scandal away with me. So I accepted. I sold my commission and took up residence.

"I had business in Edinburgh a few months into my time there. And that's when I saw her. I looked out of the carriage and there she strode, bold as brass, between her father and her brother. Her hair was pulled back from her face, but was otherwise loose, tumbling down her back in a dark cascade, and her eyes bigger and brighter than any star. I had the driver stop and I jumped out after her, making up some excuse that I thought she was my sister's dear friend, but she knew I lied. She pitied me, though, and the next thing I knew, I was calling at her father's townhouse. But the moment I looked into her eyes, it was like a thread inside of me grew taut and pulled us together."

Evie swallowed, averting her gaze to her hands where she idly rubbed at her fingers with those of the opposite hand. Had she not thought the same thing when she had seen him in the bookstore?

"I don't know how to describe her other than… I never wanted to be away from her. I wanted to know everything about her and then know it all over again. My infatuation with Lady Mary melted away, and had you asked me her name, I wouldn't have been able to tell you. When Elizabeth and I were together, it was as if… it was as if there was no one else in the world."

He cleared his throat, as if it had gone dry, but Evie suspected there was some emotion there.

"We were married less than a month later. No one objected, not really. Her brother seemed off-put, but he always had a sour disposition when it came to me. This amused her father. Her mother was long dead and she was raised beside her brother. She was... brash, headstrong, full of ideas about the world and equality.

"You have to understand, I grew up in a different time. It was a man's world. A white, wealthy man's world. It has taken me a lot of time to see that, but I was born of vast privilege. I just never felt I was because I was the youngest son; I wasn't a duke or an earl or even a baron. I had no land of my own and my well-being was entirely dependent upon my brother's goodwill. I know differently, now, but then... After our first argument, I believe I told her 'no wife of mine would...' I don't even remember what it was she suggested. She told me she was my partner. She would always be my partner, in every way, but the moment I tried to 'lord myself' over her, she would take herself right back to her father's home.

"I was so smitten, I was terrified she would make good on her promise. I fell all over myself apologizing, wanting nothing more than to please her, to show her she had made the right choice. And when I was most honest with myself, I knew I would have her no other way than exactly as she was.

"And then the winds of war grew stronger. She was an ardent Jacobite. If I hadn't known any better, I would have said she orchestrated the entire uprising from her own desk. She knew all of the movements, all of the logistics. She sent notes and letters all over Scotland, her fingers always stained and smudged with ink. It was she who convinced me to join the cause. We were standing in one of six grand salons and she was waving her hands around saying 'this could all be ours,

228

Alistair. You could be more than your brother's steward."

He huffed out a bit of a laugh. "She insisted on calling me Alistair. Said it made me sound like a warrior instead of a fop. She knew my weakness and exactly how to use it. She knew I was resentful of my position. That I hadn't brought my new wife to my home, but to my brother's.

"And so I took up the sword, again. I knew how to be an officer, and there were plenty of my brother's tenants who wanted a free Scotland. We joined with her brother and father's men, and she was right there, by my side. She would have stormed the battlefields with me. Wanted to."

He got a far-off look.

"She, uh, she was there. Well, not there, but not far away. In Inverness. I'll never know how I convinced her to stay behind. She was hell-bent on joining the men on the battlefield, had even gone as far as securing breeches and a musket. I was appalled. Not because a part of me didn't think she could do it, I knew she could. But… it was my job to protect her. I told her as much. Told her that she made me feel less a man, that I was ashamed of her, that she didn't have a female bone in her body."

"What is wrong with you, Elizabeth, that you cannot act as a woman is to act?"

The mouth stiffened and her eyes narrowed. He knew that look far too well. It was the look he was digging for.

"Don't call me that!"

"Your name? Elizabeth. Elizabeth. Elizabeth. Why must you challenge my manhood at every opportunity?

Why must you force me to look upon you with shame?"

Her head jerked back and tears brimmed in her eyes. "You fill me with such contempt, I cannot even look upon you."

He took a steadying breath, remembering the last words he said to his wife, the woman he loved beyond all else, before he left her for battle. "I wanted to break her spirit, just… just enough to keep her from doing whatever fool thing she was setting her mind to. It worked. For a time, anyway."

He cleared his throat and stared off into the hazy distance. "We were overrun incredibly fast. I took a musket ball to the leg and my femoral artery was nicked. I knew the moment I went down it was over. I would bleed out on that gods damned field. I lay there, my life's blood pouring out onto a stinking bog, my only thoughts of Elizabeth, my *Ailsa,* and my last words to her. I knew I deserved to die for the things I said to her, even if it was to protect her. I told her those things when I should have been telling her she was my everything, that I loved her. I could feel the darkness start to pull me under… And *she* appeared to me amongst the carnage. I'll never forget the way she stepped over the carrion, as if she walked across a fresh carpet laid only for her, her black shroud flowing around her. Like a beautiful mirage. She placed her hand on mine and my pain lifted away. She offered me a drink and told me that if I accepted, I would see my Ailsa again. I accepted." He closed his eyes. Drew in a long breath.

"I could barely remember my own name, and my memories of my wife? Gone. I was consumed with *her.* Mora. I was her lover for… seasons. A member of her guard by day, her personal pet by night. I stupidly thought I was the only one, the truth was, we were scattered around the Otherworld. When I realized, I began to notice the inconsistencies with the story of my life. That I couldn't remember anything but my time with her. I began refusing the little vials she fed me, and bits of my memory started to seep back in.

"One evening, on patrol, I came in contact with an Ellyll caravan. We usually harassed them and then sent them on their way, but I knew they held some knowledge of magic, and I asked one for help with my memory."

"Everything you need to know is already inside of you. You simply need to dig until you unbury it."

"But how?" he asked anxiously, gaze darting around to be sure his partner for the evening didn't hear. But the other man was on the other side of the ring of wagons, barking orders at the travelers.

"Stop looking for others to tell you who you are, and be yourself." She stepped away, dismissing him in a way that few women ever had besides Mora and...

The name was on the tip of his tongue. He could almost see her, smell her. A scent of the earth. He closed his eyes and savored it, dug for the memory of her, whoever she was, but still came up with nothing more than the knowledge that she was there, somewhere.

And, for the first time, he murmured his heartfelt thanks to a woman.

"The memories came back, but slowly. The more I concentrated on the person I wanted to be and not what I was expected to be—by anyone, not just Mora—the more the memories came to me. The more I saw about that world, not just what Mora wanted me to see. She was angry, though I never really learned about what. One of her other pets, Iain, was constantly coming and going. At first I was jealous he had so many privileges, but I slowly began to see she was running him into the ground."

Evie sat up straighter. "Iain. He was the one you mentioned in the journal. You were jealous of him…" She thought about that night in the back of her father's car, of Iain's hands on her body, of hers on his. And she swallowed as a new sense of shame wash over her.

But Alec continued as if he hadn't even heard her. She wasn't sure he remembered he was speaking to her at all, so lost in his memories.

"I overheard her yelling at him one night…"

"If you don't have Ailsa here by the full moon, I will gut you from neck to cock, Iain. Do not doubt me."

Air left his lungs with such force he could have been punched in the gut. Ailsa. His beautiful, vibrant wife. Her blue-green eyes bright and her dark tresses pulled over her shoulder. The challenging tilt of her chin, the promise in her sly smiles. How could he have ever forgotten her?

The pain, the shame, that ripped through his heart was unlike anything he had ever felt. The emptiness left by her absence was now a gaping hole he could never fill. How was he surviving without her?

He pressed back against the cold of the stone and sank down onto the floor, muffling the sob that rent his soul in two.

"I followed Iain the next morning when he left the castle. That's when I learned how to make the jump from the Otherworld to mortal Earth. When he never returned with her, I planned for weeks how to get back to her on my own. I convinced myself Mora was making good on her promise that I would see my wife, again. That she had done me a favor by obscuring my memory until she could bring her to me. I told myself Ailsa refused to go with Iain and, instead I needed to be the one to go to her. I only imagined she waited for me or thought me dead. I dreaded the pain the latter must have inflicted upon her. I found myself back on that bloody moor."

He jolted awake and almost lost the whole of his last meal, which hadn't been much. The bodies littered the ground around him, and as he took them in, the bile rose. He struggled to his feet when the cold steel of a knife pressed to his throat.

"Keep quiet."

He knew the man's voice from the eavesdropping at which he had become so adept. "Your enemy is still swarming these parts."

The flat open field where they crouched appeared rather abandoned.

"Take your bloody knife away," Alec demanded. "I'm not here for you."

Iain obliged, sliding the small knife into his belt. "You think I don't know that? I just need to be sure you don't get yourself killed."

Alec glared at him. "What do you mean?"

Iain raised an eyebrow and clucked. "You think you were stealthy, don't you?" His eyes shone with mirth. "You charged through those woods like a bear." But then they became darker, clouded and he looked away. "I wish you hadn't come. There is no saving her."

Time, the wind, movements, all stopped around him, his whole world pinpointing on that simple statement. "What?"

Iain scanned the field once more. It was growing dark and fires dotted the horizon.

"She thinks you dead. She will attack a party of British soldiers, and when she does, she will be taken captive and hanged."

"Why? Why would she do that? It's madness. It's... it's suicide!"

Iain ran the tip of his tongue over his front tooth. "Yes," he agreed.

"Then what are we doing, here? We must go to her, stop her at once, we should—"

The other man shook his head. A floppy lock of hair broke free and brushed his forehead. He didn't bother to brush it away.

"It's too late," he said with something akin to regret. "I've been trying, but it's too late. Her soul has already passed through the kingdom of Annwn. To see her now... you will be met with an empty shell going through the motions. She will not see you, will not know you are there."

"I didn't believe him. I thought that if I got to her in time, I could turn the tides. But he was right. When we reached her, she... she wasn't there, anymore. She went through her tasks as if neither of us were there. Seeing her that way broke me. I begged with her empty body to come back, to show any flicker of knowledge of my identity. I threw things—a chair through the window—just to see how she would react. She didn't even blink. I traveled back and back and back, and I could never change her. Just as Iain said.

"That was my first real lesson in how time works as one passes through the Otherworld, breaking all worldly laws. I once told you it exists on a separate plane, which is true. But our timelines, our life threads… They cannot be altered. We can pass through the veil as our mortal selves, but once death claims us, there is no altering the path. It's as if a knot is tied and everything before is sealed into the tapestry in which it was woven.

"My only option was to find her deep in Arawn's kingdom. I would have stayed in hell with her forever. But she had already gone. She had believed, it seemed, that she thought it was her only option of ever finding *me,* again. In the next life."

Evie expected to see hurt and sadness and brokenness in his eyes. But none of that there. Instead… love. And pleading.

She frowned, not understanding how he could tell her of his dead wife, of her sacrifice, his pain, and then turn to her as if it was all for her.

"Evie…" He reached for her hand.

She moved it out of reach, not wanting him to touch her. Her pulse roared in her ears, because she knew, somehow, she knew what he would say next.

His head dropped back against the headrest, his shoulders slumped, and he sighed through his nose. "I searched through the centuries to find you. I honed myself into both a warrior and a healer, someone worthy of keeping you safe. I spent lifetimes living without my heart, without air, drowning, until I could find you."

"I'm *not* Elizabeth." But a whisper in the back of her mind reminded her of the portrait hanging inside.

"I'm not," she murmured again, trying to convince herself. "I can't be. All of this is… it's impossible."

"All this time, I thought it was me Mora was after. After my encounter with Iain, I believed he would be coming for me, to bring me back to her. None of her warriors left her. None. I thought Iain was there to collect my Ailsa as a reward for serving Mora well, and when I couldn't have the other half of my soul, I knew I could not be there.

"I disappeared. I was the first and I have been the last. I covered my tracks well, and I kept under her radar. But she knew where I was the moment Iain saw us in that coffee shop together, and never has she come for me. It was you she set the trap for, Evie, it was never about me. You're the one she wants."

Chapter Twenty-Two

Queasiness gripped her, stomach threatening to overturn water she drank in place of breakfast. She could have grabbed some toast or poured herself a bowl of cereal before leaving the flat, but after half a year of rising after noon, food first thing in the morning was easy to forget. By the time she realized food would serve her well, nerves kept her from doing any more than sipping from the bottle as she traveled north.

Mouth suddenly dry, she reached for the half-full bottle and gulped the remains down. Still in hand, she twisted the top on and then back off. Her hands needed something to do, the churning of her stomach impossible to ignore. She'd planned to stop for some lunch on her way back to St Andrews. Either it was good she was half-starved—she wasn't vomiting a toasty onto the gravel parking lot—or a terrible mistake.

She fidgeted under his gaze. He waited for her to say something. Anything. But she had nothing to give him. Her entire identity was crumbling around her, chipped and hacked away until she didn't even recognize herself. What was she supposed to do with all of this?

Curling up in his lap didn't seem like the right answer, though it held a certain appeal. Being with him was easy, and it would be nothing to forget fighting with him on the street only a few days prior. All he would have to do was wrap her in his arms and soothe the fear away. Perhaps they could travel back to the cottage in the forest and never leave. Lost away from time, hidden from Mora and Iain, from history and the future.

But how could she ignore Elizabeth or Ailsa or whatever her name was? Accepting that she was linked to the woman took a considerable leap of faith. And if she did, what did that mean for her and Alec?

Who did he really want? Evie? Or Elizabeth?

Maybe she wasn't ready to find out.

"I think I need to be alone, Alec."

"Evie."

"I just... I can't do this right now." She turned watery eyes to him. "I can't be who you need me to be right now. Ever. I can't be *Elizabeth.*"

"Evie, I don't want you to be Elizabeth. I want—"

The desperation in his voice tore at her, but she held a hand up to stop him. "I just need time, Alec. I need time to figure all of this out. Alone. You being here... I can't wrap my head around it with you breathing down my neck."

Her words came out far harsher than intended. She heard it the minute they passed through her lips but couldn't take them back. Wasn't sure she wanted to.

Alec deflated before her eyes, the color draining from his face and the brightness in his eyes dimming. Slowly, he nodded and then leaned down for his bag. He pulled out a skein of red wool wrapped tightly in a sandwich bag and placed it on the dashboard. "I hope that someday you follow this back to me."

He opened the door and walked into the coming

storm.

As Alec disappeared from view, Evie wondered if she would ever see him again.

****

Evie stared at the yarn for a long moment before plucking it off the dashboard. Rolling it from one palm to the other, she tested its weight as it passed over the plastic. What hurt more? She cupped it in her left hand. Losing Calum? It fell into her right. Or intentionally pushing Alec away?

The yarn didn't have any answers. She huffed, dropped the bag into the passenger seat, and reversed the car. Sarah's preferred music—electronic dance music—played over the speakers, the bass vibrating up through the seat upholstery. The tracks on the playlist all sounded the same, but Evie turned the volume up, anyway. Losing herself to the rhythm and her thoughts might distract from the dull ache somewhere in the vicinity of her heart.

Ailsa. Was she still there? Could she reach into the dark recesses of her mind and find the other woman curled up and hiding like a sleeper cell? Would she hear her voice? Her thoughts? Would she be like some sort of spirit guide, pushing her from one otherwise ill thought out decision to another? Or were she and Elizabeth one in the same?

That gave her pause. *Was* she this other woman, slipping through life by another name? Evie wished she'd demanded more information about the dead who pass through the Otherworld's solstice kingdoms.

Or perhaps there was the third possibility. None of it was real.

Why she couldn't latch onto *that* option? Knowing

in some way she was once Elizabeth Meyner Carlisle gave her a sense of peace she hadn't expected. And the thought of it all being a fairytale left her unnerved. Her fingers gripped the steering wheel as the snow began to come down harder and faster, obscuring the markings on the narrow country road. She considered pulling over but knew as long as she could keep the center line in her field of vision she would be okay. She was close, just the Leuchars roundabout stood between her and the last stretch of road that would take her back to the flat on Hope Street.

Outside, the wind whipped the long grasses covering the hills into a frenzy. They buckled and swayed, shuddering as strong gusts heaved up the coast. The wheel jerked in her hands as the car rocked against them. Only a few more miles.

She slowed as she came to the roundabout and carefully checked all directions for traffic. But she was the only driver stupid enough to be out on the roads during a winter storm. She and a small flock of crows staring her down from the grassy center of the intersection.

Alarm bells rang inside her head.

Beware the crows.

No sooner did the memory fill her mind than a pair of headlights flashed in her rearview mirror. She slowly pulled into the traffic circle, and the other car settled in close behind.

She tried to keep her eyes on the road, but the rearview mirror taunted her, and she flicked her gaze up to it.

Mora had found her, that much was certain.

But why? What was so special about Evie? Why

was Elizabeth of such value? Nothing Alec told her was enough to form a theory,

She sped down the road, slowing only as she entered town to creep down the street. She pulled in next to the rose garden outside the flat and turned off the car. The bright lights followed her, the soft purr of the other engine rumbling in the quiet, snow-strewn street a few car lengths back.

She would never know what her value was to Mora.

Unless she asked.

Chapter Twenty-Three

Evie awoke to the sound of rustling leaves, the skein of red yarn clutched to her chest, the empty bag flung to one side. Her bones ached from the cold seeping in through the heavy clothes, muscles tightening in waves of shivers. She huffed out a breath, watching it as it swirled above her into the frigid air, disappearing into the bare arbors of the forest above her.

"What are you doing, Eve?" She pushed herself up and turned toward him.

He perched on a fallen log.

"Whatever do you mean, Iain?" she asked with feigned sweetness.

His long legs uncurled with feline ease as he stood. He looked different, and not just because he'd traded in the cargo shorts and tank top for leather pants and a hooded cowl. Perhaps it was the assortment of knives hanging from his belt, the pair of criss-crossed swords on his back, or the grace with which he moved as he stooped to retrieve the plastic bag.

"You know exactly what I mean." Iain looked pointedly at the red yarn, motioning for her to hand it to him.

She obliged, dropping it into the bag he held open.

"Why are you following me?" She slid her frozen fingers into the gloved hand he offered.

Iain yanked her up, steadying her when her leg didn't immediately accept the weight, and then shoved the zippered bag into her chest.

She dropped it into her bag and then brushed at the snowflakes clinging to her hair. "Why were you following me?"

He gave her a long-exasperated look. "You know why."

"You were supposed to bring me here, weren't you?"

At first he didn't reply, just looked at her lazily. Another long sigh. A nod.

"Yes."

"Well, here I am. You did it. You win." She threw her hands out and allowed him to inspect her.

Iain crossed his arms over his chest. "I know you, and I know it's not that easy."

Evie wrapped her arms around herself and looked around. "That's so weird, because I don't feel like I know you at all." She pursed her lips. "Talk."

He glanced up into the twisted branches of bare trees. "Not here."

"Prying eyes? Ears?" She wiggled her eyebrows.

He lifted his. "No. It's just hellishly cold." He rubbed his hands together. "And your lips are turning blue."

With a hook of the arm, he motioned her forward. Evie fell in step beside him, thankful he kept his stride to a leisurely stroll so she could keep up.

"Where are we?"

"The northwestern edge of the continent in the Myrkvior. You're lucky you passed through here. There is a tavern around the bend."

"Tavern?" she said more to herself than to him.

"Like an inn, but with ale and food. Haven't you ever heard of them?"

She glared at his back. "Of course I have. I just didn't expect to find one here."

"In the Myrkvior?"

"No, in the Otherworld."

Iain snorted. "Let me guess, you thought it was just an uninhabited, wild world dotted with peasant farms and little cottages in the mountains?"

Evie frowned. That was exactly how she envisioned it. How long had he known about the cottage? And more importantly, did Alec know he knew? "What is it like, then?"

"Vast. Far more vast than you could possibly comprehend. It extends in every direction for eternity."

"You've seen it all?"

"No. That would be impossible. But I know every inch of this land; I have traversed it for my own eternity."

She eyed him. How old was he? Was it even possible to know in this place? She doubted he would answer if she asked, so she kept her mouth shut.

"You, too."

She snorted,

He glanced down pointedly at her. "Yes, you."

Now that was a laugh. Even when both legs worked, she had never been one for exploring the great outdoors. Her idea of camping was a three-star hotel.

The small footpath they followed turned sharply, and up ahead wispy gray smoke rose over the trees. She was relieved to see it; she couldn't feel her fingertips or her toes any longer. The forest to their left disappeared and all that remained in its place was the sharp drop of a cliff into a churning, tumultuous sea. It stretched right out into the dark blue-gray horizon, the white crests upon the surface flying like birds across its depths.

Settled along the junction of wagon rut running along the bluffs and narrow path they followed, the tavern was long, its stone walls milky white. Outbuildings crowded it.

Iain shot a glance over his shoulder as he strode to reach the door before her, pulling it open to allow Evie to enter first.

A dark taproom greeted her, the shadows deep despite the fire roaring in the soot-covered hearth. It smelled of cedar, and stale ale, the remnants of several meals long past and warm, yeasty bread.

No one looked up as Iain marched into the room, hood drawn low over his brow. She slunk in after him. Chair legs scraped against a water-warped floor as dragged a chair out from under the table closest to the hearth. He dropped into it, leaning back as he eyed the door. With his foot, he pushed a second chair out.

She sat awkwardly, back straight. He had an open view of everyone and everything in the room, and all she could see was him and the fire.

He signaled to someone behind her, not putting her any more at ease.

"Why are you here, Eve?"

"Why Eve? Why can't you just call me Evie? Is the extra syllable really that difficult?"

The corner of his mouth twitched a little, but he didn't humor her with an answer.

"I saw the crows, so I knew you weren't far behind. Why fight it?"

He frowned a little. "I'm… sorry about that."

She started in surprise. "Oh."

"I never thought to find you, again. And then you walked into the bar with Evan of all people. You cozied right up to me, and I thought maybe you must have remembered. Maybe not everything, but enough. You were just like your old self, cocky, self-assured, you got right down to…" He cleared his throat and his gaze met hers. "Anyway, I just thought it was that thing we do, playing it up, perhaps. As we got closer, I thought you would give up the acting, but you didn't. So I was angry when you weren't taking things seriously. By the time I realized you hadn't been playacting, *she* was there and I got desperate to save face and… I'm sorry."

Evie examined her fingernails, wondering what she was supposed to say. She hadn't expected him to apologize, but so much still confused her.

"We knew each other?" Flora had said they did, but…

He nodded. "For quite some time. We were in the summer palace together. Knew each other well before that, as well, but it's been some time."

"Until we went to Annwn with Flora." She leaned an elbow on the table and dropped her chin into her palm.

His eyes glittered and the corner of his mouth turned up. "You *have* been busy. What else do you think you know?"

"Think?" She raised her eyebrows.

He chuckled. "Humor me."

"You knew Alec. Here. On this side."

The mirth died a little and seriousness washed over his face. "Mmm. That was a long time ago. Even by

Otherworld standards. Many events have passed since the interaction on Drumossie Moor transpired."

Over her shoulder, a pair of battered pewter tankards appeared. She turned, accepting one, and the meaty hand of the proprietress plopped the other in front of Iain. Evie smiled her thanks, taking in the golden hair woven around the other woman's crown, the plain brown tunic belted over an even browner skirt that revealed a ham-like ankle. Even the woman smelled of roasting meat, the stink wafting around them as she turned away.

Once out of earshot, Iain leaned forward across the table. "Tell me, Evie, why are we having this conversation here and not in that little bar a block away from your flat?"

She ignored him, taking a sip of the ale, instead, and finding it rather good. Much better than she expected, anyway. Once the tankard was back on the table, she turned it in her hands, a splash of the amber liquid sloshing over the rim. Absently, she brought it to her mouth, sucking it away as she leaned back in the chair.

"Because I need to know who I am. All of me. And some of that identity, I think, can only be uncovered here."

"Why? Why is this important to you?"

Evie canted her head. "Why am I important to Mora?"

He didn't say anything, just considered her. There was no surprise in his gaze. No shock, no contempt, no joy or love or lust. Just curiosity. "If you go to her, there will be no going back, you know."

She nodded. "That's why I stopped fighting it and

came to you. So to speak."

His eyebrows shot up. "You must have a rather elevated impression of my worth or knowledge, then, milady."

She snorted at the endearment.

"And what do you want from me, Eve?"

She wrinkled her nose at the nickname she hated. The name of the woman he had perhaps loved.

She saw it there, that little slip of sadness, the wistfulness of what had been and was now… gone. "Did you really love me?"

He shook his head and looked toward the heavens. "Another question." A sigh trailed his muttering.

"What do I need to do to get them answered?"

He rubbed one thumb over the back of the opposite hand. "I can answer all of your questions, but I need something from you first."

"What? Anything?"

"I need you to let me take you to her."

"Are you nuts? You *just* told me that was a bad idea."

He pursed his lips. "Have you considered you might not want to leave once you learn the truths you're looking for?"

She leaned forward conspiratorially, her lips playfully lifting at the corners. "Why don't you tell me and let me decide?"

"Let me bring you to her. And if you decide your fate is taking you somewhere else, I will help you leave."

The hint of her smile fell and she narrowed her eyes. "How do I know you aren't lying?"

He held her gaze as he fell back against the chair

and pulled at the fingers of the glove on his left hand, inching them up before yanking the leather off. His fingers were pink from the cold beneath and he held the back of his hand flat against the table as he withdrew a hunting knife from his belt with the other. Calmly, he drew the tip across his palm then flipped the knife, offering the handle to her.

Evie looked from his bloody knife to his face.

"Should I break my promise, that knife will not hesitate to plunge into my heart should you will it."

Evie grimaced and gingerly took the handle, holding it aloft between thumb and forefinger like a dirty sock. "Well, isn't that… something." She wasn't sure what she should do with it, and she certainly didn't know how to wield it. "What do I do with it now?"

He let out an annoyed sigh and held his hand out. She hurriedly passed it over and instantly wiped her palms across the thigh of her jeans.

"I'll have it. For safekeeping. But you're going to learn how to use it."

"That seems rather counterproductive for you, doesn't it?"

"No. Because I don't break my blood oaths."

Chapter Twenty-Four

Wearing the uniform he left folded on the narrow bed, Evie emerged from the little room Iain rented for her. The leather fit like a damn glove, as if the measurements of the pants, the boots, even the reinforced, padded bodice were made specifically for her. Supports were even sewn into one leg, minimizing her limp and the pain that accompanied it.

She'd stared at herself in the little sliver of mirror over the wash basin and wondered what Alec would make of her. Flinging the dark cloak Iain also left around her shoulders, she figured he would be pissed she had made a deal with the devil.

And it stung, just a little, knowing she might be disappointing him. She didn't want to... but she needed to know. She *had* to know.

Yet, she held that red yarn in her hand, as if touching it, even through the plastic, was a connection to him. She closed her eyes and let herself savor the thought of him. Imagined his warmth and his scent. And then she gently tucked the yarn into her small purse and pulled the strap over her head and one shoulder, pushing the little leather satchel to the small of her back under the cloak.

She left the clothes she arrived in a neatly folded stack on the lumpy bed. Guilt over the wastefulness of just leaving them gnawed at her, but perhaps someone else would be able to use the raggedy jeans and second-hand sweater. The coat was more problematic seeing as how it wasn't even hers, but Sarah would forgive her. Maybe. If they ever saw each other again.

As she came down the stairs, she found Iain already lounging at the table they occupied the night before, an empty bowl in front of him and a steaming serving of porridge set at the opposite place setting. She wrinkled her nose as she plopped into the chair. No brown sugar or milk graced the table, and the lump of oats was an unappetizing gray color.

"The ride to the nearest outpost is long. Eat."

She didn't say a word, but glared at her breakfast as she wordlessly spooned the watery sludge into her mouth.

He allowed her a silent meal, but tapped his fingertips impatiently on the tabletop, the gloves muting the punctuated *thunks*. No sooner was the last spoonful in her mouth than he stood to leave, the chair legs scraping against the floor. Evie followed behind, meeting the gazes of their fellow patrons. They stared unabashedly at her, all conversation fizzling into quiet whispers. She swallowed as nervous flutters seized her gut and heat rose to her cheeks.

She wrapped the cloak more tightly around herself as they exited the warmth of the tavern for the frigid edges of the Myrkvior. The twisted limbs of the trees shimmered with a thin layer of ice in the murky gray light, and she shivered.

Iain took them north, following the wagon ruts up the coastline. Below the cliff, the sea churned mercilessly, white-tipped waves crashing against the rocks, retreating, only to attack again. The water appeared almost black from the overcast sky, and the salt air was painful to breathe. Evie struggled to keep up, though the built-in brace making the quicker steps easier than they had ever been before.

"How long did you have to play soldier just to try to get to me?" she asked when the silence became too much to bear.

He glanced down at her briefly before turning back to the road. "I told you, I wasn't there for you, finding you was a convenient accident. But not long. A few months."

She frowned. "How did you even do that? It takes years to get rank. Did you just walk in, ask to be a captain, and then show up at work the next day?"

"Something like that."

She stopped in her tracks, watching after him as he strode away.

He spun around, backpedaling slowly until she caught back up to him. "I have an unlimited amount of time at my disposal, as well as a magic portal between worlds that allows time travel." He wiggled his fingers in the air.

"So, what you're saying is you cheated."

"Absolutely."

"Did Alec use time and space to cheat his way in, too?"

Iain snorted. "Him? No. He's a rule follower down to the core."

"But he joined the Jacobites."

"Only because of Ail—Elizabeth."

"You mean me?"

He didn't answer at first, the crashing of the waves below an eerie soundtrack between them.

"Yes. It's always been for you, even when you didn't need him." Iain's words sounded bitter.

That hit her like a punch to the gut, had she used him? The thought twisted inside her.

She remained quiet, her thoughts turning inward. She knew Alec was in love with her. He'd been on the verge of telling her that night in Atlanta, and when she stopped him, he had done everything in his power to *show* her. But were those feelings for her or the woman he knew lifetimes before? Would discovering they were one and the same change things? Maybe it would make things worse. And then she might never be ready to hear it.

Fear might always keep her from being able to accept him loving her. And loving him back might require more strength than she had. Losing Calum did her in. Used her up. Made her useless for anyone else… ever.

"I know who you're thinking about," Iain murmured. "He was never meant for you, Evie."

The words cut like a knife. Because as unsure as she was about Alec and her own feelings and what the *hell* she was doing… the thought of him not in her life was agony.

****

Twilight was upon them when the small keep rose out of the distance. Its dark stone weathered, the fortress was a sentinel looking out over the waves as they rolled into the gentle curve of beach below. Torches flickered brightly at even intervals, and Evie counted them as they approached the gates.

"Where are we?"

"Imeall Thalami Ar," Iain answered, the name a

253

song.

"Is-is *she* here?"

"No."

"Oh. Then why are *we* here?"

"Do you want to sleep in the snow?"

She shook her head.

"I didn't think so," he retorted.

They walked through the thick archway, their boots slapping through sticky mud, after the portcullis lifted, metal clanging against rock and chains rattling. Iain moved to speak with a straight-backed man waiting for them just inside the wall, arms at his sides, eyes narrowed. Evie flicked her gaze around. It was smaller than the ruins of the St Andrews castle, with no more than a cropping of outbuildings and a long, low structure that must be the barracks.

When she turned back, it was to find all attention on her, just as it had been in the tavern. Iain gave the other man a sharp look and a quick shake of the head as the stranger's gaze drifted her way. He wore the same uniform as the others, leather, a tunic of mail, and an over tunic of black with three silver, swirling rings embroidered across the center forming a triangle. When he caught her staring, he executed a swift bow. Iain rolled his eyes and threw up his hands in defeat.

"Come with me," Iain murmured.

He escorted her through a side door and up a narrow set of stairs to a surprisingly spacious chamber. The same black and silver that graced the people in the courtyard the room. Iain stood on the other side of the threshold.

"A meal will be sent up, but I suggest you get some sleep. We have a long day tomorrow."

"You won't stay and eat with me?"

He seemed to contemplate the invitation, but ultimately shook his head.

"No." He turned on his heel, pulling the door closed behind him.

Evie stood in the middle of the room, taking it in. A few bookshelves piled high with leather bound tomes, all stuffed haphazardly onto the rough wood of the shelves; a lone window, panes thick and bubbled; a small, stooped desk with a lone candle standing sentinel over the inkwell and stack of parchment paper; and a simple wardrobe looming over the rest of the room from the opposite wall. The latter was flanked on one side by a full-length mirror spotted with age and on the other by a dummy holding a full suit of armor. The three-swirled symbol was etched across the chest.

She ran her fingers over the symbol, and then opened the wardrobe.

Inside hung some more leather leggings, reinforced leather tunics and white underthings. Her eyes grew wide as she took in what was displayed around the clothing: knives of every size, a long, intricately hilted sword, and a beautifully crafted bow with matching leather quiver. She quickly shut the doors. She would feel much safer with those out of sight.

A knock on the door came, and a young man entered, carrying a battered tray laden with food. He probably wasn't any older than she, but he shuffled in, head lowered, as if he were waiting for her to beat him with a stick. She tried her softest, friendliest smile, but he didn't even look up as he set the food down on the desk.

"Thank you," she murmured. Her stomach knotted

and she realized how hungry she was.

He bowed low and backed out of the room.

Evie lifted a brow as the door clicked shut, and then dug into the roasted fish, potatoes, and warm bread. The food was accompanied by a large mug of ale, and she gulped it down, throat straining when she swallowed too quickly.

Full to bursting, she stripped down to the white underclothes, tossed the leathers over a chair, and fell into the bed. It was fluffy and warm, the quilts covered with a heavy white fur. She nestled into the down pillows, closed her eyes, and found she couldn't sleep.

Only when she imagined Alec, his hands running down her body, that she drifted off to a sleep filled with him.

****

It was dark when she awoke, but if there was one thing she remembered about her time with Alec in the Otherworld, it was that time made no sense.

Muffled voices echoed up from the courtyard, and curious as to why Iain hadn't already begun banging on her door, she threw off the bedcovers and quickly pulled on the clothes she'd worn the day before. She wished there was water for a bath but had a sinking suspicion the basin and bowl on the cabinet in the corner were the closest thing to bathing she would be seeing in awhile, and she just couldn't bring herself to freeze to death first thing upon waking.

Evie opened the door and looked out into the hallway. It was dark and empty but for the single torch stationed outside her door, and another down the stairwell. She followed the little circles of orange light until she found herself back in the main hall, and then used the sounds of chanting to guide her into the courtyard.

Men and women lined up performing what she assumed were morning exercises. With each move came a chant, a repetition of what their exercise leader called out. She counted the number of people in each row and decided there couldn't be more than one hundred members out there, all wearing the same uniform she saw the day before; leathers, chain mail, black and silver colors.

Iain stood off to one side, hood pulled down over his brow, obscuring his eyes, but she knew the moment he spotted her by the little jerk of his head. He left the shadows, striding over to her and taking up a spot directly behind her right shoulder.

She frowned. She felt exposed like this, him putting her in front of him, and fought the urge to duck behind him.

"What are you doing?" she muttered over her shoulder.

"Watching morning training."

"Why?"

"Would you prefer we be out there with them?"

Her eyes widened as the soldiers broke out into smaller sparring groups. Some took to the far side of the courtyard with bows and quivers. "I wouldn't know the first thing about any of this."

He snorted. "Let's see if you remember anything." He took a couple of sparring sticks from a soldier. "You were rather good with the dart, if I recall."

"Remember?" she echoed dumbly and took the one he offered her.

The words were no sooner out of her mouth than

he swung the end of his stick toward her. She yelped, dropped hers, and held her hands up in front of her face as the long, rounded bit of wood slammed into her stomach.

Air knocked from her lungs as she fell backwards, her back hitting the soft mud behind her. It wrapped around her in a cold embrace, splattering her face and squishing between her fingers. Her breath returned in a wheezing wail as she stared accusingly at Iain.

He leaned forward casually against his stick, grasping it between both hands, his lips quirked to the side.

She narrowed her eyes and rolled to her hands and knees, kneeling in the muck. Slowly, she rose to her feet, fingers already aching with cold, and realized she would have use that bowl of cold water, after all.

She flung her hands out, trying to shake off as much of the mud as she could. "What the actual heck, Iain?"

He let out a long sigh and bent to retrieve her stick. "It looks like we have a lot of work to do."

Chapter Twenty-Five

Alec snapped the cover of his journal closed and slid it away. He'd kept journals since before arriving in Otherworld with Mora and continued once out of her thrall. Though he used them to ensure he never crossed his own path twice on the mortal side of the veil, the writing was therapeutic, and scouring the most recent notebook allowed him to relive the days since he first found Evie at the bookstore in Aggieville.

It was Delyth who directed him to Evelyn. She was unwilling to reveal her source, her pride hurt over a failed mission. The location would help him well enough if he planned accordingly and kept his eyes and ears open. He should have thanked her for her help when he saw her.

"Iain and his ilk are on the move. They have a great many leagues to cover, but you will do best to bide your time on the one where wildcats play on fields of royal purple." She'd then snapped a slip of paper into his palm, a year written in her straight, stick-like hand.

Evie's accusation still haunted him. He understood her fear. She wanted to be seen as herself, not the wife he had lost lifetimes ago. But her hurt and desperation to leave him was as good as a knife poised to rip through his chest. He'd tried with every fiber of his being to see her as no one but Evie. But there was no denying who she was. The moment he saw her, standing in the back doorway of her parents' house, hair sticking out and stained shirt drooping over her shoulder, he knew he finally found his missing half.

He'd tried to separate Evie Blair from Elizabeth Meyner Carlisle. He'd thought he had even succeeded. In so many ways they were the same. And in so many they were different. Evie had a vulnerability to her that Elizabeth never possessed. Elizabeth allowed him to play at protecting her, but he'd always sensed it was an act; she didn't need it. Elizabeth was a wild thing, a contained chaos, her edges sharp and her mind always turning. He'd loved her for her wildness, her brilliance. But she never curled into him, her innocence shining on her face as she slept. She never looked at him with tears in her eyes and begged him not to tell her he loved her. Elizabeth had been a storm, fearless. A force. Evie was so much more.

Seeing her again in Manhattan only confirmed everything he already knew. The connection, the invisible tug pulled them together, again and again. She was the mate of his soul. Finding Iain with her outside the coffee shop only confirmed it. For him, there was no turning back. He was hers for eternity, just as he'd always been.

At first, he thought Iain followed her only to find him. Laid her out as bait to track him down and drag him back to Mora's stronghold in the heart of the Otherworld. He'd kept his eyes on the skies, his senses trained on the crows. But they didn't trail him. Didn't watch him as he passed. Didn't care when he sent them scattering.

Because they were not after him. They wanted her.

And yet the look on her face, of fear and betrayal

and, dare he say, the vestiges of disgust, made him question every moment they spent together.

Anxiety and fear left him in the little cottage in the wilds of the Otherworld, reading over his own clumsy writings about love and fate and destiny, contemplating whether he should wait in the shadows, ready to protect her at all costs, or whether he should leave her alone as she asked.

Both options threatened to shred him apart from the inside.

****

Evie loosed the arrow. It pierced the center of the target. She grinned, grabbed another, and took aim. The second took up the space a fraction of an inch from its twin. A third impaled the target between them, the fletching flicking in the breeze.

Her gaze shifted to Iain's target. She'd done just as well as he had. "Tell me again how I will need years of practice."

"What makes you think you haven't done just that?"

He handed the bow to one of the soldiers standing behind him. She ignored him and did the same. The woman who accepted it was a handful of years her senior, with mousy brown hair and a wicked scar across her left cheek. Evie bounced as she joined Iain, her leg hurting not a bit.

"This feels exhilarating," she said cheerfully, her face still bright with her accomplishment.

She didn't know how long they had been there. She supposed it didn't really matter, though occasionally she wished she'd had the foresight to do as Alec did and write it all down. Perhaps seeing it on paper would help her make sense of time. What she did know was that for every morning since she had been there—whatever morning meant, it always seemed different—she met Iain down in the courtyard and they had sparred, practiced knife throwing, fought with swords, and pushed each other through target practice. He'd been patient with her at first, becoming more stern and demanding the more familiar the weapons felt in her hands.

She'd been a disaster at first, and Iain wouldn't let her train near any of the others. Her days were spent in the mud and dirt until she found she was more than adept, and only then did he bring the others around. She could now best every one of them so long as she kept her mind clear and muscle memory to good use.

The bow and arrow was her greatest talent, though she quite liked the throwing knives, as well. They were like darts, and the quicker her fingers, the more accurate they were, planting themselves just where she wished them to go.

The sword's weight gave her the most trouble, though she held her own against Iain, even when he wielded two. Knowing she had infinite amounts of time slowed her pursuit of truth, and for the time being, she enjoyed being honed into a weapon.

None of the others ever spoke to her, and though loneliness often crept in, she was often too exhausted to care. She took her meals alone most days, but Iain occasionally joined her. He was her sole companion.

She stared up at him. He had shaved that morning. Usually, his jaw was shadowed with stubble but he left a bit of a mustache and a sinister-looking triangle of hair on his chin. It was almost dashing. Almost.

"Flora told me we were companions. Once."

His eyebrows rose. "You saw Flora?"

"You didn't know?"

He shook his head as they entered the main hall.

"Hmm" she murmured. "You were the one who tipped me off. I was starting to wonder if you had done it intentionally."

They turned up the stairs and she waited for his response. "Well?"

"Well what?"

"Tell me about us being companions."

"You mean in the solstice kingdoms?"

She nodded. "Where else?"

Something in his eyes flashed, but it was quickly gone and he leaned against the wall outside her door. "Yes, we spent some time with King Hafgan before traveling with Flora to Annwn."

"And?"

"And what?"

"Tell me about it." She sauntered into her room, leaving the door open in invitation.

Evie pulled the laces loose on her uniform as she approached the wash basin. It was mysteriously filled with warm water every morning after their training sessions, and sometimes a silver tub would be waiting for her next to the hearth, but it was noticeably absent.

Iain entered behind her, quietly shutting the door behind him. She turned away to splash water on her face before scrubbing away the grime with a small hand towel.

"You were there for Flora. I was there for you."

"For me?" She patted her chin dry and turned to him.

"Mmm."

"You can't just talk in grunts and sighs," she complained as she dropped the towel and sat down on the edge of the bed to unlace the boots.

"Can't I?"

"No. You promised you would tell me what you know."

"And I will. After I bring you to her."

She rolled her eyes and kicked off the boots, then stood to pull the black tunic over her head, revealing her breast band. It would have been amusing to drop it on the floor with the rest and watch him try to avoid looking at her, but she took pity on him and left it in place.

"Flora said you were in love with me," she said as she returned to the wash bowl to sponge away the sweat collected under her arms and across her lower back.

Iain stared at the ceiling, but his cheeks warmed to a pretty shade of rose.

"Is that why it didn't take much to get you to sleep with me in Kansas?"

"I don't remember any sleeping," he grumbled.

She laughed. "Well, were you?"

He turned his gaze to the tips of his boots before taking a deep breath and letting it out slowly. "Perhaps I thought myself so for awhile."

"Really?" She was thoroughly shocked he answered her.

"Why is that so surprising?"

He crossed his arms over his chest and leaned back against the heavy wood of the door.

She paused mid-scrub, the hand towel poised over one elbow. The water ran in rivulets down her flesh, dripping onto the floor, slipping between her skin and the leather pants she had loosened.

"I don't know... I suppose I see you as a silent automaton."

"A what?"

"You know, a machine that just does as it's been programmed..." She flushed and twisted her mouth to the side.

"I suppose you would see that."

"Iain, I didn't mean—"

"It's fine," he murmured. "I've been... serving her for so long, I suppose I have perhaps lost a bit of my..." He stopped, as if thinking of the word he would like to use. He lifted up a finger and ran the back of it along her cheek. "Humanity."

Her lips parted, but words stuck in her throat. His eyes grew soft, his gaze dropping to her mouth.

Did he still desire her?

She swallowed. He was certainly beautiful, and despite her brief fear of him, she supposed they had become friends. She'd certainly come to enjoy her time with him, their competition, jokes, the way he had made her forget... everything.

Her brows slowly drew together as she met his gaze. But did she want him like that?

The resounding answer in both her heart and mind was no. She didn't feel a draw to him, she never really had. She had pulled him into the backseat of her father's car because she was finally feeling again and needed the release. Perhaps he was looking for that, too, and they found the sex mutually beneficial.

But Alec had ruined her. She didn't want Iain. Not again. Not ever. The hands she wanted on her naked form were Alec's hands. The mouth she wanted on her own was Alec's. The arms she wanted wrapped around her when the world didn't make sense were Alec's arms.

Evie jumped across the veil looking for answers and Alec was her answer. Did the rest really make a difference?

No, it didn't.

Because she no longer cared. She didn't care if Elizabeth or Ailsa or whatever her name was shared her soul. She didn't care why she was important or why Mora wanted her so badly.

But the hurt she had seen on Alec's face mattered. Wanting to make up for it mattered.

"Iain."

He leaned forward, his lips brushing her cheek where his finger had just been.

"I know," he whispered softly.

A lone tear trailed down her cheek, skimming around the curve of her jaw.

"I'm sorry." Her whisper was barely audible.

He gave her a gentle smile. "For what?"

Cold wrapped around her as he moved away, taking his warmth with him. She shivered.

"We'll leave at first light," he murmured then left her to the grand, empty room.

****

First light didn't mean what she thought it meant.

She thought there would be time for a nap, perhaps a meal, but she'd barely had time to redress before Iain came knocking on her door, again.

"You just left." Evie squinted at a fully changed and clean Iain.

He nodded toward her window. "Yes, and light is already straining across the horizon."

She tossed a look over her shoulder to the window and seeing he was right, stuck her tongue out at him. "How do you get used to it?"

He pushed into the room. "Used to what?"

"Time not making sense."

Iain shrugged. "It makes perfect sense. It's your side of the realm that's off."

"How long have you been here?" she said more to herself to him as she pulled on a leather cuirass.

He only looked at her blandly. She should have known better than to ask.

"You do know you have a whole wardrobe full of those things, right? You don't have to keep wearing the old dirty ones." He nodded to the large wardrobe she hadn't opened since arriving.

"I didn't want to mess them up for whomever they belong to." That, and despite her new penchant for throwing sharp objects, the multitude of daggers and knives still made her uneasy.

Iain canted his head but didn't say anything. Instead, he sighed with exasperation, went to the wardrobe, and pulled out a pack. Each of the clothing items hanging inside were unceremoniously yanked down and dumped inside the leather bag.

"Put it on."

He dumped it into her arms, and she shrugged the straps over her shoulders as he returned to the wardrobe. Extracting several of the knives from their rests, he then tucked them in her belt and slid one inside the shaft of her boot.

"You'll need this, too."

She took the sword and baldric he held out. "Really?"

He merely raised an eyebrow and hoisted up her archery equipment.

"Is all of this really necessary?" She struggled to get the leather strap under the pack already on her back.

"Yes."

"Why?"

"You never know what—or who—you will meet out there. And it's better to be prepared than sorry. Besides, she will expect to see you like this, so it's better to just… do it."

Evie rolled her shoulders, testing the weight of it all. "I think I might fall over," she complained.

"You'll get used to it." He handed her the bow and quiver of arrows.

"But what about my leg?"

He stopped to consider, as if he had forgotten about her injury altogether. "We'll be on horseback."

She recalled how stiff she became when sitting in one position for too long. And the strain riding put on her body *before* the accident. "I don't really think that is going to make much of a difference," she grumbled.

"Well, it's going to happen one way or the other. Just let me know if you need to stop or slow down or walk."

Didn't he just have an answer for everything? She nodded, though, and looked around the room once more. It was as good a home as any. She might even miss it. Then she followed Iain out, down the stairs, and into the courtyard.

Two black stallions waited for them, blanketed and saddled, their reins held by a young man—no, a boy—

as they approached. The entire garrison was out in the courtyard, their colors spotless, weapons to their sides, their stances in what she could only describe as standing at attention.

She looked at Iain and wondered who exactly he was to get this sort of send off, but he didn't meet her gaze or any of those around them. Instead, he stood next to one of the horses, his hands cupped to help her into the saddle. She felt incredibly awkward putting her foot in his hands and then having him hoist her up. She was so nervous about it, she nearly fell off the other side of the poor beast. Her face heated, and she gazed down at her hands, fingers lacing through the reins.

Iain mounted the other horse and nodded to the commander standing before her troops. The woman said something guttural in a language Evie didn't understand, and her soldiers changed stance as one, their fists going to their chests as they bowed to Iain. He gave a curt nod, clicked his tongue, and kneed his horse into a walk. She did the same, and they exited under the portcullis side by side. But once the wide-open road spread before them, he nudged the beast into a gallop and sped off.

Not one to be left, she did the same, shooting out behind him, and into the sea grass fields edging the Myrkvior.

Chapter Twenty-Six

The moon was full and high in the heavens when she spotted the great fortress. It sat atop a rolling mountaintop, the stars its backdrop, an endless tapestry of winking lights. One tall, central tower rose up like a beacon in the night, many smaller towers flanking it. She couldn't see how many there were, but the lights, little flickering dots against the dark stone, lit it up eerily. She could almost smell the fires as the wind whipped down the mountain, the faint smell of freshly baking bread.

Evie had never seen anything like the sky.

The constellations suggested she was on the other plane of existence Alec had described; nothing looked even remotely similar to the Greek figures she had grown up looking toward. No Orion, no Cassiopeia, no Pegasus. These stars charted different stories, different gods. She wanted to know their names, every last one of them, and their stories. She had always loved stories, especially those of times long past. She felt so small, a speck in a vastness greater than she could even imagine. And if what others had told her that was exactly what the Otherworld was: an infinite realm of land and sea and mystery.

She wondered if anyone had ever tried to reach its far corners, or if it was as great as the universe, stretching beyond imagination.

"We'll be there by the mid-morning meal," Iain said.

They hadn't spoken much since leaving the sea fortress. They hadn't needed to. She wasn't sure how they had landed themselves in the companionable silence, but the longer it stretched, the more comfortable it became. She hadn't thought about keeping track with pen and paper until the hours had already flown by, their horses skirting the wood to the north and moving inland. And now, as their journey to Mora was ending, she felt compelled to break their silence. Perhaps it was the funny feeling in the pit of her stomach; the nerves, the fear, the excitement. Or perhaps she was tired of her own thoughts. Her own wonderings of where Alec was and if he would welcome her back with open arms. Or if he would turn away from her after the hurt she caused him.

"Why did we stop before? And for so long?"

"She didn't want me to bring you to her until you were ready."

"Ready for what?"

"I don't know."

"What do you mean you don't know?" she demanded.

"I am not privy to her every plan."

"She has more than one?" she said sarcastically.

"I am but a single needle in the great tapestry she weaves."

Evie wasn't sure she didn't hear a bit of sarcasm dripping from his lips, too.

"And your role?"

He was silent for a moment, the sounds of the night and the thud of hooves on the ground whirling around them. "Damage control."

She turned to look at his silhouette, his straight nose and strong chin against the backdrop of stars. "What do you mean?"

"I'm the clean-up crew."

"Does that make me the mess?" she drawled and raised an eyebrow. "Tell me, am I fraternity house vomit or just post-football game litter?"

He shook his head and chuckled. "Yes and neither."

"Mmm. Dinner dishes?"

He laughed. "Unswept floors, maybe?"

She snorted. "I guess it could be worse."

"And why was I a mess that needed to be cleaned up?" she pondered aloud.

"Because the one meant to find you and bring you back… failed. Miserably. A couple of times, it would seem."

She blinked. "Oh. Who was it?"

He gazed up at the fortress. "I think you know."

She frowned. No, she really didn't. He couldn't mean Alec, could he? That made no sense. Alec didn't want to be anywhere near Mora…

Wait. Alec had thought she was after him, not her. He had said as much. Was it possible he had misunderstood and he had been brought into her service to bring Elizabeth? Perhaps *he* was bait?

"Why does she want me?"

"Those plans are not mine to tell."

"But Flora was part of them."

"Yes."

"And what was Flora's role?"

Perhaps if she knew why Flora was brought into

the Otherworld, she could figure out what her own role was. The women of Culloden were clearly a piece of whatever was going on. She, Evie, representing Elizabeth Meyner Carlisle. Flora had to be Flora Macdonald. And the third, Lady Anne Farquharson Macintosh. Who was her player?

"She is falling into it."

Evie rolled her eyes. Why was giving her information so difficult for these people? She tried another tactic. "Owen's part then?"

She could just make out the lift of his lips in the light of the moon, as though he were proud of her for working it out. "He was merely an insurance policy."

"An insurance policy for what, though?"

"Something she has been planning for a very, very long time."

"You've been with her for a very, very long time," Evie pointed out..

"That I have."

"And what is her plan?"

He shot her a bored look, one eyebrow slightly cocked, his head canted toward her. But his lips were sealed, even if slightly upturned.

Evie groaned in frustration. "You really are no help, you know."

"I know."

"About the promise you made…"

He kept staring off toward the castle. It was growing larger, looming over them.

"Will you… get in trouble for helping me?"

He shrugged. "If you want to go."

"You think I won't."

"I do."

She didn't want to tell him he was wrong. But she'd been biding her time, only fulfilling her part of the bargain to get back to Alec. It was what kept her going. Especially now that her leg was starting to twinge. Shifting in the saddle she tried to stretch her leg out but failed miserably.

"Will you?"

He shrugged his shoulders. "It's likely."

Two heartbeats passed. "How?"

"I'm sure she has a special hole carved into the wilderness just for me." He chuckled.

"You almost sound as if you like her," she accused.

"Is that such a bad thing?"

Evie wasn't sure how to answer.

As they approached the first fiery cresset welcoming them to the enormous fortress, light peeked over the horizon to the east, painting a thin golden line across the mountains, the first fingers reaching toward the citadel.

Closer now, she could make out the smaller towers built into the massive wall. She gazed up at them, guessing they had to be at least ten stories tall, guards patrolling the top of the walls set between them. Ebony colored stone, as smooth and glossy as a mirror, reflected the torchlight. Each massive brick was taller and longer than her horse. The fire eerily bounced off the surface and the fortress glowed in the dawn.

"It's magnificent, isn't it?" Iain murmured.

Evie could only nod dumbly.

They travelled up the mountain, drawing ever closer as they took the switchback trails, the torches lighting the way. They settled back into that silence, Evie's awe sucking the words right out of her. The winds died down, the chirping of birds quieted, even the flames licked with less ferocity. The sun lit the sky by the time they reached the great portcullis, and she wondered if the whole of the sea fortress could sit in the gaping maw of the dark castle.

Soldiers lined the tunnel through the thick outer wall. It was as long as a lap pool, the torches lighting it into a long mirror. Evie couldn't help but gaze at her form in the reflective black stone. She cut a rather impressive figure, she thought for the first time. Her face had thinned out and her eyes were large and bright. And yet she appeared strong. Powerful. She had never felt strong and powerful anywhere but a library or a classroom. She could have been mistaken for a warrior.

When she turned back to Iain, he was watching her, a knowing smile playing along his lips. He knew what it was like to see oneself for the first time. The surprise. The pleasure. The excitement.

They emerged from the wall's entrance into the courtyard. It stretched in a wide circle around that central building, the heart of the castle, its tall tower shooting into the fading stars. Its mistress clearly valued the night sky. And a vantage point.

A guard wearing an intricate helmet met them, bowing low before waving over a set of grooms.

Iain jumped down from his mount as one of them took the reins and he circled the horse to come to Evie's side. She took the hand he offered for support and swung her leg around to drop into the dirt beside him. She realized he made it appear a show of deference to her rather than offering himself as a crutch. But the moment her leg buckled under her weight, she was glad for it. The pain shot through her sore limb and she sucked in a breath.

He leaned in.

"All right?"

She shook her head. "I need a minute," she said through clenched teeth.

"I will keep saying nonsense until you are ready. Keep your face serious, do not show any sign of emotion or weakness."

She gave a curt nod.

"They are all watching you. No, don't look at them. They are beneath you. Remember that. Do not look at them, do not smile at them. You answer only to her. Say something obnoxious if you understand."

"You're a bastard."

"Nice, though not terribly clever."

She glared.

"Good. You certainly look the part."

"The part?" she demanded.

"Of Ailsa."

Before she could question him, he threw his hands up and took a step back, as if she had threatened him.

"Better?" he asked, mouth barely moving.

She pursed her lips, assessed, and faced away from him.

He lowered his hands. "Straight up the stairs into the throne room. Go."

Evie pivoted toward the main building, carefully, and strode steadily, working through the stitch in her leg. Iain fell in step behind her, and she relaxed her face into an unreadable mask despite the desperate speeding of her heart. She could do this. She just needed to get through this, whatever *this* was, and then she would be back on her way to Alec.

She replayed their reunion she had been constructing in her head. She would probably cry because she always did. Beg him for his forgiveness. He would be angry. Hurt. And she could swipe at her tears and choke through how much she loved him, but that she was just so unsure of everything.

Yes, that sounded about right. He would forgive her, though. He had to. She just couldn't imagine a world where he wouldn't forgive her the time she needed. Granted, she'd spent it in none of the ways she expected, but it had still brought her back to him.

The large double doors swung open, and she trudged into the hall as the sky lightened to a robin's egg blue.

One step closer to Alec.

His name became her chant. Every step, every painful movement, was a step to Alec.

The hall was vaulted. Black and silver banners, the three rings glinting in the candle light, hung from the arcades. The passage stretched further than the thickness of the outer wall, its white carpet a sharp contrast to the black stone. A dais was surrounded by people in dark clothes, all waiting. Watching her.

Evie swallowed. She was almost there. Almost to Alec.

She glanced up at the dais. Her breath caught in her throat and the dizzying pace of her pulse tripled.

Because, next to the most beautiful woman she had ever seen stood Calum.

Chapter Twenty-Seven

Iain prodded her forward.

"They are all watching you," he muttered.

But she could focus on nothing but Calum. Calum was standing there. Calum, who had died.

Her heart was in her throat.

Calum.

He was taller than she remembered. And far, far bulkier. His straight shoulders were massive, his arms thick and corded with muscle, the inky edges of a blue tattoo criss-crossing his bicep. His chest was broad, covered by a black leather jerkin, the laces pulling it taut. Her gaze skimmed lower, past the dark leather breeches and to where his left leg was missing. He balanced himself with his one intact leg and a scarred wooden peg.

She had spent many a night wrapped around Calum's body, but this was not it.

Her gaze snapped to his face.

He flushed.

Yet his face… his face was the same. His black hair flopping over his forehead, hanging down over his collar. Longer than she remembered it. It had always been shaggy, making him seem academic, unconsumed with petty fashions.

How many times had she dreamed of seeing him again? How many times had she replayed a reality in which he had survived through her head? How many times did she beg for just one more minute with him? It seemed like an eternity ago. All of it. The accident, the dark depression she was forced to climb out of, learning he existed to no one. No one but her. And here he stood next to the woman holding her whole future hostage.

Evie didn't know what she felt. Elation to see Calum there? Or was it dread?

His gaze caught hers and his mouth opened, as if he wanted to call out to her, but knew better than to utter a sound. Instead, he swallowed, his neck bobbing with the effort. But his aquamarine stare didn't leave hers. And she could swear she could see his heart breaking in them.

Evie had to look away.

She—Mora—smiled deliciously, her red lips curving languidly, pleasure oozing from her. Her black hair was swept to one side, slipping over her shoulder to pour almost to her waist in obsidian waves. She wore all black, the ebony gown draping over her every curve, the folds soft. A full mantle of crow's feathers fanned out around her, the clasp at her throat made of those three silver circles. No jewelry adorned her neck, her fingers, her wrists.

She drew no undue attention to her assets, instead allowing the sheer power oozing from her to command the room, not the flaunting of her body. Her only decoration was a simple, slender diadem in the shape of a crow, its wings spread across her brow.

"Ailsa. You have finally returned to me."

Evie didn't know how to respond. Should she bow? Correct her name?

"And Iain, you succeeded in leading my little battle

bird back to me." Her smile turned sour as she glanced at Calum. She turned back to Iain. "It took you quite long enough. I was beginning to wonder if I had saddled myself with another useless warrior." The ire dripping from her words was enough to make Calum flinch.

"Forgive me. Ailsa has always been... tempestuous." Iain bowed deeply. "But she has returned willingly and is well-prepared to continue her service to you."

Evie's frown deepened.

"Yes, she has." She swung her attention to Evie. "Have we put the Carlisle boy behind us at last, dear Ailsa? Your distraction last time is exactly how we ended up in this little situation, How *you* ruined all of our well-laid plans."

"I-I don't understand." The voice didn't sound like hers. It sounded like someone else's, someone who was far braver, far more worldly. A harsh voice. An angry voice.

The woman shook her head. "Don't worry, my dear. I blame Calum. He was there to keep you focused and he let his jealousy get the better of him. Didn't he?" She shot another disapproving look behind her like a mother furious with her offspring.

Evie swallowed, the movement loud in her ears. All the pieces were in her hands. She could see all of the bits, all of the edges and the colors, but she couldn't fit them together.

Iain must have sensed her distress, for he cleared his throat. "If I may..." At the woman's nod, he continued. "I don't believe Evie quite grasps your meaning, Your Eminence."

A soft, knowing smirk. "Perhaps it would be easier to hear it from my lips," she murmured as the beautiful young woman melted into Mrs. Baird. She stepped lightly down the three steps of the dais to stand before Evie and took her hands lightly in her soft, worn hands.

"Darling lass," Mrs. Baird murmured. She wore the clothes of Mora, but she was greatly softened. "Do you remember nothing of our exploits together?"

Evie gave a jerky shake of the head.

One of those soft hands brushed down her cheek. "Oh, dear. You were always so headstrong. Always rushing in before really thinking about the consequences of your actions." A motherly pursing of lips. "It's what made you such an effective weapon."

She turned, edging Iain out of the way and slid her arm through Evie's. She pulled her away from the others, strolling slowly down the aisle upon which Evie had entered. Those who stood around the platform, watching silently with curious eyes tracked their mistress's movements. None seemed surprised by the transformation into sweet, motherly Mrs. Baird.

"That rising of the Jacobites was to be the first step in a plan we hoped would span generations. You, my dear, planted the seeds. You bided your time, waiting until just the right moment for the unrest. You orchestrated the entire thing brilliantly, from that young, foppish prince returning to a home he had never seen to the rampant patriotism of those who rose up behind him. You were clever enough to surround yourself with a gaggle of men who were all too willing to be controlled."

She chuckled as she glanced at Calum.

He flinched.

"Even that boy you collected. It was brilliant the way you manipulated him, the youngest son of one of the most powerful households in the British Empire, begging after you like a dog."

Alec. She meant Alec. Evie's stomach clenched.

"I was so proud of you… Up until you allowed him to keep you from the battlefield. *Your* battlefield. You never swept across it, crushing Cumberland's troops and rallying the Scots. You allowed yourself to become distracted by human emotions. Love." Her tone turned to one of anger, of disgust.

"And the worst of it, the absolute worst part of your betrayal, was when you thought him dead on that battlefield. You did something so incredibly stupid as let *yourself* be killed." Her gaze turned fiery, and she leaned in, her nose inches from Evie's. "Did you even look for him in the solstice kingdoms or did you race through them, waiting to be reborn?" she growled.

Evie had no idea. But she stared right back, clenching her teeth, refusing to break under the accusations.

Mrs. Baird turned around, fingers kneading her temples, and when she pivoted back, she was the beautiful young woman, Mora, again.

"It pained me to have to wait so long for you to return to us. Never did I imagine my most trusted guard, the one I took in when no one else would have him, would betray me."

She swung her gaze to Calum, and Evie had to give him credit; he continued to hold his head up. She tried not to let her sympathy for him show, clenching her teeth down so hard it hurt.

Mora paced, her feet silent on the black stone, her

skirts a whisper. They swirled about her like a cloud, the diaphanous material floating as if a midnight fog.

"What is to happen to him?" That voice again, the one that didn't belong to her.

"Oh, he'll continue to serve me. As I see fit." She sounded rather magnanimous. "I have reclaimed my gifts, however, and they will remain mine." She looked pointedly at the peg where his leg had once been.

For the first time since Evie entered the court, his head sank as if to hide his shame. Had Mora restored it for him? As some sort of payment for services provided?

"And me?"

"You?"

"What of Ailsa's punishment? Am I to receive it?"

She knew it was a stupid thing to ask the moment the words were out of her mouth. But she couldn't understand how it was fair for Calum to suffer while she was left unscathed? She had loved him, or at least the parts of himself she shared with him and she owed him... something. Even though she should have felt something for the man she had thought to marry, she felt only sadness. A soft mourning for the dream she once had.

Yet, dreams change and her new dream lay across the Otherworld in a small cottage in the forest.

"I am not some heartless tyrant. I won't heap Ailsa's transgressions against you, same soul or no. It does no good to punish one for a crime she does not even remember committing, am I right?" She didn't wait for an answer. "However, now that you have returned, I have great use for you and I expect you to take up your—Ailsa's—duties posthaste. Your soldiers are at the ready?"

"My soldiers?"

"Yes, Eminence, they are at the ready. Evie and I spent this last season training with them."

"Mmm," Mora smiled prettily. "I did always love that little holding of yours on the sea."

"Mine?" She turned to Iain.

He nodded.

"Hmm," she said, taken aback. "And what duties will I be accepting?"

"Ahh, yes, I suppose you don't remember, do you? Ailsa has always been an important general in escorting my enemies to the Spring and Summer Kingdom, to King Hafgan. Why else do you think I had you awaiting the arrival of Flora MacDonald? You were to escort her into battle as you have escorted so many in the past."

"But she was in the land of the dead. And she isn't dead."

Mora chuckled. "No, nor was she meant to be. She played her part perfectly. You simply took your duties too literally and escorted her back across the veil. It was a risk I was willing to take, knowing you had only a tenuous grasp here. I had hoped to keep you longer. No matter, you are here, now, on the eve of the greatest war this or any world has ever seen." Her eyes twinkled brightly. "You and I have waited a long time to see our plans through, my dear. We will see it come to pass. That I promise you," she murmured quietly, as though they were the truest of friends, as close as any two women could be. "All the work we have done will not be in vain." She leaned forward and brushed her lips across Evie's cheek. "It will be done."

And then she stepped away.

It was on the tip of Evie's tongue to ask what would happen if she refused. If she turned tail and ran just as she had thought to do the moment she had walked into the fortress. It was tempting to entertain that as an option, leave all of this behind, let it be a very strange dream, and return to a world where she met a smart, handsome doctor at a bookstore.

She could go back to studying history, spending her days in dusty libraries and musty castles. Her adventures could include plane rides to her parents' house for Christmas dinners, engagement parties, weddings. She could live by her alarm clock and what to make for dinner. Dream of having babies and fights about whose turn it was to change the diapers.

Or she could stay and do all of those things when she was done racing across frozen plains, sparring with her friends in the mud, and exploring enchanted forests.

She turned to Iain. He must have seen what she was planning, for his lips curled up, the smile reflected in the spark of his eyes.

And then the world exploded.

The castle shook with it, blue light pouring in from the windows, shouting from the guards outside. Those who had crowded around the dais, faces she still didn't know, took defensive stances, some laying hands over their swords, others reaching for their knives.

And Mora whirled, her face shining with excitement. "It's begun."

Calum was on Evie in an instant, sweeping her right off her feet then whirling her around until her back pressed against the hard wall of his chest. How he had moved so quickly while missing a leg, she didn't know. But there she was, the dagger sheathed at her side now in his hand, angled up toward her throat.

He backed away, the wooden peg thudding heavily against the obsidian floors, and he pulled her sword free from her baldric with his other hand, the well-oiled metal singing against the scabbard as it was released. He held it up in defense.

Iain stood there, looking stunned and Mora's attention was still on the fading blue light pouring through the windows. Evie twisted, trying to break loose, but his grip didn't waver. She noticed the strange tattoo that was even more visible from the back of his arm. It looked old, like something she had seen before, but she didn't know where.

"What are you doing, Calum?" Iain demanded.

"Getting myself out of here and away from her." He lifted his chin toward Mora. "I'll not be her whore any longer." Against Evie's hair he murmured, "I am so sorry."

He now had Mora's full attention. She looked positively murderous, her eyes growing dark.

"You think kidnapping my most trusted general will somehow ingratiate yourself to me?" She let out a bark of laughter. "Do you think she will want you now? Ailsa didn't want you when she knew what you were. Even if Evie hadn't already given herself to that Carlisle boy on the other side of the veil, do you think she wouldn't find out eventually? You think she will just change her mind? After all this time?"

The words were nasty, cruel. They cut through Evie like a knife, and behind her, Calum trembled with anger.

"Remember the first time you begged her for her love? How did she repay you? She forced you to play her brother. You had to stand by and watch while she married another, you playing the doting kinsman." Another laugh.

Calum had been there all along; at Elizabeth's back as she wed Alec. What had Alec said? Calum hadn't been happy about the marriage.

"Should we tell her about how you stood over her chosen and watched him bleed out on the field? How you slinked back across the veil and came crawling back to my bed?" Her eyes were full of amusement. "Oh, I suppose I just did."

Evie's heart shattered, sending an ache through her chest. Calum, whom she had loved, left Alec to die on a battlefield so that he could have her to himself? He'd tried to keep them apart by getting to her first?

But then anger took over. How could he do that to Ailsa? How could he do that to her? She endured his death, and he dared hold a dagger to her throat? She wanted to make him pay for what he had done to all of them. She imagined reaching down for the knife then sliding it into his flesh.

She jerked to loosen her arm to do just that, but he held her firm.

"No." His voice sounded hollow. "Evie—Ailsa, I—"

Iain withdrew his own daggers, turning them once, slowly.

"Evie," he called, cutting Calum off, his voice strong. "You know what to do."

In a single motion, she dropped to her knees, sweeping the hand holding the blade to her throat away and kicking out at the peg.

She barely felt the pain in her own leg at the

sudden motion, her fingers brushing against the cool floor to keep her balance.

But Calum was too quick, and he deftly outmaneuvered her sweep. She palmed her knife, but Iain lunged forward, daggers a whirl around him. Metal clanged against metal, Iain moving in a flurry of jabs and slashes, all of which Calum blocked and countered despite his obvious handicap.

One of the onlookers, an older man with a bushy beard and plaits on either side of his temple moved to join the fray, but Mora held a hand out, stopping him in his tracks.

Iain's left blade slashed deeply through the exposed flesh of Calum's forearm, just below the tattoo, and blood sprang forth like a new river, running a line down the cords of his muscle. He cried out in anger and pivoted, bringing the larger blade down toward Iain's spine. The smaller man twisted out of the way and Evie saw her opening.

She flicked the knife, aiming for Calum's sword arm, but he blocked it, and the small blade clattered to the floor. But it was enough to catch him off guard. His gaze caught hers. She read betrayal there, the deepest of betrayals, the kind that feels like the tip of a knife piercing the heart. A betrayal like the ones he heaped upon her.

Despite her own hurt and anger, his look of utter heartbreak nearly sent her to her knees.

Iain was on him in an instant, dagger to the throat.

Mora motioned for some of the guards. They clapped Calum in irons and hauled him up.

"Oh, Calum, you know how much I hate a dirty floor." Mora clucked her tongue and sighed heavily. As she swept by Iain, she paused and murmured, "You know what to do with him."

Chapter Twenty-Eight

Alec let the water heat up. He stood over the kitchen sink, studying the spray as it hit the pile of dirty dishes, dislodging bits of food.

He'd put off cooking until his stomach wasn't able to hold out any longer. After coming back to the summer warmth, he did not want to unnecessarily heat up an already hot house, but that was just an excuse, one he needed to tell himself as his mind wandered back to the cottage in the wood. If he wanted to be honest, he had been waiting for Evie to return, and cooking for just him was the worst kind of reminder that she hadn't come.

He took the brush off the side of the sink and squirted a bit too much dish soap over the skillet and empty plates. His return to a Kansas summer came just minutes after he and Evie left for the Otherworld. His hope was that she would be there shortly after. He even fell asleep in one of the chairs in the front room waiting for her. Yet, she never came.

It meant driving to work the next morning, muscles aching from sleeping at an odd angle. Physical training didn't help, either, and the hot, muggy air suffocated the already parched landscape as the sun rose. But he still ran six miles on the outdoor track, hoping to sweat the depression out of his system.

He showered, changed, spent a whole shift in the

emergency room, and went out of his way to ride by her parents' house on the way home to his own. But she wasn't standing outside the house marked with her last name, and she wasn't waiting on his own doorstep.

He hadn't wanted to consider she wouldn't come back to him, but with each passing moment, he began to prepare himself for another lifetime without her. Up until this point, it had always been about finding the other half of his soul, but he'd never thought the other half would... walk away.

He wondered what she found, what Mora offered she just couldn't refuse. Mora certainly had worlds at her fingertips, he just... he'd thought maybe he could be enough.

Eggs peeled away from the non-stick surface as he began to scrub. The last meal he had made in it was potatoes for Evie, but that was nearly six months past. Coming back to summer made the most sense; he wouldn't tie her up in knots of time if they just picked up where they left that first trip across the veil.

He rinsed off a plate then turned off the faucet with the back of his wrist before shaking off the last drops of water and sliding the plate in next to the skillet. He dried his hands on the cloth hanging over the side of the sink and tossed it back down before turning.

"Shit."

Evie grinned from where she sat perched on top of his kitchen table. She wore a leather bodice with three intertwined rings—rings he knew all too well and had tried to forget—etched into the smooth center of the chest, just over the swell of her breasts.

"I didn't think you would come back."

She swung her legs like a kid at an ice cream

parlor. "I may have overshot a bit." She held up hand, in it the skein of red yarn.

"Did you know several cultures have mythologies about the tapestries of man? Many depict the fates sitting at their looms, weaving the threads of a life with those of another then intertwining them and bringing them together?" She pulled a bit of the yarn out from the skein, examining it.

"No, I didn't."

"Alexander Carlisle, we have long been connected by a thread. Through time and space, through worlds, we have found each other, and I have no plans to let you go. If you'll still have me, that is."

He lifted an eyebrow. "And if I refuse?" he murmured as he stepped closer, coming to stand between her legs.

"Then I suppose I will be having dinner with my parents alone tonight."

His lips brushed against hers. She pressed herself into him as she crushed her mouth to his, twining her arms around his neck.

He pulled away, breathless. "I suppose I could work dinner into my schedule."

She nipped at his bottom lip. "And after that, how would you like to help me take over the world?"

CPSIA information can be obtained
at www.ICGtesting.com
Printed in the USA
LVHW081914171119
637611LV00016B/473/P